BUOY

An Alex M. Mystery #2

Maggie Seacroft

www.maggieseacroft.com

For my parents.

CONTENTS

CHAPTER 1

I *f I get outta this, I'm going to tell him how I feel... one day.* It's amazing how a brush with death, the thought of dying, can play with your mind and embolden you like never before, isn't it? Bobbing up and down on a navigational buoy, completely drenched and chilled to the bone, I rolled over onto my left side to find the same cold steel would be just as unforgiving as it had been to my right.

My name is Alex Michaels and this is how I got myself into my latest predicament. I say "latest predicament" because the last five years or so have been one predicament after another. To put it nicely. To put it less nicely, it'd been a real kick in the nuts. If I had any, but Alex is short for Alexandra and, I can assure you, I'm all woman. Now, if I'd broken a mirror somewhere along the way, I could have at least prepared myself for some bad luck, but when it comes unannounced, it really is surprising and seems so much harsher

7

for some reason.

Let's see, in chronological order, because that's the A type of gal I am, in the last five years, I'd been widowed after eighteen months of marriage, been orphaned, and—just this summer— one of my best friends, Nat Grant, became terminally ill and, while he hadn't passed, he left to parts unknown to ride out his final days. And left me to fend for myself, or so it felt at the time. As it turned out though, I don't know what I would have done without the rag-tag bunch of miscreants who live at the marina I now call home.

Home. I knew it was there, off in the distance, among those faint lights on the shore. I just couldn't see it. Teeth chattering and body aching, I wondered if I'd ever lay eyes on it again. *It* is the Marysville Marina, nestled in a little town close to Monterrey, California where I happily reside on my converted double decker tow tug and namesake, the *Alex M.* She'd been left to me by my father about two years ago, along with a small annuity and some interests in his businesses including a boat brokerage which I happily took on after telling my corporate bosses to shove it. So now, instead of towing the company line, I could, in my boat/home, literally tow the company line. However, since I'd taken up residence on her, I'd converted the *Alex M.* from a work tug built for a crew of five to a liveaboard built for one woman, plus spoiled cat and dog. The transformation would have made for a great reality show. Converting five tiny bedrooms to one master suite, and a salon area with a space carved out for my home office from which I sell surplus marine inventory, broker boats and barges, engines and chandlery-type items to commercial marine buyers. Sometimes, I even throw in the odd pleasure boat sale just to spice things up a bit.

I had been wrapping up a correspondence with one of my customers—more precisely to one of the throwbacks who had referred to me as "Sir"—when I heard familiar voices on the dock. That fact, combined with the pleading eyes from my black lab Pepper, told me it was a good time to stretch my legs and for him to take a nature break. As I peeked out the stern door, surveying my little neighborhood, I could sense the change in the air. Fall. Gone were the last vestiges of the "weekenders". Couples and their entitled spawn who could be found on the decks of their boats, necks craned toward their phones, thumbs tapping out SOS messages to those they'd left in the city while dinners burned on barbecues and what passed for music replaced the whispers of the wind and cries of the gulls. From the brass hook near the stern door, I grabbed the latest in my hoodie collection, tied it around my shoulders, and Pepper and I made our way toward the voices.

Those voices, and the bodies that went with them, belonged to the dapper group of sexagenarians who had congregated near the *Summer-wind.* There they stood, my homies, my crew, the group of men I list among my closest friends. Though they are about forty years older than me–my last birthday I turned the big three-o— in the close to two years I'd been living at the marina, this group of men had become like family in the truest sense of the word–cantankerous at times, corny jokesters often, and always ready to pitch in, if only with their opinions. They shared the common bond of having served together in the navy under the same commander, our mutual and now AWOL friend Nat. And *we* shared the common bond of knowing that Nat had, rather than bear the pitying looks and burdensome feelings that were the side effects of his terminal illness, headed off into the sunset. The thing was, in the spirit of the true old film fan which he was, he'd faked his own death and, once I'd figured it out, I was sworn to secrecy by the gang. Something I happily obliged. Outside of our circle, while it had been de-prioritized in the news headlines, the paper still contained the odd tip about the "senior sailor" missing from the Marysville Marina. The last tipster claimed that Nat had parachuted out of a plane over South America and that they'd shared cocktails in Rio.

"Oh, hi kiddo." Jack Junior issued me his standard greeting once he'd noticed I'd sidled up to him on the dock.

Jack was standing, arms crossed in front of his chest and squinting winsomely as he watched the activity on the stern deck of the *Summerwind.* At close to seventy, though he won't disclose just *how* close, Jack Ross Junior is a fixture at the marina. With a twinkle in his eye and an endless supply of pep in his step, not to mention occasional bouts of wisdom, Jack Junior has stepped in where Nat stepped out, as sort of the unofficial mayor of the marina and head of our gang.

"What's going on?" I asked.

Jack glanced down at his watch and shook his head. "Oh, we're just getting Shears off to meet his airport transfer. He's been back and forth inside that damn boat twenty times in the past five minutes."

"Oh, that's right." I nodded, scolding myself for somehow forgetting the news I'd been told at least a dozen times. Robert Shears had let it be known that he was going on a European vacation. And, since he hadn't been overseas since his stint in the navy, he was particularly giddy about it. David Sefton, one of his pals from our group who, along with James Seacroft, referred to themselves as the "S-troop", had already been on the same month-long tour and seemed to have liked it despite referring to it as the "ABC tour", as in the Another Boring Church tour. The plan, as we had all been advised at a number of preceding poker games, was for Shears to meet his cousin Chester, who was flying into Rome from Florida and thus would begin their trek around twelve European hotspots. We were each promised a postcard. I asked if he'd bring me back some olive oil, Jack was hoping for booze, and the rest of the gang weren't specific but didn't want anything too "churchy".

Robert Shears popped his head out of the stern doorway, squinting into the sun. "Hey, do you think I need to take my French press?" he asked, the coffee carafe in his hand.

"You-you-you-you're going to France!" Jack shouted, his dark blue eyes wide, his voice rife with frustration, though I'd bet he was going to miss his friend terribly.

I smiled to myself. Jack Junior is so terribly cute, and the amount of stammering he does is a good indicator of his frustration level. It's like the kind of early warning system you need for violent weather events. Getting Shears on his way was a four out of five.

Shears nodded and, through his coke bottle glasses, he shot me a wink then disappeared into the stern salon and emerged a few minutes later. Luggage in hand. Well, one in each hand to be exact. The kind with wheels on the bottom, that in no time I could picture getting caught in the cracks between the weathered dock boards.

"Want some help?" I asked.

"No thanks, dear," Shears responded with a crinkly-eyed smile. "You could carry this for me, though," he said, handing me a slip of paper I realized was the confirmation for the airport pickup.

Jack Junior nudged me with his elbow and muttered, "We've been asking him if he needs help all morning, but you know how he is." He shook his head. "Now, will you come on, you're going to miss your flight and we've got to get to that thing."

I walked beside Shears as he made his way down the dock. "Anything you need doing while you're gone?" I asked as we neared the end of the dock and the United Airport transport van.

"No, just hold down the fort and keep an eye on the gang," he said. The same word-for-word response he'd given me the other times I'd asked. He had no pets to be fed, no plants to be watered, and if his dock needed tending to, he could count on good ol' Bugsy to enlist my services to supervise. In fact, Bugsy was even lingering by the van ready to wish Shears a safe trip.

Ahh, Bugsy. Our newbie of a marina manager had arrived on the scene some three months earlier. His real name is Bill Beedle, though I call him Bugsy because it's just too irresistible not to. He pretends he doesn't like it, but I'm not convinced. When I first met him, he had the personality of a housefly, but since I've gotten to know him, he's risen from insect status to something more like a friend. He keeps my dock in good repair and I keep my petty complaints to myself. *Mostly*. I smiled at him as the gang and I got closer. Bugsy looked like he'd just stepped off the pages of a blue-collar calendar. Caramel-colored hair whisked by the wind, sea-blue eyes and dimples like you've never seen, wrapped up in jeans and a t-shirt and work boots that had finally lost their lustre.

In short order, farewells were given to Shears like he was headed off to the navy again. Sefton and Seacroft reminded him of the places he *must* see, Junior slapped him on the back and told him to have fun and to watch out for the French girls, I gave him a big hug, and he checked his bag one more time for his passport and wallet before the door of the transport van finally slid shut and we all watched as it made its way up the hill and out of the marina.

"Be back in a sec, Jack, I have to hit the head," Sefton said and trotted toward his boat.

It was then I noticed that the gang seemed suspiciously overdressed for the occasion. "You're all looking debonair today. This can't be just for Shears. He'll be back in a month, right?"

"Oh, yeah, sure, sure kid," Jack said, nodding. "Funeral today," he added and glanced down at his watch one more time.

"Oh, that's too bad. Anyone I know?"

Jack smiled and shook his head. "Nah, I don't even know him."

I arched an eyebrow at him.

"He was with the Rotary," Jack tossed in as if it

explained everything.

"Ok?"

"Rotary guys have the best looking wives," Seacroft piped up from beside me.

"And?" I asked, waiting for the tenuous link to be made.

"*And* there's bound to be some cute chicks there," Peter Muncie chimed in.

"Umm..." I winced and the gang turned their eyes on me. "Never mind." I'd thought for a moment about letting the guys know that many, if not most, women don't take kindly to being referred to as "chicks", but I decided that may be a lesson they could learn best on their own. I looked down at Pepper, who looked up at me with an uncanny expression of understanding behind big brown eyes.

Seacroft came bolting down the path, zipping up his fly. "Sorry, guys."

"Wish us luck," Peter Muncie said as he put his hand on my shoulder. Peter rounded out the group of navy vets and, if I had to choose who among them was most spry, it'd be a toss up between him and Jack Junior. However, all of them could pass for younger with their white or grey hair—tamed on this day for the funeral—sinewy limbs, bright eyes, and big smiles.

"Good luck," I called out to the troop as they headed off then piled into Jack Junior's Buick SUV, dapper older gentlemen in suit pants and white shirts set off by their deep tans. I smiled, a little jealous of the chicks they were going to run into at the funeral.

✻ ✻ ✻

"Mornin'," I called out cheerily as I crossed the threshold into Aggie's place after taking Pepper for his constitutional walk and sniff uptown.

Ags must have caught sight of my blonde head bopping up the stairs to her store because she was already poised at the counter waiting with an apple fritter on a plate and a coffee carafe in her hand.

"Hey, girl. Shears get away ok?"

"Oh yeah," I said and took a seat on one of the red and chrome vinyl stools at the counter, the swivelling retro kind. Ags poured me a cup in an equally retro, thick ironstone diner mug.

"Good," she said and poured herself one as well. "I gave him a little care package for the flight, and for his bag. You know how he likes his black licorice," she said, shuddering.

I giggled and blew on the steaming cup I held to my lips before taking a sip and looking up at Ags doing the same. I wondered if, when we are older like the guys, we will still be best buds. Ags, or Aggie, is short for Augusta Wind Bellows, if you can believe it. I certainly couldn't the first time I met her, until she shared the stories about her colorful parents. She is a transplant from the Canadian province of Quebec, and when she gets really fired up, she goes on a rant in French... I think. She's a dark-haired beauty, free-spirited, and perpetually in a good mood. Her store, the not-so-ingeniously named Aggie's, is a one stop shop for everything from sunscreen to dish soap. She serves up sweets from the bakery in town and a small offering of items she prepares in her kitchen, but mostly it's whatever she feels like eating that day, though she does have her regulars like yours truly who stop in religiously for a roast beef sandwich and some of her famous freshly-made potato chips.

I looked up to find a studious expression on her face as she gazed at the aisles. "I'm going to re-jig the cleaning products section," she said, nodding thoughtfully.

"What? Again?" I asked and felt myself screw up my face. In the short time I'd known her, Ags had *re-jigged* her store displays at least a dozen times, like a woman who couldn't quite settle on a hairstyle, though it looked fine to everyone else already. In fact, Aggie's place looked great —a classy combination of white-washed walls, nautical fixtures, and gallery type displays of sepia-toned prints of boats and beaches. There's even a little lounge area carved out at one end of the store with five club chairs surrounding an electric fireplace and a big-screen television where most mornings my gang of older gentlemen can be found debating the headlines on the twenty-four-hour news station that's usually on.

"Wanna sit out front? I need to make my list for dinner," Ags said, having ceased the mental redecorating for the time being.

"Sure," I said, scarfing down the last bit of my fritter before toting my topped-up coffee in the direction of the door then settling into one of the table and chair sets in front of the place. The November sun was just enough to warm my shoulders through my hoodie but not strong enough to warrant unfurling one of the beer-logoed umbrellas all but tucked away for the season.

"So, how many are coming for dinner?" I asked.

"About twenty."

"Can I take a look?" I smiled eagerly and nodded toward the list Ags had started.

"You're still in that crazy writing analysis class, aren't you?"

"Maybe," I said. Though it was indeed true. Just for kicks, I'd enrolled in a writing and communications analysis course at the college. It was an intro to analysing everything from handwriting to texts to email. Ever since, I'd been on the hunt for samples to dissect and personality orders to diagnose.

Ags tapped the end of her pencil on the table then scribbled on the pad again. "Onions. I never buy enough onions," she said before laying her pencil down. "Oh, and I need new napkins," she said, making another note while I studied her scrawl.

Despite Ags being a Canadian transplant, she had adapted to U.S. traditions quite handily, including hosting a (later than Canadian) Thanksgiving feast in her store. She sets up a big table in the lounge and invites the regulars like me to pig out on turkey while the college football game makes us all feel lazy. This would be my first year attending. Though I had been living on my boat at the marina this time last year, I hadn't been in much of a thankful mood, what with the passing of my father and, shall we say, leaving my job in a rather unceremonious but at the same time memorable and satisfying fashion. My resignation letter was a post-it note, and my choice of language was true to my upbringing near the docks. But time has a way of making you mellow, and I considered I had more to be thankful for this year. Good friends, a thriving business that had saved me from corporate cannibalism, and an overall sense of serenity.

Aggie's phone buzzed and she glanced at the screen. "Chris," she said unexcitedly, and I watched her eyes scan the message on the screen.

"Not *thee* Chris? The same one as before?" I searched her eyes for the truth. I'm generally good at that.

"No, another Chris. It's a lucky name for me."

That I found debateable. The last Chris that

Aggie dated was our former marina manager. And, due to some less-than-stellar vetting by the dating maven of Marysville, Ags had failed to notice that *that* Chris was married. And, in what amounted to an extortion deal between Mrs. Chris and the marina owner, Mr. Bob Beedle, the offending Chris was relocated within the company and the marina owner's son Bugsy entered the picture. More my type than Aggie's. Hers being ten years her junior, impossibly fit, and they get bonus points if they have a couple tats and a bad boy streak.

In fact, Bugsy's more boy scout than bad boy. However, to his credit, with the sum total of zero marina management experience, he's taken on the challenge of running the place. Actually, I don't think he had much choice in the matter. The spit and polish, ex-army, dimpled one had received his orders from his father, the commanding officer of the clan, and we'd all been witness to the evolution of Bugsy, mellowing with time and even providing some comic relief along the way. Oh sure, he still holstered his cell phone on his hip like a modern-day gunslinger and spoke using military time, but he'd grown on us. That is, once we got over his questionable taste in female companions with painted on dresses, and once I'd convinced him I was not, in fact, responsible for the disappearance of my friend Nat. And, to top it all off, this summer, when he'd told me he was staying, he kissed me.

In my engine room. I mean the engine room of my boat, not some weird colloquial sexual term for female anatomy. It was on the lips and it was one of those kisses that makes your toes curl and your spine tingle. But that's as far as things had gotten in three months. Bugsy isn't a speed boat; he's a canoe.

I was stirred from my daydream by the sound of footsteps, and when I looked toward them, there was a man I'd never seen before. He proceeded to drop his duffel bag with a huff then looked around. When I looked at Ags, I found she had perked up parts of her I didn't know she could, and she was eyeing him like he was lunch.

"Hi," he said in a youthful voice with just a touch of rasp that hinted at a rough night.

Ags was speechless, her mouth fell agape, and her eyes seemed fixed.

"Good morning," I said toward the man-boy as I sized him up. He was roughly twenty-five, about 5'9, with short dark hair, hazel eyes, and some scruff on his face. Actually, he looked like the kind of guy who had five o'clock shadow no matter what time it was. He also looked like he was hiding a six pack, and the tight jeans he wore left little to the imagination—sort of reminiscent of the too-old member of a boy band. He looked like someone you meet only once but remember for a long time to come.

No, scratch that, he looked like trouble. I can't explain why. And, as it turned out, his arrival at the marina marked the beginning of a chain of events you won't believe.

CHAPTER 2

"H-h-h-hi," Ags finally managed to eke out. Her cheeks were flushed and, for a moment, I wondered if she was having a stroke. There was a pregnant pause which seemed fitting given the pheromones flying between the two.

I rolled my eyes. Hard. And when I looked back at Johnny Dangerous, the young man who looked as though he'd just stepped out of a designer jeans ad, he approached the table.

"Can we help you with something?" I asked, my tone friendly but cautious.

"Uh, yeah." He looked around. "I'm lookin' for my grandpa."

"Oh?" Ags squeaked.

I slid the side eye to my friend who had suddenly been reduced to single syllable sentences.

"I'll bite. Who's your grandpa?" I cocked my head, trying to guess the answer just from the resemblance. I was stumped.

"Robert Shears. He's got a boat here some-place," he said and rested his hands on the back of the chair adjacent to Ags.

"Shears?" I asked, and I know my voice went up wondering why Shears hadn't mentioned him. I'd also taken note that our stranger wore no wedding ring and sported no tan line for one, which boded well for my short-winded pal who was still eying him.

"Do you know him?" the stranger asked.

"I do." I nodded and glanced at Ags who knew him too but seemed too distracted to answer.

The man-boy glanced down at his watch. "Oh, don't tell me I missed him before he left?"

"Left?" I asked, baiting him. Naturally.

"Yeah, he's going on a trip." He rocked the metal chair back and forth nervously. When he caught me watching him, he abruptly stopped. "Sorry. I guess he's gone already, huh?"

I nodded. "Was he expecting you?" I forced myself not to give him the squinty-eyed, dubious look I felt gurgling up from inside.

"Yeah, well, he said I could come by anytime and that he'd be going away soon but it'd be ok. Damn, I guess I messed that up too. Don't sup-pose he left the key for me?" he asked and turned down the corners of his mouth in disappoint-ment, which I couldn't tell was real or not.

I shrugged my shoulders and made a hope-lessly unhelpful facial gesture.

"Alex–" Ags began to say, and I kicked her under the table.

I cut in, "Well, he might have left a key with one of his pals. They'll be back in a bit," I said and shot Ags a knowing look. The knowing look that says, *I know that you know that I know Bugsy has a key for every boat in the marina. But I also know that you know that I watch a ton of* Dateline *and that this guy could be anyone.* You know?

See, it's written in our lease contract. You have to give the marina manager a copy of your key just in case some emergency dock repair or unforeseen marine catastrophe should take place. As if Bugsy would know what to do. However, I wanted to wait for Jack Junior and the boys to come back and vet the legitimacy of this so-called relative. To be honest, I'd known Shears for less than what, two years, and mostly interacted with him at poker games and at Aggie's place while I scarfed down my daily fritter and cuppa joe. And, though I'm incredibly nosy, in that time I hadn't gleaned any information regarding his family tree. The man in front of us could have just as easily been some stranger looking for free waterfront accommodations.

"Why don't you sit down. You look a little beat," I said as I stood up. "Ags… can I see you inside for a sec?" I tugged at the hood of her hoodie and turned toward our latest arrival. "Oh, sorry, I didn't catch your name?"

"Russ. Russ Shears," he said before rolling his

shoulders and pulling out the chair he'd been rocking earlier. "Thanks, I drove all night to get here." He plunked himself down.

"Do you want a coffee or anything?" I asked, faking a smile and a little hospitality while I pulled Ags further toward her store.

"No, ma'am," he called back.

My smile, albeit fake, dissolved instantly. If there's one thing I hate, it's being called ma'am. It's a salutation I'd always reserved for teachers and old ladies at church, and I was damn sure I hadn't quite wandered into that demographic.

Three angry steps into Aggie's store, I let loose in a loud and incredulous whisper, "Did you hear that guy?" I hitched my thumb in the direction of the culprit. "He called me ma'am. I'm not a ma'am!" I rushed to the sunglass carousel, crouched down, and looked up into the mirror to assess the situation. "Ags? Do I look old enough to be a ma'am?" I turned and asked in earnest.

"No. Pfft. You don't look a day over a miss," she replied, and I was thankful she'd regained the ability to form sentences and was finally making sense again.

"Thank you. Now what do ya think of that clown?" I asked as my distracted friend craned her neck to look over my shoulder at the dude from the jeans ad. "Ags! Pay attention!"

"Sorry, did you get a look at that guy? To think... Shears' grandson." She sighed. "You know what that means?" she added dreamily.

"What?"

"Shears has that thick head of hair... That guy's going to grow old looking good."

"Yeah, in about fifty years, Ags."

"Who cares. Look at him."

"That's not the point. How do we really know that's Shears' grandson? He sure never mentioned it when he was saying his bon voyages today. I think that'd be the kind of thing Shears would bring up, don't you?"

"So, it slipped his mind. He's getting up there."

I shook my head then looked over my shoulder to see Russ Shears, or whoever he was, sitting at the table leaning on the back two legs of the chair, angling his face toward the sun. I'd bet my life he wasn't wearing sunscreen.

"I don't know, Ags. Maybe Jack and the guys recognize him or knew he was coming, but—"

"Alex, of all the people who could be impersonated. You think some guy who looks like *that* is just going to show up and pretend to be Shears' grandson? Let's just ask him for his ID."

"You just want to know how old he is!"

"Well, that too." Ags smiled and got a glint in her brown eyes.

"Ok, you do it," I said. "You're older."

"Nice try, girl. He called you ma'am. And you're the one who doesn't trust him, so you're on deck."

"Ok, I'll ask him." I groaned. "But until he

proves who he is, we don't send him to Bugsy for the key to the *Summerwind*. Deal?"

"Deal," Ags replied, rolling her eyes.

I rolled my shoulders a few times, limbering up for my next round with the young whipper snapper. *I'll teach him not to call me ma'am.* I turned on my heels and pushed through the screen door with Ags trailing behind. The man who called himself Russ Shears tipped his chair forward and rubbed his eyes. Trying to up his pathetic factor, no doubt. Didn't work. At least not on me.

I cleared my throat. "Look, I hate to do this, but would you mind showing us your ID? You see, Shears is a friend and–"

"Oh, no problem. Hey, I'm sure Gramps would appreciate you being so cautious," he said and leaned onto one cheek, angling his hand toward his back pocket, I assume on a dive for the wallet.

Ags gave me an "I told you so" nudge I should have expected.

The man returned his hand from his backside and met my fixed expression with a panicked look, eyes wide, biting his bottom lip pensively. "It's gotta be in my bag. Hang on."

I nudged Ags with my elbow. If this kept up, we'd be as bruised as the bananas on the counter of my galley.

Mr. Yet-to-Prove-Himself got up from the table and squatted down to unzip the blue canvas duffel he'd dropped earlier. The zipper caught on something in the bag and we, mostly I, waited impatiently for him to remedy the little luggage snafu while he mumbled obscenities. As I watched, I resisted the urge to be smug. If he did turn out to be Shears' grandson, I didn't want any resentment from my poker buddy on how I'd treated his kin. I shifted awkwardly. First, I crossed my arms in front of my chest, but I decided that might seem confrontational. Then I put my hands on my hips, which didn't seem too friendly either. Finally, I settled on thrusting my hands into the pockets of my jeans, although that felt completely unnatural. I watched as item after item was removed from the duffel bag and laid out on the gravel path until there was nothing left and the man stood and shook the empty bag. By the end of it all, he had laid out numerous t-shirts—notably a couple from Ohio U, rolls of white sport socks, a pile of boxer briefs—all of them black, three or four wrinkled flannel shirts, a tan vinyl toiletries bag, and a few pairs of jeans. But no wallet.

"Shit! It's not here," he said, looking back at us searchingly as if either of us knew where he'd last placed it.

The hands came out of the pockets and I gave Ags an elbow of vindication and raised my eyebrows at her.

She shook her head at me and sighed. Though she's only five years older than me, she has this older sister schtick down pat.

"Well…" I paused to think and glanced down at my Timex. "Mr. Shears' friends are at a function and they'll be back in a little while. Why don't you just hang tight until they get here. They'll know how to handle this."

* * *

While I waited for the gang to return, I killed some time answering work emails and phone calls—two inquiries about landing crafts and a call from a restaurant that was interested in the bona fide nautical antiques of my client in Ontario, Canada. I kept an eye on the driveway into the marina and, roughly three hours after they'd left, I saw Jack Junior's SUV return. I gave him a little time to change out of his dapper but impractical attire and then made my way toward his boat, the *Fortune Cookie*.

"Hey, kiddo," he called out to me once I'd reached his dock. He was on the stern deck sitting with Sefton; they were taking turns looking through binoculars.

"Hey, how was the funeral?"

"Dead," Jack said, pulling the binoculars down from his eyes.

"No chicks?" I asked.

"Nothin' to write home about. Peter Muncie got a number though," he grumbled.

"Ah, well, I have a feeling Ms. Right is just

around the corner," I said.

"Hmph, I wish I knew what corner," Jack snapped back and craned his neck from side to side in an exaggerated fashion as if to look for her.

"The egg salad sandwiches had horseradish in them. That was different." Sefton shrugged as he got to his feet. "See ya later, Junior, I better go take my digestion pills," he said as he winced and rubbed his stomach. "Later gator," he said to me with an unfortunate gassy expression, and I took his place beside Jack.

"Hey, ya know your boyfriend is over there." Jack offered me the binoculars. "In the helicopter."

"A, I don't have a boyfriend and B, what are you talking about?"

"Hagen, he's training for the marine unit. Came by when you were gone yesterday. He'll probably be jumping from that chopper any minute now."

"What? I didn't know that," I said. "Let's see." I took the binoculars and, sure enough, there was a police helicopter doing exercises in the distance. I shook my head. I may live and make my living in a marina, but I wouldn't jump into black water if you paid me.

"So, what's up, kiddo?"

"Well... we have a little... situation."

"Those words never sound good, especially when they come from you." Jack sighed and looked as though egg salad indigestion was creeping up on him as well.

I nodded. I had to agree with him; I really ought to work on my delivery.

"So, what is it?"

"Does Shears have a grandson, that you know of?"

"Grandson? Grandson. Grand. Son," Jack said as if this little exercise would help him remember. "Yeah, I think so. I mean, doesn't everybody? Why?"

I arched an eyebrow at the noncommittal response then nodded in the direction of Aggie's. "Well, some guy showed up after you left. Claims he's Shears' grandson."

"Oh? And?"

"And he says he's been invited to stay on the boat while his *grandpa* is away," I said, adding air quotes although I generally detest it when other people do the same.

"And?"

"And he has no ID, so I figured, since you knew Shears when he was about that age... Look, he could be anybody."

Jack Junior nodded. "Could be," he said, rubbing his chin. "You've been watching those shows again, haven't you?"

I shifted in my chair awkwardly. "Maybe. Just one or two little episodes." I could have added to that response "every day since I was twelve".

"Mmhmm. Where's the boy?"

"I told him to sit tight until you got here. Last I saw him, he was with Ags," I said and pointed in the general direction of her place.

"We'd better hurry." Jack's face morphed into one of mock horror. Aggie's reputation as a cougar was not exactly a secret. He grabbed his blue cotton fishing hat from the hook inside the salon and we made tracks down the dock, with Junior recounting the Shears ancestry to the best of his recollection and me glancing back toward the bay at the helicopter.

❋ ❋ ❋

Just behind Aggie's place and to the right a little is the marina pavilion where Ags had indicated to us that What's-His-Name could be found. It's a nice covered cement pad with a few benches and tables where marina members and visitors can spread out or, in this case, where homeless imposter types can curl up. When our footsteps didn't rouse the man, Jack Junior cleared his throat in that belaboured theatrical fashion perfected by older men everywhere. It worked, and the subject righted himself, ran a hand through his tousled hair, and rubbed his eyes.

"So, uh, you're Russ Shears, are you?" Jack asked and extended a handshake to Sleeping Beauty.

"That's right, sir," he said through a yawn,

shaking Jack's hand.

"Jack Ross, friend of Bob's," Jack said by way of introduction.

"Nice to meet you, sir."

Jack turned to catch my eyes and sent me a smile, as if politeness was an indicator of credibility, and I wondered for a moment why it is that men don't dread the ma'am treatment like women. Sir seems practically reverential in comparison. Junior paced a few steps, nodded, and then began to rub the back of his neck. His contemplative pose. As inextricably tied to his pondering as that of Rodin's *The Thinker*. Maybe he was trying to remember what Shears looked like before acquiring the coke bottle glasses that so dominate his present-day appearance. He looked at the kid. "Well, you kinda look like Bob did at your age. What are you, twenty-two, twenty-three?"

"Twenty-five, sir."

"No ID, huh?" Jack winced.

"No, sir, I must have lost it between dinner last night and this morning."

"How'd you get here?" Jack plodded on.

"Rental car. Took it back a couple hours ago."

"I see. So, your parents... You must be–"

"I'm Randy's son, sir."

"From?"

"Ohio, sir."

Jack Junior looked at me with urging eyes and I sensed he'd run out of questions already. "Well, my friend here, she doesn't trust you, so to keep her off my back, do you mind if I give 'em a call, you know..."

I raised my eyebrows at Jack, surprised at the ease with which he made me out to be the bad guy.

"Russ Shears" let out a little laugh and looked at me. "Oh, sure. Go ahead and call them, sir."

Junior shot me a smarmy smile. "Ok, what's the number, son?" he asked and pulled out his cell phone from the holster on his hip. A fashion tip he'd acquired from Bugsy.

"The number, sir?"

"Yeah, just give me the number. Haven't talked to Randy since he was a little jasper..." Jack tapped the screen to open the phone app.

"Five one three..." The man-boy closed his eyes and looked up as if that ever really helps anyone remember anything. He let out a huff and frowned. "See, it's in my phone and my phone's gone too."

Oh, that's convenient. Jack looked at me and I raised both eyebrows. It was my turn to be smug.

"If there's any way you can get in touch with my grandpa, I'm sure he could—"

Junior waved off that suggestion. "He's on a plane by now and it's a long flight. Besides, if I know Bob Shears—and I do—he's too cheap to spring for wi-fi on the plane. Sorry, son." Jack began to pace again.

"Well, did you two solve this one yet?" I heard

a loud baritone say above crunching footsteps behind me.

When I turned, I saw Bugsy. Blue-jeaned, blue-shirted, tanned, dimpled Bugsy, his dirty blond hair askew, a clipboard in his hand. It's times like these he can appear haltingly handsome, and I suddenly found myself where Aggie was not long ago in mono-syllabic town.

"Solve?" I asked.

"Yeah, Aggie told me. How are ya, Jack?"

"Good, good, just-just you know..." he said and nodded in the direction of the mystery man.

Bugsy looked at the kid. "So, no ID, huh?"

The kid shook his head. "No phone either."

Bugsy smirked at me, knowing I'd be in my element. He knows if there's one Elvis song to sum me up, it's got to be "Suspicious Minds". "How about your social media? You have Face-book? Instagram?"

"Oh yeah, sure, Facebook!" The kids eyes lit up.

Bugsy tucked his clipboard under his arm, did a quick draw to retrieve his phone, and tapped on the ubiquitous social media app icon as I sidled up to him on one side, and Jack Junior flanked him on the other. A few taps later, there it was. A social media profile for Russ Shears. Intrigued and incredulous, I let my fingers do the walking on the screen of Bugsy's phone and helped myself to some scrolling. Russ Shears kept his posts to a minimum, and his profile picture was the logo for the Ohio University Bob-cats.

Bugsy cleared his throat in an annoyed fashion and, when I looked up to meet his eyes, he gave me that look I knew well, the one I considered *faux* consternation. "Hmph," I said, recalling the University of Ohio shirts I'd seen "Russ" lay out on the ground earlier. I scrolled some more.

"Are your fingers clean?" Bugsy asked.

"Are they ever?" I guffawed and continued. Russ Shears followed various pages, including a few bands I'd never heard of, the Cleveland Browns, and a Red Sox fan page. He also listed over four hundred friends including one Robert Shears. I double clicked on that picture to make sure it was the same Robert Shears we knew. Tall, tanned, bushy white hair, coke bottle glasses. That was him alright. As I reviewed his profile, I noticed that the option to message Robert Shears was greyed out with a comment beside it. "Invite Robert Shears to download Messenger."

"Hmmm," I let out involuntarily.

"Well, there ya go, kiddo!" Jack Junior looked up from Bugsy's phone with relief. His smiling Irish eyes met my less-than-jubilant pensive gaze. Something still didn't sit right.

"So, it's ok? I can stay on my gramps' boat?" Russ looked at us hopefully and pushed himself to his feet.

"Sure, son. I'll take you there myself." Junior

slapped the kid on the back.

Bugsy re-holstered his weapon and untucked the clipboard from under his arm. "Well, now that that's settled, I've got to get going," he said and looked at his watch.

"Big afternoon?" I asked.

"Actually, I'm off to find the *Gee Spot*."

CHAPTER 3

"The-the-the-the what now?" Jack Junior gripped Bugsy by the forearm. He wasn't getting away without explaining this little nugget.

"You're what?" I hardly recognized the sound of my own shriek.

Bugsy blushed a little then smiled. His dimples punctuated his grin like quotation marks.

"The *Gee Spot*." He looked from one of our faces to the next, lingering in the suspense. "It's a boat, supposed to be showing up today in short-term dockage. Should be here by now."

I rolled my eyes and let out a sigh that was slightly aggravated, slightly relieved. Despite the fact I wasn't completely sold on how I felt about Bugsy, I didn't cotton to him discussing female anatomy and his pursuit of it.

"Oh, I think I might have seen them on their way in the bay. Couldn't make out the name.

About a fifty-footer," Junior said, nodding.

"Probably them." Bugsy looked down at the paper on his clipboard. "You, uh, want to come with me, roll out the welcome wagon?" he asked in my direction.

"First of all, that's not an expression, and second of all, why not," I replied, my curiosity piqued. I had to get a look at these people. See, since my relocation to the Marysville Marina and my latest occupation of selling boats, it'd become quite apparent to me that some folks use boat ownership as a way to advertise their creativity. Take, for instance, people like my friend Nat who name their floating refuge in homage to one of their favorite movies. The *Splendored Thing* was named for the 1955 romantic classic *Love is a Many Splendored Thing* starring the hunky William Holden. Some folks opt for a play on words, like the boat I'd sold that summer to Doctor Stephen Richards—the *Just Aboat Perfect*—and then there are the attention grabbers who name their boats things like the *Gee Spot*. It makes me wonder what, if it were socially acceptable, they would name their kids.

"I'll... I'll come too," Jack Junior said, bounding to catch up with us. "You don't mind if we make a pit stop first, do ya son?"

"No, sir," came the predictably polite response from his sidekick, and we all made our way toward short-term dockage. And no, it had not escaped me that we were going looking for the *Gee Spot* in the zone identified on the marina map as STD.

Now, just as a point of reference for you, the Marysville Marina is divided roughly into long-term or permanent dockage—comprised of year-round riff raff like yours truly and the weekender set—and short-term dockage where coastal cruisers find our little community a nice port of call on their way to places like Ensenada. As we approached STD, I could see its latest arrival, a fifty- foot trawler with European lines. Probably Dutch. She had a dark blue hull, black bottom, white superstructure with gold striping, and written in big letters that were made to look windswept, *Gee Spot*. An older woman clamored out of the cabin as we got closer.

"Well, hi there, cousins!" came a twangy greeting I was not expecting and, based on the look he gave me, neither was Bugsy.

"Hi," I was the first to say, and my greeting was followed by a chorus of similar sounds by my posse.

The seventyish-looking woman on deck was about five foot nothing with silver-blonde hair in a short trendy cut. She sported tan Sperry top siders, a long-sleeved white t-shirt, red Bermuda shorts, a navy neckerchief, and big gold hoop earrings. Her tanned skin looked as though it'd seen ten thousand sunsets, but there didn't look to be any shame in her game, and I just hope that when I reach her age I am as sporty and as adventurous even if it's only with my hairstyle. I spied a bottle of Corona in the cup holder of a deck chair. Maybe it was five o'clock where she'd been most recently.

Bugsy looked at his paperwork. "You must be–"

"Gladys," she said, bounding to the dock with more energy than someone half her age. She extended her hand out to each of us with a firm yank up and down. "Hey, Ginny, Geraldine, get your keesters out here, we got company!" she bellowed over her shoulder toward the boat.

I smiled and nodded. *Gladys, Ginny, and Geraldine. Got it, the Gee Spot.*

"This–this is *your* boat?" Jack Junior asked, his voice trickling upward.

"Sure is. Well, one third," she twanged and turned to look back at the boat to see her compatriots exit to the stern deck on their way to joining us on the dock.

"Bill Beedle, I'm the manager, and this is–"

"Why, I bet they call you Bugsy, don't they?" the twangster insisted.

"Most people don't." Bugsy cleared his throat. "This is Alex Michaels and Jack Ross Junior and uh... Russ Shears," he said, indicating toward each of us in turn.

"Oh, y'all work here too?" the twangster went on.

"No," I piped up. "We live here. We volunteer as tour guides though, if you want to see the highlights." I smiled and nudged Jack Junior who seemed a little stunned.

"You mean there's more highlights than seein' this tall drinka water?" she said with a playful grin, looking Bugsy up and down.

"Plenty," I mumbled with a smile as I observed the two women from the boat who were now on either side of Gladys.

"Ginny, Geraldine, this here's Russ, Alex, Jack, and Bugsy," Gladys gestured to all involved.

"Um... oh, never mind," Bugsy interjected then sighed. There was no use in protesting; once a Bugsy always a Bugsy.

The Ginny and Geraldine who rounded out the Gees of the *Gee Spot* couldn't have been more dissimilar, and I wondered how three such incongruous women had managed to get together and *stay* together. While it was obvious Gladys was southern, Ginny was clearly of northern descent. Her *Baston* accent gave her away when she said hello, and I couldn't tell from Geraldine's greeting from whence she hailed. She simply murmured quietly and nodded.

Not only were their greetings completely unique from one another, the ladies looked nothing alike. Ginny, the northerner, a very thin woman, wore a black and white gigantic sun hat. Peeking out from under it was a tight blonde chignon. She wore black capris, a white cotton sweater, crisp white sneakers, and her most defining accessory may have been the Jacki

O sunglasses she put back into position after making her greetings. Her skin was pale and porcelain-like. She reminded me of an older Grace Kelly, and I pegged her somewhere in her sixties or even late fifties–but definitely younger than her years based on how conscientious she seemed to be with her sun protection.

Geraldine, by comparison, looked like the quintessential flower child. She was less angular than her friends, a nice way of saying she was a little plumper, and her long grey curly hair hung down like Spanish moss halfway down the layers of blouses and necklaces she wore which topped a flowery, flowy peasant skirt. From the hem of her skirt to her ankles, you could make out shrubs of thick silvery hair on her legs which ended at her strappy leather gladiator sandals. She was somewhere between the vintage of Gladys and Ginny but I'd bet she'd lived more lives than both of them combined, and the liver and sun spots on her forearms and hands looked almost artistic.

"Are you ladies staying long?" I asked.

"Oh, round about 'til Thanksgiving or the day after. I 'spect you have some papers for me to sign, handsome?" Gladys directed toward Bugsy. Obviously.

"Yes, I do," Bugsy said toward his clipboard. I smiled when I observed the hint of red on his cheeks.

"Well, come on aboard." Gladys beckoned

with her hand. "Time's a wastin'. Say, you want a drink?" she asked as she drifted toward the gangway.

"No, it's uh, a little early for me and I'm working," Bugsy replied.

Gladys turned toward the rest of us before setting foot on the stern deck, Ginny and Geraldine in tow. "How 'bout y'all?"

"No, I can't, I've got some work to do, but I'll stop over later," I said. "If you're looking for the fifty-cent tour guide, though, I live on my tug over there." I pointed in the general direction. "The *Alex M.*, can't miss it," I said and smiled.

"Yeah, yeah, yeah, I've got to go too, right, son?" Jack said toward Russ, already pulling him away.

"Yes, sir."

"Alright, we'll see y'all later then," Gladys said. "Well, come on now." She took Bugsy by the elbow and, when I last saw him, he was looking back at me with a touch of fear in his eyes.

❅ ❅ ❅

Two hours and what felt like innumerable crazy phone calls later, I needed a break. My last phone call came from a regular. I won't refer to him as a customer because, frankly, I never expect for him to buy anything I have listed. This time he'd called under the guise of asking about a new workboat I'd featured on the website, though eventually the conversation turned to the topic of his latest conspiracy theory. One time he even told me we were all living in a simulation. I remember that day in particular, because it was the day before I got my new keyboard—his ramblings had caused me to spew out my green tea across the number pad of the old one. With crazy on the mind, I decided to go over and, to quote Bugsy, roll out the welcome wagon.

I took the steep set of steps down to the galley, plucked a bottle of white from the rack, tied a bow on it with some sisal string I keep in the junk drawer—it's right beside the scotch tape, rubber bands, thumbtacks, and old fridge magnets. "You're in charge, Georgie." I patted my black cat on the head, and he gave me the stink eye before I ventured out the stern door.

On my way down the dock, I did a quick check of *The Splendored Thing*. Nat's pride and joy, where we watched old movies on Saturday nights and discussed everything from philosophy to knot tying, and I don't mean the subject of marriage. Since his "departure" from the marina in June, I'd been appointed caretaker of the vessel thanks to his lawyer, Cary Tranmer. Truth be known, the boat would one day be willed to me, along with his vintage truck and a horrendous amount of equities and, once things were made final with the estate, I'd decide what to do with all that. In the meantime, I'd moved her from Nat's former slip to a spot close to me so I could keep an eye on things. Oh, don't get me wrong, it's not like the Marysville Marina is rampant with crime. The last remotely felonious event that took place was, I believe, the stuffing of the ballot box at the judging table of the July Fourth show-and-shine for boats.

As I made my way toward short-term dockage, I noticed Bugsy, chatting with Jack Junior on the *Fortune Cookie*. "What's the matter, you hiding from the Gee Spotters?" I chided him as I neared the boat.

"Hardly," he said flatly and got to his feet. "Thanks, Jack. See ya, Michaels," he said, stepping onto the dock and heading in the direction of Aggie's.

"See ya," I replied faintly. It wasn't like Bugsy to take off so abruptly after seeing me; usually he waits for me to say something stupid or insulting first. I stepped onto Jack's boat. "What's up with him?"

"Hmmm? Oh, he was just here to talk about something."

"What kind of something?"

"Guy stuff." Jack's eyes flickered at me as though I wouldn't understand.

"What kind of guy stuff? You guys get together and talk over strategies of how to do a one cheek sneak or discuss the best urinals in town?"

He smiled. "No, nothing like that."

"Let me guess, you were spying on the Gee Spots," I said, my eyes landing on the binoculars nearby.

"I was not *spying*. I-I-I was just looking around. You know, you never can be too careful. Why-why we don't have a neighborhood watch program here, you know. We get some shady types coming here and—"

"Jack, I think we're safe." I squinted to look in the direction of the visiting boat. While I doubted the ladies were up to no good, they were up to something. "What are they doing? Let me see your binocs," I said and beckoned them forth with my hand.

"Oh, some pagan dance ritual, I think," he grumbled.

Yeah, that was likely. I put the glasses up to my eyes. "Mmhmm, no pagan dances, sorry. Looks more like Tai Chi. Hey, why don't you go join them?" I moved my arms to shift my magnified gaze. "Hey! Is that... Is that Sefton over there?"

"Yeah, that's him." Jack shook his head disgustedly.

"Jack, the Lord hates a coward. Just go!"

He shook his head again. "Nah, if they wanted my company, they'd ask. Besides, they're not my type and they're only here for a couple weeks."

"Well, I'm heading there now," I said, handing back the binoculars and hoisting the bottle of wine I'd carried. "I hope they like white. You sure you don't want to come with?"

"No thanks, kiddo. I think I'm just going to sit here. I've-I've-I've got to finish this book and—"

"Ok, but if you change your mind, that's where I'll be. May take them uptown, you know, check out the bakery, the ice cream place, Harbor Pizza. You know, the landmarks," I said, realizing that the landmarks for me seemed to revolve around food rather than cultural sites like the Marysville Museum—which by the way contains a heck of an exhibit on barbed wire. Or so I'm told.

"No. Thanks. You go have fun," he said, offered a weak smile and opened his book to the piece of paper he'd used as a bookmark. No *kiddo*, no *sweetie*, no *dear*. That wasn't like him, and I walked down the dock wondering what was eating at Jack.

* * *

I can't tell you exactly what happened when I went to the *Gee Spot*. The next morning, it all seemed like a bit of a blur. After Sefton and I took the ladies on a tour of Marysville, they took us on a tour of Jamaica via rum, Russia via vodka, and Ireland via some whiskey sour drink they whipped up onboard. One thing I do recall is the nature of the common bond that unites the women. They were all three, at different times, married to the same man. And each invested part of their divorce settlement into the boat that would become their floating home, steadfast in the notion that they'd never see their ex-hubby again since he'd never had any luck finding the g-spot in the past. Sefton had walked me back to my boat that night, and I was surprised to see him looking so sprightly the next morning when I ambled into Aggie's.

Ags tipped a coffee mug upside down, placed it in front of me, and filled it to the absolute brim. I guess she could tell I needed it. Smelled fresh. A fritter or possibly two would have gone nicely with it, but I didn't see any in the baked goods case. "No fritters today?" I asked woefully.

"Not yet, bakery must be running behind," Ags said and looked up at the clock that's set into a brass port light.

"Hmph."

"Want an omelette?"

"Mmm no. I have a bit of a stomach thing today," I said and took a sip of coffee. I'm not sure what she puts in it, but it started acting on contact with my throbbing head and rotting gut. Dejected from the culinary disappointment, I swiveled, slowly mind you, on my stool to face the gang in the club chairs. Peter Muncie was handing a cell phone back to Jack Junior.

"Not bad," he said.

"What are we looking at, guys?" I asked.

"Now, now, now, it's nothing," Jack said, and his cheeks went a little flushed. Intrigued, I took my coffee toward the nook.

"Junior and Lisa, sittin' in a tree," Sefton teased his buddy, lyrically, and I wondered what made him so impervious to the side effects from our bender the night before.

"Oh, that's real mature," Jack griped.

"Ok, tell," I said, plunking my derriere on the arm of Peter Muncie's club chair. "Who's Lisa?"

All eyes turned toward Jack Junior, and he blushed a little more. Even his ears got red. It was cute.

He swiped at the air dismissively. "Oh, it's no big deal."

"Jack's got a cougar after him," Seacroft said.

Jack Junior shook his head.

"How many times do I have to tell ya, a cougar is when the lady is older than the man. This babe's younger," Muncie moaned.

"Which babe?" I asked, looking up at the clock, still hankering for that fritter and wondering when the bakery truck would roll in.

"It's-it's-it's nothing," Jack said. "Will you guys–"

"Jack, I know you're dying to tell me, so out with it. Who's Lisa and why's she after you? You hit her car or something?" I asked before taking a sip of java.

"No, *I did not hit her car or something,*" he said, mocking my tone and making a childish facial gesture. "Just so happens she has a yen for me."

"A yen?" I asked.

"Isn't that Japanese currency?" Peter Muncie squinted.

"Will you shut up!" Jack groused. "Look, kiddo, Lisa is a woman who contacted me on, you know, on the Facebook."

"Oh. Right. On *the* Facebook." I nodded. "And what'd this Lisa person say?"

"She asked if I remembered meeting her at the Rotary gala a couple years back in Hamilton. Just so happens she was at the funeral yesterday and it jogged her memory."

"And did you? Remember her?"

"No, she must have mistaken me for some other devilishly handsome blue-eyed Adonis."

Peter Muncie guffawed. "Yeah, that's it."

Jack noticed me wincing.

"What? It happens," he said.

"Ok, so assuming all that's true, what of it?" I asked.

"Well, so far, we've exchanged a few messages."

"Any pics of her, uh, you know..." Sefton began to say and gesture with his hands what he was thinking. I'm so glad he stopped.

"No!" Jack Junior let out a huff.

"Mmhmm. Hey, did you ever hear back from Shears? About whether that kid is his grandson?" I asked.

"Shhh!" Ags hissed from the kitchen. "He's cleaning out the storeroom in the back."

"Whatever." I shook my head at her. I was still

a little wary of the man who drifted into town without two cents to his name, looking for a place to stay.

Jack smirked. "Not yet, you know how Bob is, just upgraded from that flip phone last year. He's a little slow on the uptake," said the man who referred to *the* Facebook.

"Well, let me know, will ya? I've got five bucks riding on it," I said and winked at Sefton with whom I'd made the little side bet the night before.

"Mmhmm. Say, why are you so suspicious anyway, kid?" Jack asked.

"Me?"

"Yeah."

"I prefer to think of it as being careful."

"Oh, puh-lease," I heard Aggie say from the direction of the kitchen.

"What?" I pretended to be offended. I can't help it if I was born with a curious streak, though I'm the first to admit the proliferation of mystery and murder shows I binge watch on rainy days doesn't help my condition. "What's the time difference in Rome anyway?" I asked.

"Nine hours ahead," Peter Muncie piped up. In Shears' absence, he'd apparently assumed the role of resident encyclopedia.

"Oh, geez, speaking of time." Jack jumped up from his chair.

"Oh yeah, you have to get ready." Peter tapped the crystal on his watch.

"Ready for what?" I asked, looking down at Peter. "Ready for what?" I asked again.

"He's got a date," Peter said.

"Already?" My voice went up. Not that I was necessarily surprised that Jack would have a date; he is awfully cute and could pass for a man years younger, but I was a little surprised that things moved that fast. I suppose, though, in the age of texting and dating apps, combined with the fact that you've got less time on the planet, things tend to move exponentially faster. Then again, I also didn't want Jack to act out of desperation or sheer loneliness.

I cleared my throat and my voice slid down to the octave I'm used to. "You mean you have a date with this Facebook floozie?" I kidded. Sort of.

"My dear, you are sweet and wonderful and I love you for it, but that doesn't exactly keep my toes warm at night."

"Or the other parts of you either," Sefton chimed in.

"Or the other parts of me," Jack nodded. Vigorously.

"Ok, where are you going to meet her?" I asked.

"The Grind."

"The coffee shop? Jack, you've had enough caffeine already to run a marathon backwards," I said, knowing Jack's caffeine habit.

"Make you a deal, kiddo—you let me go on my

date and I promise I'll have decaf."

"Ok, but I want you home before the street-lights come on, young man." I smirked and watched as Jack slapped on his fishing hat and adjusted it to a jaunty tilt. "If you fine folks will excuse me. De-dee-de-dum-de-dum-dum-dum," he belted out what I believe is the only "song" he knows while he danced his coffee cup to the counter.

I was so engrossed watching him that I hadn't noticed the police cruiser that pulled up out front. When I looked toward the ringing bell at the door, there he was. In his uniform. Officer Ben Hagen, or Officer Handsome, as Ags refers to him. All six foot two of him, his jet-black hair parted sharply, the light shining on it like the moon on the water at night. Hagen had been a fixture in my life that summer when Nat went missing and certain people, who shall remain technically nameless (i.e. Bugsy), had tried to point the finger at me for being involved in said disappearance and, when it turned out that the only involvement I had was being named as Nat's primary beneficiary, Bugsy ate crow and Hagen served it up. With a square jaw, green eyes, and perfect bright white teeth, Hagen could charm the stars out of the sky if he'd a mind to, but he seemed to like hanging around the marina from time to time and credited Aggie's superior blend of coffee for his regular visits. *Right.*

"Oh, hi," I said and felt a few butterflies inside

my queasy stomach; they were probably flopping around in there, drunk on rum. My hand instinctively went to my hair and I did a quick check of what I was wearing. Most times I run into Hagen, I'm usually sporting some mysterious stain or paint splotch from doing maintenance around the boat or helping Ags around her store. On this particular occasion, my fashion faux pas was how the tinge of green in my complexion courtesy of a teensy little hangover clashed with the yellow of my sweatshirt.

"Good morning." He smiled, nodded, and made his way toward the chrome and red vinyl stools at the counter.

"How about a cup?" Ags asked, her hand already on the carafe, poised for a pour.

"Thanks, been a heck of a morning," he said.

I sauntered over to where he was. "Oh, got any dirt you can share?"

Hagen took a big sip. "Guess you'll find out soon enough. The bakery on State was robbed last night."

CHAPTER 4

"**W**as anyone hurt? Did they get them on camera? Much damage done? What about the fritters?" My questions came rapid fire while Hagen, bleary-eyed, took another sip.

He held up his index finger as he swallowed. "No, I don't know, I don't think so, and they're coming." He smiled.

"Geez." I plunked myself down on the stool beside him. The sound of the air whooshing out from under my behind made me a little embarrassed, and in mixed company I always feel the need to look down at the seat as if to blame it for what sounds like a very rude noise.

"So, what did they get? Cash?" Ags asked.

"Actually, they took the whole safe and, the way Ash described it, it sounded like a big one," Hagen said and looked around Aggie's, I'm assuming for its vulnerabilities.

"Who knew there was so much dough in the bakery business," Jack Junior quipped as he approached the counter, paused beside me, and handed Ags his empty cup.

"Jack, not funny," I groaned.

"I know. Sorry, kiddo." He smiled and didn't look sorry whatsoever, though I was happy to see "smilin' Jack" was back.

My eyes flicked from Jack to Hagen. "He's just giddy because he's got the prospect of getting laid."

"What is it, as often as Halley's comet comes along, Junior?" Muncie bellowed from the TV nook.

Ignoring the comment, Jack practically skipped toward the door. "See ya, suckers," he said and saluted his gang on his way out.

After Jack Junior's bouncy exit, Hagen was subjected to interrogation by the rest of the fellas. And, in his typically good-natured fashion, he apologized for his inability to offer much in the way of details. For my benefit, he offered to deliver some fresh fritters once things were back to normal at the bakery later that morning.

"You have an alarm system here, right?" he asked Ags when she topped him up.

"Absolutely," she said, smiling and raising her eyebrows at me. I remember she dated the guy who worked for the alarm company and, when they split up, he tried to remove the system but didn't get very far with that notion.

I turned to him. "Hey, you haven't met Russ Shears yet," I said, and when I looked up, Ags was suddenly glowering at me.

"Who?"

"Russ Shears. You know Shears, the older guy with the boat here?"

"Yeah. Thick glasses, right?"

"Yes. Anyway, his grandson," I said, for the sake of telling the story though I still didn't quite believe it.

"No, I *haven't* met him." Hagen responded in a way that told me he knew there had to be something to my wanting him to meet Russ.

"Ags, is uh, Russ still here? Couldn't hurt for him to meet the local constabulary." I smiled at her.

Ags flitted her eyes. "Lemme get him." She shot me a crooked smile and disappeared into the back.

"So, who's this guy?" Hagen leaned toward me and asked lowly.

"Some guy who drifted into town with no ID looking for a place to stay. Check his fingers for powdered sugar and cinnamon," I whispered.

"No ID?"

"Zippo, zero, zilch, nada, bupkis." I continued whispering so Hagen would continue leaning in.

Ags reappeared. "He must be running an errand," she said and shrugged.

I raised my eyebrows. He was running alright, from something. I just knew it.

Hagen looked down at the blue face of the shiny silver diving watch on his tanned wrist and made a disappointed expression. "Damn, I've got to run."

"I'll walk out with you," I said and echoed Jack's salute to the gang on my way to the door. With his hat in his hand, Hagen and I slowly made our way to his cruiser where I finally had the opportunity to broach the subject of Hagen's sanity, at least indirectly. "Hey, I didn't know you were going to be training for the marine unit. When did you decide on that?"

"Oh, I'd been considering it for a while now. Someone I know got me into this boat thing." He winked at me. "Plus, there's an opening in the unit, thought I'd take the plunge."

* * *

I walked back down the dock, head getting clearer and ready to tackle the easier emails I'd spotted that morning. I did a mental recap as I felt the sun warm on my face. Jessica King was looking for a liveaboard in New York, and Eddie Richards wanted me to list a couple of propellers and... *What is that smell*? My olfactory senses were immediately and without warning brutally assaulted, and my eyes began to water. Mixed with my SPF moisturizer, the stinging nearly blinded me, and mixed with the alcohol in my stomach, the odor was putting me on the door step of hurling. I looked around for the offending source; it wasn't the dead fish smell that sometimes rose up from the channel. It was more of a putrid sharpness that intensified the closer I got to the *Fortune Cookie*. A cross between a tannery, a dead skunk, and the cosmetics counter of the department store.

"Hey, kiddo!"

I turned and pinched my nose to keep from suffering permanent nerve damage. There was Jack Junior walking toward me in a cloud of smells, reminding me of the old Pepe Le Pew cartoon with the greenish yellow haze trailing behind him.

"Jack, is that you?" I asked, waving my hand, blinking through stinging eyes, and trying not to choke or toss my cookies.

"What?" Jack asked as he sniffed the air, and I swear I saw his own lip curl. "Uh, yeah, I wanted to get your opinion."

"On what?" I asked nasally.

"On, uh, which cologne you like best."

"Did you bathe in them?"

Jack winced. "Too much?"

"Not if you're trying to cover up the smell of a dead body... You're not, are you?"

Jack waved his hand toward me, dismissing the notion. "Nah. Not today. I just uh, you know, wanted to pick a nice cologne for my date with Lisa. Could you sniff my spritzes?"

"I'll try," I coughed. "Where'd you spritz?"

Jack pulled a slip of paper out of one of the pockets of his cargo pants. This turned out to be the legend. "Ok, right neck, Black Leather," he read.

I flitted my eyes at the name and got as close as I could to Jack's neck, weathered with age and tanned like a vintage purse. His grey hair still had the sharp line from a fresh haircut. "Kind of musky," I said and wiped a tear out of my eye.

"Good musky or bad musky?" he asked hopefully.

"There is no *good* musky."

"Ok. That one's out." With a little pencil it looked like he'd nabbed from the mini-putt place uptown, he put a strike through the first item on the list.

"Let's see here, uh, left neck... Savage."

"Savage?" With trepidation, I put my nose on the left side of Jack's neck and immediately recoiled at the spicy scent. "No, just no. I don't even think that's a cologne."

Jack arched an eyebrow at me and put a swift strike through Savage. "Moving right along," he said, a little frustration in his voice. "Left wrist, Sucre by Pierre," he said and held his wrist up to my nose.

"No," I shook my head. "Too sweet. Makes you smell like a cupcake." I pulled Jack's right wrist up to my sniffer, assuming this'd be my next option. "I like this one, it's perfect. Subtle and clean."

"Clean, huh?"

"Yeah, clean."

"Well, it ought to be, it's Irish Spring." Jack crumpled up the list in his hand and shoved it into one of his pockets.

"I'd go with that one. Look, Jack, if you have time...or even if you don't, go take a quick shower. You're a catch. You don't need any fancy colognes."

"You think?"

"Of course. You're spunky and sweet, you can speak on any topic, you have an incredible sense of humor. You're kind and–"

"Ok, kiddo, you better stop there or I'll ask *you* out." He smiled and gave me dancing eyes and waggled his eyebrows at me.

"Shower. Date. Then de-brief me. Got it?"

"Got it. Say, how about you? Are you and Hagen or Bugsy ever going to—"

"Jack, will you just go? You don't want to keep her waiting."

"Yes, ma'am!" he said and, while I am generally loath to hear that word, from Jack Junior it didn't sound so bad. Must be all in the delivery.

* * *

The day played out pretty much as normal—emails here and there and a poker game on the agenda for that evening where, rest assured, the gang and I would get the low down on Jack's much anticipated date. See, a couple times a week, Jack Junior, the S-troop, Peter Muncie, and I get together for poker. Sometimes their former navy buddy turned lawyer, Cary Tranmer, comes by to sit in, and Doctor Richards is also a semi-regular. Something Nat Grant had introduced me to—bonding over cards, a drink or two, and what passed for junk food at their age. And so, after walking my dog, tidying my office, and highlighting a few emails to address first thing in the morning, I headed off to Jack's boat with a few vodka coolers and a peach pie I'd thawed and baked.

"Ready to lose your shirts, fellas?" I asked as I boarded the *Fortune Cookie*. Peter Muncie and Sefton were sitting on the stern deck, binoculars angled toward the *Gee Spot*.

"Hmmm?" they asked distractedly and in unison.

"Oh, never mind. Anything good happening over there?"

"I think they're dancing," Peter said.

"Maybe it's some kind of Jazzercise or that twerking thing," Sefton added.

"There's a big difference between those. Let me see," I said, put down the items I was toting, and Peter handed me the glasses.

"Well, what are they doing?" he asked. "Some kind of tribal dancing or what?"

"Nope, yoga," I said and handed him the glasses and headed indoors, where, to my great surprise and consternation, I found already seated at the poker table none other than Russ Shears.

"Hi," he greeted me in a tone as if we were friends.

I forced a smile and nodded and briefly studied the room to make sure none of the expensive stuff was missing.

"Oh, hey, kiddo. Cheeseball? Russ here brought 'em," Jack said as he strutted into the salon with a bowl of round orange puffs of what may pass for food on college campuses.

"No thanks, Jack, I just ate," I said, trying to be polite while I slid the real food I brought onto the sideboard. Jack relieved me of the coolers in my hand and headed toward the galley, trusting me to be temporarily left alone again with Russ.

"How are you?" I asked, relying on the default question of folks everywhere who feign politeness and don't know what else to say.

"Oh, fine. Hey, I hope you don't mind me crashing the poker party. Junior invited me."

I smiled back and wondered when "Junior" would reappear with a drink for me, and I also wondered when Russ and he had managed to get so chummy. "Oh no, it's fine. I just didn't think you had any money. Did you find your wallet?"

"I wish. Aggie gave me an advance on the work I'm doing for her, and I sold my watch uptown at the jewellery store. The battery was dead anyway."

I nodded and hoped Russ would never consider a career in wealth management or financial counselling. Selling a watch for want of a ten-dollar battery seems like folly to me, but then again, I've been hanging on to the same Timex since college. Fiscal responsibility is my specialty.

Jack returned from the galley, handed me my long overdue beverage—which I downed almost immediately and in a most un-ladylike fashion, and he rubbed his hands together anxiously. "Well, I guess we can get started." He went to the stern door and hollered out. "Hey, you guys, stop ogling those chicks and get in here."

Russ' presence aside, I was happy to see Jack back to his old self, with snappy lines and twinkling eyes. I proceeded to take a seat as far away from Russ as possible. ensuring this fact by counting the number of chairs between us, and I watched Sefton, Seacroft, and Muncie file in the salon. A thudding on the deck and a few footsteps later and Doctor Stephen Richards was also on the scene.

"Oh, hi, I didn't know you were back," I said to the good doctor who couldn't be considered a year-rounder, though I think he longed to and one day will be. At something close to fifty, he's still a little young to pack up his practice.

"Here until after Thanksgiving, barring any emergencies," he said, placing his contribution to the eats on the sideboard—guac, and if I knew him, low sodium tortilla chips—then taking the chair on my immediate right. "I don't believe we've met." Richards extended a hand to the new face at the game. "Stephen Richards."

"Russ Shears. Nice to meet you, Steve," said the interloper.

I cleared my throat, hoping to clear away my agitation with the ill-mannered punk. Even I didn't call the man Steve, and he'd seen me at my worst, sick on my bathroom floor. Besides that, he is definitely a Stephen and not a Steve.

"Shears? As in *our* Shears?" Richards' voice went up as he turned to me to verify and, receiving no confirmation—I can't give what I don't have—he searched the other faces at the table.

"Yeah, grandson," Junior piped up, shuffling the cards.

"Oh? I don't remember him mentioning you," Richards said aloud what everyone else had been thinking over the past couple days.

I shifted in my chair and accidentally on purpose kicked him. "Sorry."

Russ Shears shrugged nonchalantly. "Guess he forgot."

I flitted my eyes and Junior dealt the cards. A few hands in, the conversation got rolling but the ride wasn't overly smooth.

"So, what do you do for a living, Steve?" Russ asked.

"I'm a doctor," Richards said, sorting the cards in his hand.

"Oh yeah. Good money in that I bet," Russ lent us the benefit of his insight and I raised my cards up to hide my pained expression. "Got any kids?" he persisted, and I wondered if he was hunting for a new family.

"Two boys," Richards returned.

"Married?" Russ continued.

"Not anymore."

"Amen!" Peter Muncie exclaimed.

And before Russ had the chance to ask Doctor Richards additional personal questions – I'm not sure why I find curiosity in others so darned offensive – I changed the subject. "Speaking of women, how'd your date go today, Junior?" I asked, looking over the tops of my cards across the table at Jack.

"Oh, didn't ya hear? They're going steady," Sefton answered for him.

"Really? Do tell." My voice went up with playful intrigue.

"Now, now, now, let's just see what happens," Jack said, and he blushed all the way to his ears.

"How about you, Peter? You got a number from the funeral, didn't you?" I winked at him and felt a little awkward when Peter didn't answer, scowled at his cards instead.

"Oh, didn't ya hear? It was a dud," Sefton seemed happy to volunteer.

"A dud?" I asked.

"Yeah," Peter grumbled. "The number she gave me was a fake. 867-5309. How was I supposed to know that was a song?"

I sucked in through clenched teeth trying not to laugh. I'd used that one in the past myself; I think I'd even told the poor schmuck that my name was Jenny. "So, you like this Lisa person?"

"She's-she's ok."

"Well, what's she like? Where's she live? Does she have any significantly memorable features?"

"You mean like a tramp stamp?" Seacroft asked.

"No, she means, does she have a rack?" Peter Muncie chimed in.

"I did not mean *any* of those things. What I meant was..." I glanced to my immediate right for inspiration. "What I meant was, does she have nice hands or nice blue eyes or does she smell good?" I asked and, when I looked back at Jack, he was looking back with raised eyebrows and a knowing look.

"Look, if you're good little boys and girls, I'll bring her around. Dealer takes two cards," he said, and laid a couple cards face down on the table. "But I expect you all to behave."

"So, you have another date with her?" I asked.

"Tomorrow." Jack nodded and he tried to act discreet while at the same time beaming like the hottest commodity in town.

"Tomorrow, huh? Well, I happen to be free," I said.

"You're not coming," Jack mumbled.

"Jack, I have no intention of chaperoning your

next date with... What's her name again?"

"Lisa."

"Ok, Jack I have no intention of chaperoning your next date with Lisa. So, where is it going to be?"

"No sitting and spying either."

"Ok, no sitting and spying. Where's the trust, Jack? Geesh. Far be for me to spy on you and your girlfriend."

"She's not... now she's not my girlfriend."

"Maybe just friends with benefits, huh, Jack?" Peter Muncie jabbed at his friend.

"Huh?"

"You know."

"What benefits?" Sefton was intently curious.

"Look, now...the only benefits I'm after fall under her drug and dental plan." Jack played with his cards a bit.

"Benefits. You know, sexy benefits, sexy time," Seacroft said and popped a few peanuts into his yap.

"The horizontal mambo," Peter Muncie added for clarification.

Jack Junior's look of wonder turned to one of concern. Maybe he was doing a mental check of the last time his equipment had been tested for function, or the last time his chassis had been up on the hoist. "All we're having is coffee."

"And maybe a tart?" Sefton cackled.

"You're one to talk. You've been spending an awful lot of time on the *Gee Spot*," Jack Junior griped.

"The what now?" Doctor Richards perked up and turned to me, his go-to gal for filling in the blanks.

I nodded then put my hand on his forearm and glanced into his inquisitive eyes. "It's true. But what you need to know is..." I paused for effect, relishing in the suspense à la Bugsy. "The *Gee Spot* is a boat in short-term dockage." I smiled wide though I still felt a little weird every time I used the name of the boat in mixed company.

"Are we gonna play cards or what?" Jack said.

"Yeah, come on, guys," Russ Shears scolded us for no good reason, other than to ingratiate himself with Junior. It soured the mood instantly and the topics of conversation changed to less personal content and more current events like the fall festival in town and, when we got around to discussing the robbery at the bakery, I took note that Russ Shears excused himself to use the head.

"How about we meet on the *Summerwind* next poker night, Russ?" Doctor Richards asked once the kid was seated again.

My eyes were locked on Russ for a response or reply of some kind. There was none.

"Russ, the doc asked if you want to host the next poker night," Junior said.

"Oh, sorry, I must have zoned out. I've really been putting in the hours," he said.

Liar, liar, pants on fire. I tried not to roll my

eyes.

"Sorry, but this isn't my thing after all, guys. This is fun, but I don't think I'm cut out for it," he explained.

And, like every other statement he'd made over the past two hours, Russ' words provoked in me a tiny involuntary throat clearing. Either a tick or an allergic reaction to total bullshit. Because the guy who claimed he wasn't cut out for poker was up a hundred bucks and, try as I did, I couldn't figure out how he kept consistently winning. And the way he dodged wanting us to play the next game on the *Summerwind* made me suspect there was something on the boat he didn't want us to see. The safe from the bakery perhaps? The evening wrapped up shortly after.

I was in the galley of the *Fortune Cookie*, drying the highball glasses at the end of the evening, when Stephen Richards joined me, a cocktail plate in each hand.

"Too late?" he asked, an impish smile on his face.

"I'll take 'em," I said and ran some water over the plates while Richards leaned against the galley counter and helped himself to a forkful of pie.

"So, you going to Aggie's for Thanksgiving?" I asked while I wiped a plate dry.

"Probably." He nodded and downed another forkful. "Hey," he said, put down the fork, placed his hands on my shoulders, and squared me up to him. The motion took me by surprise. "Open up," he said, though his pretense of seriousness was kyboshed by the smile I saw forming.

"Why?" I asked and, although I was taken off guard, at the same time I didn't altogether mind searching into his crystal blue eyes for an answer.

"Because you're either coming down with a cold or you *really* don't like Russ Shears."

I rolled my eyes and resumed my volunteer dishwashing duties. "Am I that obvious?"

"You're pretty obvious." Richards reached around me and dropped his fork into the sink.

"Well," I began to say in a voice just above a whisper before Jack sauntered into the room.

"All set in here? Say, thanks kiddo, for washing the dishes. Nothing like a woman's touch to spruce things up."

I turned and raised my eyebrows at Richards. Jack's smitten kitten routine was going to take some getting used to. "Anytime, Jack. Well, I'd better be going," I said and placed the tea towel on its hook in the galley. "Night."

"Me too," Richards said. "Night, Jack."

"See ya, kids." Jack walked us to the stern door and waved us off.

A chill had settled in our marina over the past few hours and the moonless night yielded a vista of bright stars. The gentle lapping of the current against the side of the boat was interrupted only by a brief, distant screeching of tires uptown.

"So, what's the deal with Russ Shears?" Richards asked once we were on the dock.

"Do you have a sec?" I motioned in the direction of my boat.

"For you, always."

On the walk toward the *Alex M.*, I explained to Doctor Richards how Russ Shears had arrived on the scene with nothing but the clothes on his back and a few spare outfits in his duffel bag. How he'd won over Jack Junior with some saccharine politeness and Ags with his tight-fitting jeans. How he seemed to skimp on the details of his life while he unabashedly asked personal questions of others, and then there was the disappearing act he pulled when Officer Hagen came in for coffee. "Besides that, he called you *Steve*."

Doctor Richards let out a laugh. "Well, that *is* my name."

"You're more of a Stephen and you know it," I groused and looked out at the dark night beyond my dock. It was the kind of night where you couldn't tell where the water ended and the sky began, and it only compounded my frustration. "So, what do you think?"

"I *think* there's more. Keep talking, sunshine," he said.

"Not much more to say."

Richards looked out toward the inky sky. "How about this girlfriend of Jack's?"

"What about her?"

"Well, you don't sound too keen on her and you don't even know her."

"So? What's that have to do with anything?"

"And Sefton and the women on the new boat in short-term?"

"Ok, I'm lost. Where are you going with this, Doctor Richards?"

He let out a huff. "What I'm getting at is that you're not good with change and it takes you a while to warm up to new people. Heck, I still remember the withering look you gave me the first time we met."

"I did? You do?"

"Sure. If it hadn't been for Nat insisting that I look at the boat, I'd have run for the hills." He snickered, trying to lighten the mood.

I nodded. Not in agreement so much as in understanding. There's something quietly authoritative about the doctor that keeps me in line, if only for a moment, and in the absence of the indignant reply I would have given anyone else, the only sound was the creaking of the ropes on the *Alex M.* "Goodnight, Doctor Richards," I said and stepped onto my boat.

CHAPTER 5

The next morning, after five crazy emails, three absurd phone calls, and getting the crap scared out of me by a spider the approximate size of a shoe, I was ready for some Aggie time. My last words with Stephen Richards had left me needing to chat with by bestie. And, as I left my boat and bopped down the dock, I looked in the direction of the *Just Aboat Perfect*, the boat I'd sold to Richards that summer, the 44' DeFever Aft Cabin Trawler/luxury floating home. The boat I never would have expected to sell to the man I never would have expected to endear himself to me. Our first meeting left me nonplused. While he cut a nice figure tall and broad, the hybrid sportscar and country club get-up he wore did nothing for me. It wasn't until I saw him in faded jeans and a t-shirt and rolling up in a dual diesel pickup that he got my attention, and I was reasonably happy to see the more down-to-earth version of him.

As I crossed the threshold into Aggie's, craving my usual, I called out to her. "Morning, chickee-poo!" The bell above the door that announced my arrival even sounded more cheery than usual.

"Morning," came a voice from somewhere in the back of the store.

Before I knew it, the owner of the voice was stationed behind the counter. Only thing was, the face wasn't that of the smack-talking, ride-or-die gal pal I'd come to love over the past two years. It was Russ Shears, or whatever his name was, decked out in one of the navy-blue hoodies Pike gave out. The logo of his shop on the back, his dog in a sou'wester in yellow and white.

"Oh, hi," I said, walking in a little farther at a tentative gait. "Is Ags here?"

"Oh, no, she went out."

"Oh."

"You want some coffee? She made it just before she left."

"Sure," I said and made my way toward the red stool that all but had my name on it. As I eyed Russ behind the counter, I replayed Doctor Richards' words in my head. Did I just distrust people? Was I so longing to hang onto the status quo that I excluded anything and anyone that might change it? Was my intuition about Russ Shears really that off? He looked like a normal human being. Was he *really* that bad?

I eased onto my stool and, when Russ placed

a full mug of coffee in front of me, some of the contents slopped over the side. A streak of brown ran down my ironstone mug and onto the counter. "Thanks," I said, forcing a smile. *Ok, so he's not big on presentation.* Then I watched as he slid open the door to the baked goods case. I felt my smile change from bogus to bona fide and assumed that Ags had coached the lad on how to win me over, fritter-style. I pulled off a few napkins from the chrome dispenser—Russ didn't seem the type to mess with the formalities of a plate—and when I looked back at him, my hand ready to receive my usual, there stood Russ Shears with shards of cinnamon sugar in the corners of his mouth and a half eaten fritter in his hand. The last one in the case. My theory about him was gaining ground again.

I cleared my throat and hit the reset button. "You, uh, takin' a break from all that hard work?" I asked, glancing up to see my half-masticated fritter bouncing its way around Russ' mouth.

"Something like that."

I took a sip of the too-hot coffee and tried not to show that it burned. My tongue felt for the scald on the roof of my mouth. We two were quiet for a moment, save for the sounds of Russ licking the sugar from *my* fritter off his fingers. "And what is it you do, *Russ*?"

"You mean, like, for work?" He wiped his fingers on a raft of napkins he pulled from the dispenser.

"Yeah. Work or *like* work. What's your occupation?"

"I'm, like, just trying to find myself right now."

I nodded. I was at half-smile by this time. At twenty-five, Russ was old enough to have found himself, and I considered the merits of giving him one of the old map books from Nat's truck if that'd speed up the process and get him on his way. "What courses did you take at the University of Ohio?" I asked as though I had any interest in being his career counsellor.

"Oh, you know, math... geography."

I fixed my gaze on the counter to keep him from seeing my rolling eyes, wondering if he truly grasped the irony of the bozo with the geography background trying to find himself.

"What time'd you say Aggie'd be back?" I glanced up at him to ask.

"I didn't," he said coolly, the words delivered in a flattened voice that made me wonder if he'd chopped her up and put her in the deep freeze. There was a buzzing noise and Russ pulled a cell phone from his rear pocket, looked at the screen, made no facial expression whatsoever, and returned it to his backside.

"Oh, I see you found your phone," I said, taking a sip.

Russ shook his head. "It's a new phone," he said flatly, turned his back on me and went to the refrigerator to suss out some breakfast I presume.

The air between us was quiet. The only sounds in the room came from the cooler units in the corner of the store, Russ rummaging in the fridge, and the sound I made when I sipped my coffee. You know how it goes when you try to keep that quiet and it ends up sounding like you're slurping ramen. "Thanks for the coffee. Tell Ags to call me when she has a chance, please," I said in Russ' general direction, my cup still half full, my suspicions topped up, wondering where Russ got the funds for the new phone.

It was a couple days before I went back to Aggie's. I had texted her, you know, just to make sure she wasn't in fact in the deep freeze, and she reminded me that she was helping her cousin move apartments a couple hours away. Her part-timer Bailey would work a couple of shifts—which I interpreted to mean that Bailey would be checking in on Russ. Ags was sheepish about asking me if I'd also keep an eye on him and her place and she said she'd be back as soon as possible. So, while I avoided my usual coffee and (sometimes) fritter routine, I did take note on my daily walk or jog that Aggie's place was still standing. On the third day of dodging my hangout, Jack Junior approached me just on my way to walk Pepper around town; he was on his way out of Aggie's place looking caffeinated.

"Hey, kiddo."

"Hi, Jack."

"How, uh, how come you haven't been in

lately for coffee and your fat bomb?"

I shrugged. "Just not in the mood, I guess. Hey, have you heard anything from Shears yet? About whether—"

Jack was already shaking his head. "No. Still don't trust the boy, huh?"

I kicked at the ground, debating which part of my Gemini would surface for this round. Turns out it was the brassy one. "Well, does anyone other than me think it could be more that *just a coincidence* that the bakery was robbed just as this man claiming to be Russ Shears comes to town?"

"Oh, that-that-that's nonsense," Jack groused.

"Is it?" I asked

"Sure, it is. Look, kiddo, I was in Dallas in November '63. That doesn't mean I shot Kennedy, does it?"

"Probably not." I sighed. "See ya, Junior. We have some walking to do," I said, and Pepper and I headed up the hill out of the marina. We were not long into our walk when a young lady named Morgan Kennedy added fuel to the fire that Russ Shears had started.

We were on King Street, an area of Marysville that conveniently has automotive specific establishments clustered together. On one stretch of King you can have your car serviced by Kelly's Auto Master and Collision, and if those repairs were going to take a while you could rent a car at the Enterprise franchise a few doors down. If things really went south with your vehicle, you could even shop for a new one two doors down from there at the GM or Ford dealerships on opposite sides of the street. Pepper was enjoying a good sniff at the base of the tree in front of Enterprise when I saw a familiar face. Morgan Kennedy, the daughter of the local vet, Marcy Kennedy, was taking down some information on a rental car on the lot.

"Hi, Morgan. How's the new job going?" I asked. At seventeen, Morgan, the eldest of the Kennedy kids, had already graduated and was working for a year to save up for college. Her proud mother had given me the scoop during Pepper's last vet appointment.

"Oh, hi there. Hi, Pepper." Morgan bent down to Pepper's eye level. He's a hit with the ladies. "I actually love this job," she looked up at me to say. "Everybody's got a story when they come in. Some reason they need to rent a car. It's interesting."

I smirked. I'd never imagined the car rental business to be so stimulating. And it was then that I remembered the day Russ Shears came to town and that he said he'd returned the rental car that he'd driven all night. "Hey, Morgan, do you happen to remember a guy a few days ago, about five foot nine, dark hair, five o'clock shadow, early twenties, and sort of looks like an Abercrombie and Fitch model?"

Morgan's eyes got wide the more I described

Russ Shears. "No. Do you have his number?" She smiled.

"Trust me, your mother wouldn't approve." I flitted my eyes. Marcy keeps a tight reign on her daughters. "He said he returned a rental car and that he may have forgotten something in it," I fibbed, a tiny bit. "This is the only rental place in town, right?"

"That's right." She nodded. "We have a lost and found box in the office, but the guy you described hasn't been in."

"And you've been working every day this week?"

"I've been working overtime actually. Every day for going on nine days now. Really banking the hours, but it's good for my college fund." She shrugged.

"I bet." I nodded. "Well, I'll let you get back to work. Tell your mom I said hi," I said, and Pepper and I went on with our constitutional. A thoughtful one at that.

❉ ❉ ❉

Now, I've always been the type who could entertain herself. Even as a child, I remember my babysitters splitting their earnings with me because they felt so guilty about what little work was required of them when they were summoned to the house I grew up in. I'd either read or work on building some Lego masterpiece, and if it was during the evening hours, I'd gaze up at the stars with the telescope I got for my ninth birthday. On this night, restless and hot on the heels of having new information about Russ and the rental car he lied about, I opted to entertain myself with a little spying. I told myself it was in the best interests of Ags and the rest of the gang.

From the darkened wheelhouse of the *Alex M.*, I aimed my binoculars out the stern porthole toward the *Summerwind.* Nothing much happened at first, but the wait was worth it. There was Russ in the salon of the boat sitting in the banquette just off the galley; for the longest time he had his neck craned toward his phone. Then I watched as he got up from the bench seat and headed toward the stateroom. I've played enough poker on the *Summerwind* to know the layout like the back of my hand. The curtains in the stateroom were almost entirely pulled shut and I couldn't tell what he was doing in there. A moment later, he reappeared in the salon with something in his hand. I slid the lever on my binoculars to zoom. Russ looked down at what was in his grasp and used his other hand to count it out—like you'd do with money. When he was done counting, he tidied the stack and put it on the table in front of him, then folded his arms behind his neck and leaned back, looking contemplative or satisfied, I couldn't tell which from that distance. It could have just as easily been gas. A moment later, his head snapped toward the stern door. I followed with my binoculars to see that someone had boarded the boat.

Russ hastily grabbed for what he'd laid out on the table and stuffed it behind the toss cushion on the banquette. I'd given Robert Shears that cushion for Christmas the prior year in our Secret Santa exchange—navy blue and screen-printed in white on the front were the words "Work Like a Captain, Party Like a Pirate". I saw Russ mouth something and turn and look back at the banquette before heading to answer the door. I was hooked, watching the *Russ Show* in magnified view with my binocs—good thing I'd opted for the lightweight version—when my cell phone went off. I jumped and turned to look toward it, finding the screen now casting an upward glow on Pepper's face where he lay on the wheelhouse bunk. The effect made him appear like someone about to tell a ghost story around a campfire.

"Jesus!" I said and thought my heart would leap out of my chest. The phone buzzed again and I looked at the screen. Aggie. I tapped to answer it.

"What are you doing?" she asked.

I froze. "What do you mean?"

"It's a pretty simple question. I just wondered what you're doing."

"Can you *see* me?" I asked.

"No. Why? Why are you acting so weird? I just want you to come over."

"Oh." I let out a sigh of relief and went back to the stern porthole to see what I was missing. "Sure, I'll be there in a few minutes," I said, tapped the screen to end the call and watched the lights go out on the *Summerwind* before Russ went down the dock with his visitor.

I took Pepper down the main level of my boat, tucked my family in for the night, and headed off to Aggie's where, as soon as I crossed the threshold, I could smell fresh coffee wafting from the kitchen, and a roast beef sandwich lured me to the counter as if I were being pulled by a string.

"Ok, what is it?" I groaned, knowing the sandwich was clearly a bribe.

"How'd you like to help me paint?"

"How about your man-child? Can't he help you?".

"He said he has some things to take care of. You don't think he's seeing someone else, do you?"

"Who, that catch? Not likely." I rolled my eyes. As far as I could tell, Russ' lifestyle was being funded by his grandfather who had provided for him a place to stay, the gang and I during our last poker night, and Aggie and the odd jobs she gave him. Though I did wonder if it was cash he had counted out on the banquette table. "I don't know what you see in that kid. What could you possibly have to talk about?" I asked as I went to the counter and poured myself a coffee.

"Girl, we don't get together to *talk*." She shot me a roguish smile and spread a drop cloth on the floor.

"So, it's just sex."

"It's not *just* sex. It's two people who enjoy the company of one another. And don't you always say life is short? Let's hear it for a little hedonism. Think of it like my therapy." She went on, and I wasn't sure if she was trying to convince me or herself. "See what I save in psychiatric bills?"

"Mmhmm, I've always said you're the poster child for mental health. I still don't get it, though. Not with him," I said, taking a sip.

"Be nice."

"Ok, I'll be nice," I said and wondered at what point of being nice I could reveal that Russ was a big fat liar and that he had not, as he'd claimed, returned a rental car to the lot uptown. I decided to bank my concerns until I had something more substantial to offer.

"Hey, how'd you know I was going to ask you to help me paint? You even came dressed for it," she said as she shook a gallon of paint.

"Ags, I've been wearing this all day," I said, looking down at my ripped jeans, long sleeved t-shirt, and paint-splattered shoes before shaking my head at my abysmal fashion sense. "So, we're painting these walls I'm guessing?" I looked at the two walls dotted with slightly discoloured rectangles, reminders of the prints that had been removed.

"Yeah, I just want it freshened up, you know, for the dinner."

"Russ coming to that too?"

Aggie cocked her head and squinted at me. I gathered the answer was yes. "Bugsy's invited too."

"Oh yeah? That's nice."

"Even though—," she said as though the rest of the sentence had broken off.

I knew what "even though" meant. *That* "even though" was an invitation for me to ask what "even though" meant.

Ags pried open the lid of the can and poured some Cottage White into a tray for me and some for herself while I slid the rollers on their cages. The air between us was dead quiet while I debated asking what the "even though" was that she was dying to explain. After a protracted wait that was probably a solid two minutes, I caved. "Oh, for heaven's sake, *even though* what?"

"Hmmm?"

"You know damn well what I said. *Even though* what?" I dipped my roller in the paint.

"Oh, you mean about Bugsy?"

"Swear to God, Ags, if you don't just come out with it—" I waved the paint roller at her.

"Ok, ok, calm down. I was going to say Bugsy's coming, *even though* he's being evicted from his cottage."

"He's what?" I asked, searching her face.

"Yeah, he came in the other day and told me his old man is booting him out of free accommodations."

"Why would he do that?"

"Oh, he's pissed at him. You remember this summer, that land deal Bob Beedle had going?"

"Yeah."

"Well, Bugsy effed that up for him. Apparently, he knew the land was contaminated and Bob figures it was him who told the buyers and they backed out of the deal."

"Oh, I see." I nodded and started rolling on paint.

"You know the buyers were going to put a rec centre on the property for kids, big outdoor soccer complex and—"

"Well that's too bad... I mean for him." I rolled some more. "So that's why Bugsy's been kind of moping around?"

"I think so. That and..."

I looked at her. "Ags, why don't you ever just finish a sentence like a normal person?" I dipped my roller into the paint and waited for the other shoe to drop.

"Ok, well, we were talking."

"We?"

"Me, Bugsy, Junior, you know," she said while she rolled on white.

"Oh, right, the little Mensa group you've formed."

"Never mind then."

"Ags, would you just tell me."

"We were talking... and we wondered if maybe you would rent the *Splendored Thing* to Bugsy and I would rent the cottage."

"Why don't you just rent him above the store?"

"Well, Johnny Fleet wants to rent above the store."

"Really?" I asked, dipping and rolling.

"Yeah, seems Granny Fleet has a new boyfriend and she's looking for some privacy."

Oh great, another love connection in my midst. "Wow, good for her. What is she, eighty?"

"Yeah. If he stays here, he's close enough to keep an eye on her without having to listen to the springs in the mattress bounce when her beau is over. So, whaddaya think?"

"About what?" I looked at her to ask.

"*About renting Nat's boat to Bugsy.*"

"No."

"You didn't even take two seconds to think about it."

"What's to think about?" I said, although in the split second I'd *had* thought about it. A million thoughts ran through my busy female brain. I didn't want to make any rash decisions about Nat's boat. Sure, I knew Nat wasn't coming back. Everyone had figured that out. But I saw no need to rush into things. My mind ran the scenarios. What if Bugsy rented Nat's boat? That boat's docked precariously close to mine, and what if I'm subjected to a parade of women on that boat? Doing the walk of shame in the morning, carrying away their inappropriate footwear. The boat's docked close enough that I'd hear giggling or romantic music or God forbid moaning or other carnal jungle noises. No thanks. If Bugsy was going to undertake that type of behaviour, I didn't want to see it or hear it or smell it. Then again, what if Bugsy and I got together and it didn't work out? Then I'd have to collect rent from him for God knows how long. That'd be awkward.

"Well, Nat's boat is just sitting there empty," she went on, pleading Bugsy's case as though she'd been hired to.

"It's not exactly empty, Ags."

"Well..." She paused. "It could be. I mean, do you really think he's coming back?"

"Aggie, it's not for me to—"

"But you're the caretaker of the boat. His lawyer said so, didn't he?"

"That doesn't mean I can rent it out to every Tom, Dick, or Bugsy... And what if Nat *does* come back? Then what? He finds Bugsy's been sleeping in his bed and crapping in his john?"

She giggled. "We're talking Bugsy, not Goldilocks here."

I flashed my eyes at her. "Ags, it's not mine to rent out."

"Well, could you at least discuss it with his lawyer Tranmer and see if he has any *objections*?"

She paused. "Get it?" she giggled and motioned toward me with a paint roller.

"Yeah, I get it. Lawyer. Objections... I'll ask him." I feigned a smile, hoping it'd mean we could move on.

"Perfect, and if he's around he can come to Thanksgiving too, he's kind of cute. You know, in that older man way." She batted her eyelashes.

It's amazing how much catching up needs to be done when you haven't spoken to your best friend for a couple days. Fortunately, we moved on from talk of Bugsy's housing crisis. I listened to her dish a little about Russ—who had already settled into her rotation of companions, I asked her how the move went with her cousin, and I vented about a few boat deals I had on the go. We were well into the second coat of paint, had split the roast beef sandwich, and were midway through a couple spiked lemonades, gabbing like old ladies going over old times, when a late-night knock jolted us. It was well past midnight where the only logical answer to who's at the door *has* to be the escaped serial killer. Not so this time. It was Pike Murray and his dog Bear.

"Hiya. What's up? You're a little late for Halloween," Ags greeted him through the door then pushed it open for him.

"Ladies, and I use that term loosely," Pike said, smiling. At six-foot something, broad and bearded, Nordic looking and perpetually in plaid, Pike looked like an imposing L.L. Bean model. But if you're used to trading barbs with him and swapping his captaining services for dinners like I do, that imposing figure is cut down to the teddy bear who stood before us.

"You're out late. For you, I mean," I said, putting down my roller in the tray.

"Guess you don't have the local station on." He paused while he tried to make out what we were listening to and cringed his critique. I locked eyes with Ags before we both turned our curious gazes on Pike. "The pharmacy was robbed tonight. Alex, when you're ready to go back to your boat, I'll walk you."

CHAPTER 6

*W*hat was happening? I suddenly felt myself surrounded by a suffocating expanse of water. The water was cold and black and I couldn't touch the bottom, and as I struggled to swim, my clothes were so heavy and wet and thick that they fought against me in my bid to stay afloat. I couldn't catch my breath. I couldn't scream. I felt myself slipping down, losing the battle, sinking, gasping, choking. I caught a glimpse of the moon and reached for it and… And then I sat upright in my bed, my chest heaving from the breaths I could finally take. Looking around the room, the brass porthole glinted from the glow of the television I'd forgotten to turn off. My cat was peering back at me from the armchair, where I'd dropped that day's clothes, and Pepper lay outstretched on his half of my king-sized bed looking bleary-eyed. Try falling asleep after a dream like that, especially when you live on a boat.

I grabbed the hair elastic from the nightstand beside me, whipped up a messy bun, and padded across the passageway to the salon of my boat where I flicked on the electric kettle in the mini kitchenette, dropped a peppermint tea bag into my favourite vintage Hall mug, then peered out the porthole while I waited for the water to boil. So those were my choices? Bad dreams or restless thinking? As my eyes scanned the sleeping vessels near me, thoughts whirred like a propeller. Thoughts like, *What was Russ Shears doing last night?* and *Was it a coincidence that he went out on the night that the pharmacy was robbed?* Thoughts like, *I hope Ags turned on the alarm like I insisted and re-insisted and then texted her to triple insist that she turn on before going to bed.* Thoughts like, *Why all of a sudden had our sleepy little town become a hot bed of crime?* Then there were the thoughts of what to do about Bugsy and his impending homelessness. *Could we coexist as neighbors if I rented him the* Splendored Thing? and *If good fences make good neighbors, what chance would we have with no fences?* The kettle clicked off and I returned to the porthole with my mug of tea. A few docks over, I saw someone board the *Summerwind* and the lights in the salon come on. A look to the clock radio on my desk told me it was five a.m.

Stokes Pharmacy on State Street was burglarized last night. Authorities say that between nine p.m. and midnight the pharmacy was entered and a quantity of cash and prescriptions taken. If you were in the area and saw anything, you are asked to contact the Marysville police. Now sports. The Marysville Ravens outshot the—

I tapped on the radio to silence it. I'd been listening to the same announcements for the past two and a half hours interspersed between the lively conversations of 96.9's Morning Crew Roger and Marilyn, some classic oldies, and the sound effect they were running for a contest. I'm pretty sure it was the sound of a hole punch, by the way. The drizzle that started around seven a.m. was a testament to their weather forecaster who had given a forty percent chance of precip for the day. I swapped out my jammies for jeans, a t-shirt, my runners, and a slicker and headed out into the sprinkles toward Aggie's.

When I got there, the scene was chaotic. Where days earlier the disruption in my fritter supply had slightly impacted my morning sugar addiction, the incident at the pharmacy had completely discombobulated the gang. I took my usual spot at the counter and watched the discourse with rapt attention, knowing I'd become involved at some juncture.

"Can ya believe it, kid? First the bakery then the pharmacy," Jack ranted, shaking his head and scoffing as he came from the nook and took the stool beside me.

I faked an intrigued expression. I didn't have the heart to tell him I'd known since the wee hours of the morning when Pike let Ags and me know.

"I personally think the two are related. The guy probably needed some Tums after eating Ash's meat pies," Peter Muncie grumbled.

"More coffee, Jack?" Ags asked.

Jack gave an adamant nod and held out his mug. "Hey, kiddo, your boyfriend Hagen too busy taking swimming lessons to keep this town safe?"

"A, he's not my boyfriend, and also, B, he's not my boyfriend." I took a sip of the smooth, strong coffee Aggie'd poured me.

"Anyone know what they got? Cash? Pills?" Sefton asked. "I'm almost out of yellows, and my blues are getting low too. I can't go very long without blues."

Jack meandered back to the nook by the TV. "I don't know, Lee told me about it this morning."

"Lee?" I asked. *Had I blacked out and missed something?*

"Well-well, that's what I call her. Lee, you know, Lisa."

"Oh." I nodded and downed another sip.

"Oooooh," Ags let out as she craned her neck to see who owned the lug soled shoes trotting up her front steps through the drizzle that persisted. "Officer Handsome's here."

I turned to look. "Hagen. Yeah." I smiled a greeting to him when he came through the door, his tanned complexion sprinkled with rain, his hair not even slightly askew, and I watched him walk to the counter, hoping he wouldn't notice the suitcases under my eyes.

"So, I bet you had a fun night," Ags greeted him with a consoling expression.

"Long night. How about some coffee please?" he asked and sent a crooked smile my way, dimples and all.

"Coming up. Fresh pot's just about done," she said, turned on her heels and walked to the machine.

"So, Hagen, what in the Sam Hill's going on?" Peter Muncie shouted from the nook.

I watched in profile as Hagen closed his eyes, let out a breath, and swiveled on his stool to face his critics. "Peter, fellas. Guess you've all heard," he said, and I watched the bravado of the gang fade into empathy.

I nodded slowly and sympathetically at Ben Hagen. Two robberies in a short time in our little town couldn't be good for business.

"You're keeping your doors locked, I hope," he said, looking from Aggie's eyes to mine, though I noticed he lingered a little longer in my direction. Geesh, you have one little encounter with a prowler and everyone thinks you're incapable of taking care of yourself.

"Me? Oh, sure, sure," I said. Lying. Convincingly, I hoped. It's not like anyone could abscond with my two-hundred-and-eighty-ton floating home, and most of my worldly possessions are either bolted to that behemoth or are inconsequential to anyone but me anyway.

"How about you, Aggie? Your alarm working alright?"

"Yep."

Hagen nodded and sipped. "And, uh, what would you do if someone tried to rob you while you were here?" he probed.

"Well, I– You mean if he tried to grab me?" she asked after a moment's pause.

"Don't get your hopes up," I said tartly.

Hagen looked serious, and it was kind of sexy in an officious way. "Listen, we're having a self-defence class at MacDonald Park tonight. Five-thirty. Supposed to clear up by then." Hagen looked over his shoulder at the gang in the peanut gallery. "You guys can come too." He turned back to Ags and me. "I think you should both come."

I locked eyes with Ags, shrugged, and felt the corners of my mouth turn down.

"Yeah, we'll be there," she said, and I looked at Hagen and nodded through a yawn.

❋ ❋ ❋

That morning practically flew by. After completing my rainy-day abbreviated jogging route —State Street was a mess anyway due to the activity outside the pharmacy—I showered and swapped my sweaty running clothes for my work uniform, jeans and a t-shirt, opting for a retro Snoopy number. And then I got down to business. The business of selling boats. Most of my commerce is done over email and phone– I connect sellers with buyers and take my cut of sale prices of surplus marine inventory from Nova Scotia to California and the Arctic to Mexico. The fact that I work with my black cat George and my dog Pepper means that office politics are kept to a minimum and staff meetings don't get too out of control unless one usurps the other's choice spot on the couch during nap time—I've been guilty of this myself. I was staring at the computer screen, critiquing my website, when I heard footfalls on the deck, and a moment later the owner of those size twelves appeared in the open stern door.

"Hiya, Alex," Johnny Fleet greeted me in his customarily cheerful manner. I've never seen that kid in a bad mood.

"What's new, Johnny?"

"Mind if I…?" he began to say and nodded toward the interior of my boat.

"Sure, come on in. You're welcome anytime." I motioned to him with my hand toward the chair on the opposite side of my desk.

"Howdy, Pepper," Johnny said, bending to rub his soft lab ears.

"What's up?"

Johnny perched on the edge of the club chair, looking ready to spring out of it at any moment.

"I was, uh, lookin' for you at Aggie's, but she said you'd probably be here." Johnny was nervous, looking everywhere but directly at me.

"Well, you found me. What can I do for you?"

"I was wondering if you'd please do me a favor."

"Sure... if I can." I looked at him skeptically and wondered what *I* could possibly do for the young man who was already surprisingly self-sufficient. Johnny Fleet had turned seventeen a few weeks earlier and was already quite the junior corporate captain. He owns the bait business at the marina, a rustic and cute structure that has been grandfathered in over generations of property owners, and he delivers bait to other places around town in his customized bike and trailer set up. Johnny, I'd come to learn, had parents in Maine but ventured west to live with his grandmother four years ago when she'd broken her hip. Granny Fleet isn't one to be coddled, and she probably won't leave her house unless she's in a pine box, so Johnny stayed and they each believe they are taking care of the other. Johnny does maintenance and keeps her company, and Granny Fleet shows up most days to bring him lunch and a jacket if she feels the weather is turning.

He looked at me as though he were about to impose. "Well, I was just wondering if you'd please come with me tomorrow?"

"Where? What's happening tomorrow?"

"Well," he said, looking at the top of my desk and nervously adjusting the brim of the baseball cap he wore over his thick crop of ginger hair.

With all this lead up, I was mentally dreading him asking me to the prom, and the meagre contents of my closet flashed through my mind. I have nothing suitable, one summer dress and one all-purpose black dress I usually just pull out for funerals.

"I, uh, I'm going to see this boat tomorrow." He pulled out his phone, tapped it a few times, and angled it toward me. "And, uh, seeing as how you're so good at negotiating and selling boats and—"

"You want me to go with you?" I asked, relieved but surprised. I'm still relatively new to the biz.

"Would you please?"

"Of course. I don't know how much help I'll be. Where's the boat?"

"Evanston," he said, reading it off the phone screen as if he hadn't memorized that fact already.

"Sure, no problem. One question, though. How are we going to get there?"

"Oh, I guess you didn't see my new truck," he smiled with his entire face.

"*You* got a new truck? Congratulations!"

"Well, new to me. Not as nice as Nat's truck, but... you know..." Johnny's words trailed off solemnly, he'd been close to Nat too. He pivoted to look toward the garage where Pike stored Nat's wheels.

Nat's truck. The very essence of Americana, a tribute to the once glorious auto industry. A 1956 GMC step side truck painted light blue with a white cap on the roof. We took that truck on countless adventures. Nat would drive me when I would go see a boat, or gather information for a listing from a potential client—insisting that there were too many sketchy people for me to go out on my own and do it. Wherever we went, we'd make a day of it, stopping at a flea market or some little town we'd never been to, singing to the oldies the entire time courtesy of a modern sound system, the only modification he'd permitted on the truck. Somehow, in the months since Nat had been "missing", I had managed to avoid any out-of-town trips, opting for my bike and the two feet God gave me if I wanted to get around. The odd time I'd bum a ride, but more and more I had the feeling that my neighbors—likely sick of my off-key singing—wanted me to find a more permanent solution, and it's something I mulled over from time to time.

I smiled at Johnny. "Ok, tomorrow then."

"Oh, gee thanks. You're the best," he said, springing out of the chair.

"I keep telling people that!" I called out the door after him. If he was ten years older, I'd be smitten. As it was, I treated Johnny like the little brother I never had. "Hey, what time tomorrow?" I went to the door and hollered. He'd already bounded to the dock, no doubt with visions of a new boat dancing in his head.

He stopped in his tracks and turned. "Oh yeah. Ten o'clock!"

"Ok, see you tomorrow," I said.

Johnny waved back at me and I took a break from work and headed toward my closet wondering what the modern young lady wears to a self-defence class.

* * *

"Hey, Jack, I thought we were going to meet your gal Lisa," I shouted from the steps of Aggie's as I spotted Junior and Peter Muncie headed toward me. Straggling much further behind them were the gals from the *Gee Spot*, Sefton, Seacroft and I think I spotted Richards with them.

"Oh, I don't know, she's got a thing I guess," Jack said. He couldn't conceal the disappointment in his voice and I felt a tug at my heartstrings.

"Oh. That sounds like an invitation to me," I said, beaming at him and extending my arm for him to take while Ags followed suit with Peter Muncie, and as we walked, leading the pack up from the marina, I glanced back a few times and wondered if we didn't look like some entry from a Veterans Day parade.

We arrived at MacDonald Park in generally satisfactory shape. The only casualty being yours truly when the sprinkler in front of the bank soaked the back of my blouse—something I should have expected since I'm rarely one to show up anywhere looking any better than an unmade bed and I had left my boat feeling overly confident in my appearance. From the look of things, the news of the self-defence class had spread through the community faster than a sale on Imodium after a chili cook-off. It was a healthy sized crowd, heavy on the geriatric demographic. The contingent from the marina, led by Ags and yours truly, wove its way through the walkers and grey heads to an opening at the front of the crowd. Ben Hagen was looking both in charge and approachable at the same time— his khaki shorts made me feel chilled on his behalf, though I didn't mind the view. The navy-blue t-shirt he sported was emblazoned with the insignia of the Marysville Police, and his jet-black hair was, as always, perfectly parted to the side. He was flanked by members of the auxiliary force, similarly attired, with the exception that Hagen was equipped with a bull horn.

"Ok, ladies... and gentlemen, thank you all for coming tonight," Hagen said into the device at precisely five-thirty. "If you'll all give me your attention—" The bull horn squelched and then sent a cringeworthy piercing sound through the crowd, leaving the masses grumbling. Frustrated, he handed off the device to one of his team members, an auxiliary officer with a perky brunette ponytail who seemed to be hanging on his every word and movement.

"Shhhhhhhh," Peter Muncie shushed the gathering.

"Thank you." Hagen nodded at him and then raised his volume to address the crowd. "Now, as you all know, we have had two incidents of late and the Marysville PD know that it can make people nervous. So, the purpose of this evening is to teach you some self-defence maneuvers that anyone can do. Ok?"

A collective "Ok" gurgled back at him, and there was a buzz of chatter and a sea of nodding heads with the exception of Sefton who had a raised hand and an earnest look about him.

Hagen pointed at him. "Do you have a question?"

"Yeah. How do we know our attacker isn't here? And if he's here, won't he know what's coming once
you teach us these moves?"

I smiled. Sefton had a point, and with that thought of potential attackers, I instinctively looked around for Russ Shears. He wasn't there.

All eyes were back on Hagen and he paused for a moment. "We'll assume he *or she* isn't here tonight, ok?"

Sefton nodded. "Alright."

"Ok, are there any *other* questions?" he asked, and seeing no indication of any, he proceeded.

"Now you'll need to pair up with someone as your partner. So, go ahead and do that now."

I turned to my immediate right and exchanged a hearty handshake with Ags. "Howdy, pardner," I said, adopting Gladys' twang.

"Howdy." She smiled her hundred-watt smile.

And, like a wave through the crowd, you could see the mergers and strategic partnerships forming. Jack with Peter Muncie, Sefton with Gladys, Ginny with Doctor Richards, Seacroft with Geraldine, and so it went throughout the crowd.

"Are we all paired up?" Hagen shouted after scanning the assembly.

There was a chorus of "Mmhmms" and more head bobbing.

"Ok, now," Hagen approached Ags. He took a few steps towards her, pulled her arm to jerk her close to him, and from behind put his arm across her chest. Her reaction suggested that she hadn't been expecting it, but by the same token she wasn't upset by it either. "Now, ask yourself, what would you do?"

"I'd invite you up to my place." Aggie giggled and continued to do so uncontrollably until Hagen relented. Frustrated. Self-defence can only be taught to someone looking to fight. And he went on the search for someone less compliant.

"Ok... I, uh, might need to try a new partner. You game?" he asked me.

"Me?" I felt my face get warm. "Ok." *What was the worst that could happen?*

"Thanks, I owe you," he said lowly and positioned himself in front of me while he shouted a play-by-play to the crowd. "Ok, so pay attention. An attacker comes at you like this," he said and raised my arms in what felt like an unnatural position, though I've never actually assaulted anyone so I can't say for sure. His hands were big and warm and easily closed around my wrists. "Now what do you do?"

"Depends on what he looks like!" shouted a twangy voice from the crowd. Had to be Gladys.

"I'd say you're screwed," Jack Junior offered up.

"Are you sure?" Hagen volleyed back, and I felt my body suddenly in motion.

"Wha—?" I began, not even getting out the entire word before the damp fabric on my back was suddenly on the grass, my heart thumping, and Hagen was crouching beside me. For some reason the crowd applauded as if they felt I had it coming.

"Are you ok? I didn't hurt you, did I?" he asked me, his green eyes piercing.

"No. I could have used some warning, though," I said, arching an eyebrow as I looked up at him.

He extended his big, warm hand to me as he pulled me from the ground while he addressed the crowd. "Ok, now she's going to show you what I did there, and you'll all replicate it."

A flash of panic ran through me like a lightning bolt. "Maybe you should pick someone else," I said just above a whisper. I had a flashback of the fourth grade where, in the spelling bee in the gymnasium, I flubbed on *pachyderm* while I had my eyes on Ryan Dougherty in the front row, two grades above me, and he rode motocross on the weekend. This time, I'd been too consumed with the scent of Hagen's body wash and warm hands to concentrate on his self-defence choreography, and it had all happened so fast.

"Listen, you can do this." Hagen ignored the pleading in my eyes. "Ok, ready?"

"She was born ready," Ags piped up. God love her for her confidence in me.

I let out a deep breath, then Hagen motioned in the attack pose and, somehow, I leveled him. It wasn't textbook, and I don't imagine it was pretty, and he probably gave in just a little, but Ags told me later that it looked convincing. A smattering of surprised sounding "ohs" and one or two cheers rose from the crowd and I took a bow. When I looked down at Hagen, he had a goofy grin on his face like a proud father. He got to his feet and dusted his backside with his hands, and I re-joined Ags, assuming my work was done.

"Thank you, Miss Michaels, excellent work. Now, there are other ways to disable a predator, especially if it's a man. You can kick or punch him in the family jewels, so to speak," Hagen went on.

"You done?" Ags mumbled toward me while Hagen went on about how to disarm a predator.

"Done what?" I turned to her, screwed up my face, and asked just as lowly.

"Whatever little dance you two were doing up there."

I rolled my eyes at her and turned my attention back to Hagen.

"The main thing is to be aware of your surroundings," he said.

"What if they have a gun?" an older woman called out.

"Run... or walk as fast as you can." Hagen corrected himself after his eyes drifted down to the aluminum walker the old lady leaned on.

"What if he's after my body?" Gladys shouted.

"He won't be!" Jack Junior retorted.

"Jack Junior, you little smart aleck, you keep your comments to yourself, you hear," Granny Fleet hollered out.

"If he wants your body, consider yourself lucky and buy a lottery ticket while you're at it," Jack retorted and high-fived Peter Muncie.

"Ladies and gentlemen, if we can just behave like *ladies and gentlemen* for a moment. If you don't feel safe or you can't perform any of the moves I'll be showing you, you may want to carry mace or pepper spray."

"How about a Glock?" Granny Fleet shouted.

"No!" Hagen was getting flustered. "Now look. If you are going to walk, walk in pairs. Leave your Glock at home, Mrs. Fleet."

"What if he gets me on the ground and gets on top of me?"

"In your dreams, Ginny," I heard Gladys remark.

Hagen closed his eyes and sighed. He was having a moment. "There's always a way to get out of that situation. Here, let me show you. Alex, do you mind?" He reached out and pulled me by the arm.

"Do I mind *what*?"

Hagen laid down on the grass. "Get on top of me."

"Excuse me?" I heard myself crow.

Hagen propped himself up on his elbows and addressed the crowd. "She's going to help me demonstrate how to get out of a vulnerable situation."

"Oh, I think maybe..." I held up my hands in protest or surrender, wondering how I'd gotten into *my own* vulnerable situation.

"What, uh, what's the matter, kiddo?" Jack said, and when I looked back at him, he was beaming.

I let out another deep breath, squinted, and nodded slowly at him in the "I'm going to get you later" fashion. It only fanned the fire; his smile grew bigger. I got closer to Hagen; I couldn't leave him just lying there.

"Ok, just straddle me here."

"In the name of public good, of course," Ags said without missing a beat.

My cheeks were on fire and I gingerly put one leg on each side of Hagen like he was a bucking bronco I didn't want to touch.

"Uh, uh, uh," Jack stammered.

"Oh... Mylanta," Gladys groaned. "Everybody, shush." And when I looked up, I saw her nudge her friend. "Geraldine, are you seeing what I'm seeing? Can you video this with your phone?" Geraldine and the rest of the crowd were transfixed.

"I'm going to kill you, you know that, right?" I mumbled down to him.

Hagen stayed in character. "Ok, now everyone watch closely," he said as if they weren't doing it already. "Now this aggressor has me pinned."

"I always knew she was like that," I was surprised to hear Doctor Richards chime in.

"And, you're not, uh, putting up much of a fight there, Hagen," Jack said.

"Shush, Junior, this is just getting good," Granny Fleet said.

"Ok, so pay attention," Hagen scolded the onlookers. *Or were they voyeurs?* "Put your arm on my neck like you're going to choke me."

"Oh, so that's what you're into," someone said.

I closed my eyes and wondered what strange sequence of events got me to this place. Two years ago I would have been in my pre-furnished condo working on a spreadsheet or analyzing financial statements while I waited for dinner to be delivered. Now I found myself on public display, straddling a handsome police officer and wondering how my hair looked after I'd been tossed on the ground.

"Ok, so I'm going to lock her arm at my neck while, without her noticing, I bend my legs and get ready to roll her over with my hips," he said slowly in that way that's meant to sound instructional. His naivete was cute – no one in this crowd needed instructions so much as they did a cold shower. But in a second or two, I found myself suddenly under Hagen. "See, she had no way to ground herself and I knocked her off balance. And now I can get up and run away."

"And yet, oddly enough, you're not," I heard Ags cackle.

"Can I see that again?" Gladys of the Gee Spots asked.

"Yeah, I think I need to see that one again too," Ginny said, and when I glanced in her direction, despite the coolness of the early evening, she was fanning herself with a newspaper.

"Ok, now let's all try that move," Hagen told the crowd.

"Muncie's in the head again. I'm a free agent ladies!" Jack announced. "Any takers?" And with that invitation, Jack Junior ended up paired with Granny Fleet, sans Glock, of course.

* * *

"Well, ladies, what'd you think? Think any-one will retain any of that?" Hagen asked as he strolled toward Ags and me shooting the breeze on the teeter totter in the park while we waited for the rest of our crew to end their social hour and walk with us back to the marina.

"Oh, I know I'll have a hard time forgetting it," Ags said with a smile.

"I think it went... well," I said, trying to re-assure Hagen. I didn't tell him that afterward the ladies from the *Gee Spot* asked me some in-depth and extremely personal questions about him. From the corner of my eye, I could see Johnny Fleet approach with his gran.

"Hey, Alex," he said.

"Hi, Johnny, Mrs. Fleet."

"Just giving her a lift home. How'd the thing go?"

Hagen kept it brief. "Good, thanks."

Johnny looked at me. "We still on for tomor-row?"

"For sure. Ten, right?"

"Yep, pick you up at ten," he said then nodded and let his gran take him by the arm. She looked intent on spilling her guts about the X-rated self-defence class the town had been treated to.

"What's at ten?" Hagen asked while I was tee-tering. Or was I tottering? Well, my butt was low to the ground at any rate, and Ags was aloft.

"Oh, Johnny and I are going to look at a boat tomorrow, for his business."

"Oh?" Hagen asked, his voice rising an octave.

"Yeah, in Evanston. A thirty-footer. Aluminum number with twin outboards. Should go like stink," I said.

Hagen nodded and his furrowed brow told me the wheels were turning.

"What?" I asked, looking from his face to Aggie's. She shrugged.

"Nothing," he said, and I watched him as he watched Johnny walk away with his gran. "Getting dark. How about I walk you girls back to the marina?"

I dismounted the seesaw as gracefully as possible and let Ags down as gently as I could, then looked around for our escorts. Jack Junior and Peter Muncie were not far off. Peter was chatting up the *Gee Spot* gals while Jack stood by looking bored. I shot him a wave, which he reciprocated, and I turned to walk with Hagen and Ags. It's not a far walk from the park to the marina. In fact, nothing in Marysville seems far from anything else. A neat little trick the town planners pulled off, back in the days when walking must have been the primary mode of transportation, but if there's one negative about the town infrastructure, it's a distinct lack of public parking. With the sun sinking low and fast this time of year, it was dark by the time we got to the marina. Members of our walking group seemed to veer off one by one until, finally, it was just Hagen and me at my dock.

"Would you like to come in for coffee or tea?"

"Hmmm?"

"I asked if you'd like to come in for a drink. Something bothering you?"

Hagen paused and looked as though he was struggling with his thoughts. "Well, actually there is. I'm kind of hesitant to bring it up, though."

My mind started to wander and wonder. Was Hagen about to ask me on another date? Sure, we'd watched that movie once at his home in the tony, gated community–where I don't mind telling you I felt completely out of place. Did he consider the self-defence class foreplay? Was he about to ask me for a kiss? Because I certainly wouldn't have objected.

"Where'd Johnny Fleet get the money for a boat all of a sudden?"

Pop. There went the bubble he burst. My thoughts went from how to form the perfect pucker to how to punch an officer in the face without being charged. "Excuse me?"

"I'm just curious. And when did he get that truck he had at the park tonight?"

I felt my jaw drop. "You don't for one second think that Johnny Fleet had something to do with what happened at the bakery and the pharmacy, do you?"

Now let me tell you something about Officer Ben Hagen. He has a nice face. In fact, it's *very* nice. Square jaw, beautiful green eyes, dimples when he chooses to break them out, the full meal deal. What he does not have, though, is a poker face. At least around me.

"You do, don't you?"

"All I'm saying is that we have to look at every conceivable angle. Johnny Fleet has come into enough money to suddenly buy a truck and a boat and—"

"Whoa, whoa, whoa. Johnny Fleet is one of the hardest working guys I know. Just because he wasn't born with a silver spoon in his mouth like you doesn't mean he has to steal in order to buy things."

"Alex, I just—"

"Well, I just... I *just* remembered, I have some work to do. Goodnight, Ben," I said before boarding my boat, unlocking it, flicking on the lights, and closing the stern door without looking back toward the dock.

CHAPTER 7

When Johnny Fleet and I rolled back into the marina the next day around one, we brought with us the thirty-foot, twin outboard aluminum boat of his dreams. To my complete amazement, I'd managed to negotiate the seller down ten percent, and he even gave us a deal on a trailer he had on site. All in all, I had proven myself worthy of the adoration of my seventeen-year-old fan. I'm sure the effect will wear off when he's old enough to hit the bars. I couldn't, though, bring myself to add to Johnny's teenage angst by telling him that Hagen was suspicious of his seemingly sudden windfall. I knew after all that Johnny was a hard worker and his gran had taught him how to pinch a penny ever since he'd come to live with her. The last thing I wanted him to think was that the police didn't trust him. It wasn't long after we pulled into the marina that the aluminum trophy we were towing drew a crowd. Or as much of a crowd there can be in the off season.

Once he parked the new-to-him truck, Johnny jumped down out of the driver's side and introduced the new gal at the marina. "Isn't she a honey?" He beamed to Peter Muncie, Sefton, and Bugsy who had all been drawn to the boat as if by a magnet, but we're talking aluminum here, so that analogy doesn't really work, but you get my drift.

"Nice boat, kid," Peter said and nodded with approval as he ran his hand along the sides that'd been buffed to a polish.

"She's a beaut," Sefton added while making a closer inspection of the twin Yamaha motors.

Bugsy had sidled up to me on the left by that point and nudged me. "Hey, why do men call boats *she* anyway?" he asked lowly as if it's something he should have learned in Marina Management 101.

"Because they cost you a pile of money and they'll take you for a ride," I quipped and smiled up at him, meeting his big blue eyes.

"See the console up there, and there's lots of room for storage and nets and pails and..." Johnny's voice trailed off as he gave the tour highlights while Bugsy made small talk with me. You know, the kind of small talk that's made by people who aren't great at it. That's Bugsy. The kind of awkward small talk where he'd have said anything other than to say what was on his mind, and I take it his living situation was still *very much* on his mind. I was thrilled when, while postulating with Bugsy about the weather forecast for the next week, Johnny threw me a conversational life ring and yelled out for my attention.

"Hey, Alex!"

"Excuse me, please." I smiled at the Bugster. "What's up, Johnny?"

"The guys want to know if I'm going to name her. Whaddaya think, should I?"

"Sure, why not."

"Well, what do you think I should call her?"

"Johnny, I'm not creative enough to—"

"How about after you? You're pretty awesome." Johnny gave me that look again.

"Thanks, but I think one boat in the marina named *Alex M.* is quite enough. We don't want to confuse anyone," I said, nodding toward our illustrious marina manager who in turn arched an eyebrow at me.

"Yeah, Johnny, we've got enough trouble with this one," Bugsy fired back.

"How about you name it after your gran or a play on words with your last name?" I offered up the extent of my helpfulness.

"Fleet Feet," Sefton piped up with inexplicable satisfaction.

"*Fleet Feet*?" Peter Muncie asked in a disgusted tone.

"Sure. Didn't you say you've got the track record for the county?" Sefton asked.

"Sure. Ok, that's an option," Johnny replied in a tone that said there was no way in hell he was going to name it that.

"Fleet's In," Bugsy offered, and through twinkling blue eyes and a smile, he seemed quietly delighted with himself. "That way when you come back to the harbor, everyone will say 'Hey, Fleet's in.'"

"You know, that's not half bad," I said, a little surprised. I turned to give him a smile when my eyes landed on Ben Hagen walking toward us—uniformed, lug-soled, tanned, and if I knew him, smelling good.

Ben's footsteps halted when he flanked me on my right. "Hi, there. Wow, nice boat," he said loud enough for Johnny to hear.

"Thanks, I love it!" Johnny was still overflowing with enthusiasm.

"Hey, Hagen, you wanna give your two cents?" Sefton asked; he was still making an inspection of the vessel.

"Hagen's got more than two cents to spare," Peter Muncie tossed in, somewhat aware of the economic status of the officer.

"Go for it," Hagen said.

"Johnny's looking for a name for his boat here. And I suggested 'Fleet Feet' since everyone knows he's got the track and field record for the county."

As soon as Sefton said the words, I cringed, watching Hagen processing the notion and making the tenuous links I would have if I didn't know Johnny so well. We'd all heard that an eye-witness to the robbery at the pharmacy had seen the culprit take off on foot and word was, they ran faster than a jack rabbit.

"Ok, what are my other options?" Hagen asked.

"Well," I piped up and nudged Bugsy. "Bugsy here suggested Fleet's In, which I personally love."

I looked up and to my right to see an un-amused Hagen, though he gave it a good shot. He and Bugsy were never what you'd call friends, and as long as I stood between them, they prob-ably never would be. Though I can't for the life of me understand the attraction one bit.

"Either one's fine, I think," Hagen offered apathetically.

"Yeah, but don't you think—" Sefton began to say.

"Alex, could I see you for a minute?" Hagen interjected and tapped me on the arm. "Sorry, guys, I have to take her away for a second."

"Sure," I replied dismally, sensing Hagen was still suspicious of my young friend. "Johnny, let me know when to come over for a ride, ok?" I called over my shoulder as I marched to my doom.

"You got it. An hour or so and she'll be in the water," he shouted back, blissfully unaware of Hagen's suspicions.

Hagen and I walked in companionable silence toward his cruiser parked beside Aggie's place. When he stopped walking, I did as well. He leaned against the driver's side door of the car and smiled charmingly.

"Yes, Officer Hagen. What can I do for you?" I asked and offered him my own cheeky smile.

Hagen smirked and searched my eyes for sympathy or forgiveness, I wasn't sure which. "I want to apologize."

"Ok, go ahead."

"Go ahead?"

"Yeah, you want to, so go ahead and apologize," I said and looked down at my nails to clean the gunk out from under them.

He sighed. "Ok, I'm sorry about last night."

"Me too."

"But—" he began to say.

"Oh, come on, you were doing so well with the apology and everything," I cut in to say.

Hagen hitched his thumb toward the gang down the dock. "Did Sefton just say that Johnny was in track and field? He's a runner?"

"Well, so am I, but I didn't rob the bakery or the pharmacy. Honest," I said, crossing my heart.

"What about that hoodie he's wearing?"

"What about it?"

"One of the witnesses who looked out from her window the night the pharmacy got hit said she saw someone wearing a hoodie with a white or yellow graphic on the back."

"Ben, I have a navy hoodie just like it. Pike hands those things out like Halloween candy. You should be looking into that Russ Shears guy."

"Who?" he asked, looking back at me, scrunching up his nose in the most delightful way.

"Russ Shears," I said, using air quotes. "The guy I told you about. The one who claims to be Shears' grandson but is never around when you are."

"And I take it you don't believe him."

"Of course not! Drifts into town with no ID, hardly any money, and claims his grandpa told him he could stay on the boat while he's in Europe."

Hagen looked up and to the right, then back at me.

"Can't you take his fingerprints or something? Maybe search the boat for prescriptions he took from the pharmacy or the safe from the bakery."

"Not without probable cause, dear."

"How about if I get his fingerprints? Could you run them?" My fiery enthusiasm was doused by Hagen's wet blanket of an eye roll.

"You're just going to surreptitiously get his fingerprints? For me to run?"

"Sure. I can get them. I bet Aggie's covered in 'em."

"What's she got to do with it?"

"Oh, he's her latest. Don't ask me why. He's barely old enough to vote."

He smiled. "Then I think I know why."

"Can't you at least talk to him, give him the smell test?"

"I'll think about it," he said, and in a move that completely surprised me, he leaned down toward me. "I'd rather give *you* the smell test." He sniffed my neck, I'm sure to his great disappointment, because all he'd get a whiff of is Ivory soap and sunscreen. Speaking of smell tests, when I turned my head to the side to give Hagen a whiff, I got a glimpse of Jack Junior walking down the dock toward the *Fortune Cookie* arm and arm with a woman. Lisa, I presumed. I was staring at them when Hagen's words jarred me back to the present.

"How'd you like to go to Weener Fest tomorrow night?" he asked.

"Is that a colloquialism?" came the voice of an eavesdropper rounding the corner. Bugsy. He said the smart remark like a drive-by shooting and kept on walking.

Hagen scowled in his direction, though Bugsy didn't turn to catch it. He turned back to me. "Whaddaya say? The music, the midway, the food on a stick."

"Sure, I love food on a stick. Besides, I think I'm on deck for selling shirts for the dog rescue tomorrow," I said, smiling up at Hagen. "I'll see you there."

❋ ❋ ❋

When two o'clock rolled around and I headed to Johnny Fleet's headquarters, I quickly realized that my invitation on the yet-to-be-named vessel was not an exclusive one. Jack Junior, Sefton, Seacroft, Doctor Richards, and Peter Muncie had all assembled for the ride, and I tried to recall the capacity of the vessel. I nodded as I did the headcount. We were safe. As Johnny eased the boat away from the dock and through the channel, still overflowing with enthusiasm, he gave me a lesson, explained the features of the boat as though he'd built it himself and generally seemed ecstatic with the purchase. When Sefton asked for a turn at the controls, I indicated that I could be found on the bench seat toward the stern where Jack Junior was bouncing, the wind in his hair, his light blue fishing hat clutched in his hand.

"So, you had another date with... what was her name again?" I shouted to him over the sound of the twin Yamahas.

"Lisa," Jack replied, and his face lit up when he said her name.

"Oh yeah, that's right. Things must be going well."

"Yeah, kid, I guess you could say that."

"Well, why don't you tell us all about it at poker tonight. My night to host, right?" I did a mental checklist. Yep, the salon of my boat was clean and the head was as tidy as it was going to get.

"That's what I wanted to talk to you about, kid. I was thinking we'd change the venue."

"Change the venue?" I asked, wondering if all my cleaning would be in vain.

"Yeah, to *my* boat. You know, Lee wants to play hostess and all that. She came to see it earlier today and—"

"Hostess? After a couple dates?"

"You know how women are," he said, waving at the air.

"Well, I have a vague idea, considering I am one."

"Considering you am one what?" Doctor Richards plunked himself beside me on the bench seat.

I gave him a mildly disgruntled expression. "Considering I am... oh, I am a woman," I said.

"Well, after twenty-odd years of practicing medicine, I can't argue with you there," he said and leaned back and let the wind blow through his hair. He looked relaxed. Relaxed like I'd never seen him. My eyes lingered a bit on his rugged yet refined features. His silver aviator glasses concealed his light blue eyes and a part of me wondered where he was looking, though I was still smarting from his comments the other night about my motives.

"Woman..." Jack tapped me on the leg. "You were saying?"

"Oh, nothing. I forget. If you want to have it on your boat, that's fine. I'll be there at seven. You want me to bring my special recipe cookies?" And by "my special recipe cookies", I meant the chocolate chip and black walnut numbers I generally whipped up to the MMM Bakery to get on nights I host.

"Um, well, uh—" Jack floundered more awkwardly than usual.

"What?"

"Well-well-well, it's just that, you know Lee has this idea of making poker night a little classier. She's, you know, she's upscale." Jack's eyes flickered past me to the water around us.

"Oh. I see. Well, should I wear a cocktail dress or a formal gown?"

"Gown," Richards said matter-of-factly. I didn't think he'd been listening. "Low cut," he added.

"Just bring your money. And... " Jack's words trailed off.

"And what?"

"And, well-well-well, you know, Lee is new to the gang and I'd like her to stick around so—"

"So, go easy on her? Don't unleash all my natural charm at once?"

"I'm sorry, did someone ask for charm?" Doctor Richards leaned forward to say.

My eyes followed him with a blend of mock consternation and bemusement. "I'll behave, Jack."

"Get it in writing," Doctor Richards chimed in. He'd clearly taken his sassy pills before starting his vacation time.

* * *

I arrived at the *Fortune Cookie*, ready to behave but eager to learn more about Lisa and wondering if the two agendas were mutually exclusive. I'd never been successful at behaving–my otherwise enviable academic record was dotted like a dalmatian with incidents of truancy, impertinence, and even the odd protest. Still, my desire to know more about the new woman in Jack Junior's life, aka the hostess with the mostest, meant I should at least try to be on my best behaviour or a close facsimile thereof. So, there I was in my jeans, white cotton sweater, and Chucks, my ponytail swinging from side to side, a six pack of vodka coolers in hand. I'm never one to show up empty handed, even when I'm explicitly told to.

"Ding dong!" I sang out as I stepped onto the deck and grabbed to turn the doorknob and let myself in like usual. Except it wouldn't turn. This had something to do with the hand on the other side of it. And it was then that I was greeted by who I can only assume was Lisa.

"Good evening," came a squeakily breathy voice that reminded me of a Marilyn Monroe impersonator I saw once in Vegas.

"Good evening," I said in a normal human voice. "I'm Alex."

Lisa's eyes drifted down to the six pack of bevies in my hand, and it seemed to evoke in her a visceral reaction, and a sneer formed on her heavily made-up red waxy lips. The red of them snaked up into the rivers of wrinkles above her top lip, she must have been a smoker at one time. The sneer punctuated the artist's pallet on her face which included what I believe they call smoky eyes, with fake lashes to fan the fire. From where I stood, I could also see the cakiness of her foundation and whiteness of the contouring powder she used. Yes, although I don't myself subscribe to the necessity for makeup, I'm familiar with the theories and methodologies. I guess Lisa was relying on bad lighting or Jack's poor eyesight so she'd never have to explain the texture. Maybe she was hiding reptile skin or something? When I looked back at her, I wondered how Jack was going to react if he ever woke up beside her and saw the mudslide on the pillow.

"Why thank you, you shouldn't have," Lisa said, and I really felt she meant it. She reached out and took the drinks by the cardboard handle as though I were handing her steaming dog feces. "Won't you come in?" she said, and I followed. In fact, I could have followed her blindfolded she was so pungent. It took me a second, but it came to me, a cross between pine-scented cleaner and the cosmetics counter on the day the clerk is spritzing you with whatever new perfume just came out. "Thanks," I said, and a brief look around the salon of the boat told me Lisa was already putting her stamp on things, like a cat marking its territory. At least I'd not *previously* noticed the dusty rose napkins or fake hydrangeas on the sideboard placed between a plate of sausage rolls and something that was either a fondue pot or a candle warmer.

"Oh, hey kiddo, I see you two have met," Jack greeted me cheerily as he came from the direction of the stateroom. He was buttoning the top of what looked like a freshly pressed shirt. "Lisa Claire, this is Alex Michaels."

"Yes, Alexandra and I were just getting acquainted."

I nodded and wondered why she'd used my full name and how she'd guessed it wasn't something like Alexis.

Jack interrupted my inner monologue and possibly read my mind, though I wasn't going to break out the tin foil hat just yet. "I told Lee all about you."

"Oh?"

"Oh yes, I think I remember you mentioning her," *Lee* said, disappearing with my beverages, and I instantly regretted the decision not to have one before I left my boat.

"Remember! Remember? Why, of course you remember," Jack hollered into the galley after her. "She runs a boat brokerage and—"

Lisa reappeared. "Oh, that's right. Jacky says

you have a boat here as well," she said in that contrived affect I equated to something like nails on a chalkboard.

"Oh, is that what *Jacky* said?"

"That you even live on yours. Well, good for you, I must say."

I nodded. "Yes, I live on it."

"Jacky said he might even rename his boat after me," she went on.

"Oh," I said and nodded again. See, I read somewhere that you can't nod and roll your eyes at the same time. It looked like I was going to do a lot of nodding around Lisa. I thought for a moment of telling her that it'd be bad luck for him to rename the boat, though I got the feeling that Lisa might just be bad luck in general.

"What's the name of your boat, hon?"

Being called hon by total strangers isn't my thing, just so you know. Nodding again, I replied, "*Alex M.*"

"Oh." She nodded and I saw her eyes sweep over the horizon until they halted. Haltingly.

"That's your boat? Over there? The um, *big thing*?"

I nodded once more and clenched my jaw to keep from telling her off.

"Oh. What kind of boat do you call that?"

"It's called a tug." I looked at Jack who offered me sympathetic eyes. Ok, I'm the first to admit you don't see many boats like mine in a marina like this. You see cruisers and trawlers, sailboats and sloops, but my hundred-foot steel behemoth with the black hull and red superstructure could quite rightly inspire you to start singing that classic kids tune "One of these Things is not like the Other."

"How quaint, hon," Lisa said and disappeared toward the galley again. Mercifully. She wasn't *overly* merciful, mind you, because she came back and with her was a tray of bite-sized triangle sandwiches that made me wonder what sort of afternoon tea party she must have catered last. She urged me to take an isosceles from sandwich mountain. Crab as fake as the woman herself, I'm still not sure how I choked it down.

"So, Lisa, do *you* live around here?" I asked, just making general conversation, staying this side of controversy, for the time being, and still what I'd call well-behaved, since that was my mandate.

After a pause, she replied. "Oh, yes, I just moved here with my son. Do you know the Brentwood Court community?"

"Yeah, I think I've heard of it." The truth was I *had* heard of it. I'd even been there. Officer Ben Hagen lives there. Brentwood Court is a gated community of muckety mucks and well-to-do folks. There are security guards at all the entrances and every place comes standard with an alarm and wide crown molding. I believe there's also a bylaw specific to that part of town that prohibits dog ownership owing to their destruction of the "natural landscape".

It seemed like an eternity before the rest of the gang showed up to the boat, but the wait was worth it. A people-watcher by nature, I was engrossed in the airs Lisa put on. Watching her give the treatment to the guys as they arrived, I pegged her as the poor man's Scarlett O'Hara. Fishing for compliments and doling them out, but not as successfully as you could tell she'd hoped. When she greeted Seacroft with "What a nice young fellow," I about died. He doesn't look a day under sixty-five. And when she was introduced to Doctor Stephen Richards, I swear I saw her blush. The good doctor probably gets that a lot, though and I can only imagine what a hopping place his practice would be if he specialized in gynecology. Sefton and Muncie were the last to arrive, and each received a mock scolding from Lisa who threatened to paddle them the next time they were tardy. That was just plain weird.

As I sat at the poker table, watching the *Lisa Show*, I couldn't help but notice her attire. It's what I refer to as "yold". It's when an older woman dresses inappropriately young for her age. Subscribing to trends for the sake of trends that don't suit her at all. Now, Lisa has what I've overheard the gang call a "bulbous bow", meaning she's well endowed—either by nature or a surgeon, it doesn't matter. But what *does* matter is how you dress it. The low-cut vee neck sweater she wore over tight fuchsia capri pants screamed "Look at me!" It wasn't long before I felt a nudge from beside me.

"You're staring," Doctor Richards sort of whispered, sort of mumbled.

I stopped immediately, shifting my gaze to the window ledge where there were lined up a quartet of pumpkin-spice scented candles I'd never noticed before.

Sefton must have been taking inventory of our hostess as well. "Those are some fancy shoes," he said.

"Manolo Blancos," Lisa replied.

I nodded. Even I knew she had mangled the designer name.

As the rest of the gang got seated, and Jack doled out the cards, they got some polite chatter out of the way. "So, you live over in Brentwood Court, I hear," Sefton said.

Lisa didn't immediately respond.

"Lee, honey, Sefton asked you a question," Jack said.

"Oh, I'm sorry. I was wondering about–"

"About the ring?" Jack interjected, and he seemed bothered.

"What ring?" I asked, hoping Jack Junior wasn't lonely enough to have already popped the question.

"Oh, Lisa lost her diamond ring today. Darned thing slipped right off her finger," Jack said, shaking his head. "I told you, sweetie, that it must be because you're wasting away."

"Where'd you last see it?" I asked. I'd always considered myself somewhat good at finding things, and I was willing to give it a go, even for Lisa.

"On the boat here, today," she replied weakly.

"Oh, really?" I asked, and I noticed my tone went up an octave.

"Three carats," Jack smirked.

"Three, huh?" I nodded and I wondered how many of the carats were real.

"Well, if I see it out on the dock or something, I'll let you know."

"Oh, I'm sure if anyone sees it, they'll just keep it. You know what a world this is, hon."

I nodded. The insinuation irked me. "Well, I'd like to think that the residents here are a tad more honest than that. You had it insured, I hope?"

"Well, I hadn't updated my policy to our new town here, so no. It was voided when we moved."

I nodded again. That is to say I kept myself from rolling my eyes, because it took every fiber of my being to not call bullshit on the woman.

Peter Muncie piped up, "Hey, Lisa, you must know that cop that comes around from time to time, Hagen."

"A police officer? Now, why on earth would I know a police officer?" She seemed downright insulted. The *Lisa Show* was getting good.

"He lives in Brentwood Court, doesn't he?" Peter looked directly at me to ask.

"Yes, I believe so." It wasn't up to me to tell the gang that Ben Hagen most certainly lived there and that he made the best steak this side of Carter's Steak and Chop House.

"So, you know him?" Peter indelicately persisted.

"No, I don't think I've had the pleasure."

"Oh, you'd uh, you'd remember him," Jack Junior guffawed. "Shiny black hair, very preppy, and always smiles with too many teeth," Jack said, pointing to his mouth.

"Jack!" I griped.

"What? I don't trust people who smile with *that* many teeth."

"You're just jealous because he still has that many teeth," I quipped.

"Oh, now that you describe him a little, I do remember seeing him, I think. He's what my mother would have called 'popular' with the fairer sex, isn't he?" and when she sent that zinger sailing, she was looking directly at me, waiting for a reaction.

I changed the subject. "Jack, are you going to deal?" The heat was rising in my cheeks.

"Oh, I'm sorry Alexandra, dear, is he a special friend of yours?" Lisa sent a gloating smile at me, or were those fangs she was bearing?

Whatever they were, she didn't like me. And despite seeing right through her tactics, a part of me wondered if it might be true. The part about Ben being popular. And while I stared blankly at my cards, my mind wandered. Ben Hagen *is* a good-looking guy, wealthy. Something befitting the country club set if it interested him. What could he see in a boat nerd who can't for the life of her keep herself clean and tidy? I'd walked onto the *Fortune Cookie* feeling good, and the woman in the tight pants on the barstool in the salon, thumbing through a fashion magazine, had reduced me to a self-conscious schoolgirl.

Richards nudged me back into the game.

"Two," I said and laid down a couple cards. "Hey, anybody going to Hamilton soon?"

"Why, what's there, kiddo?" Jack asked.

"I've got to take some pictures and get information on listings. The client's away on a job and he told me he'd double my commission rate if I took the pictures and did more of the leg work for him."

"Why don't you take the truck?" Sefton asked and plunked down a hand that won the pot.

I smirked. I had a measly pair of kings. "Well, to be honest, I don't know how to drive stick, but if one of you taught me…"

"Don't look at me," Peter said.

It was a shared sentiment around the table as though this was something they'd rehearsed. I turned to my right. "How about you, Doc? Could you teach me?"

"Could I? Yes. Will I? No."

"Why not?"

"Because, thus far I consider us to be friends."

"What's that supposed to mean?"

"It means that teaching someone to drive stick can be... tricky."

I felt my lower lip extrude into a pout.

"Yeah, you need to find someone to teach you who can take your abuse," Muncie chimed in.

"Fair enough." I nodded and decided to ask *that* person the next day.

"What do ya say we take five?" Richards suggested after a few more hands.

"You always say that when you're losing," Peter Muncie griped.

"Hmm, for a guy who is looking for a new GP, you've got some real attitude, Muncie," Richards scoffed playfully.

"Ok, ok, let's take five," Muncie agreed.

Doctor Richards got up from the table and stretched his back, arching and twisting. I watched as Lisa eyed him, and by eyed him I mean looked at him from top to bottom, lingering somewhere in the middle.

"Rough day?" I asked.

"Just a kink in my back," he said, and I watched as he took a triangle sandwich from crab mountain.

I was watching and waiting for his reaction to the sandwich filling when Lisa walked to the sideboard, reached around Richards, and from my vantage point, I saw her brush her bow against his stern. I felt myself arch an eyebrow and I thought I was going to be sick.

"Oh, excuse me," she said breathily, practically panting. I then watched her pour herself a scotch and jauntily hop back onto the barstool. "What you need, sweetie, is a good massage."

I lowered my head and felt my mouth drop open, and the room went deathly quiet. From the corner of my eye, I could see Jack Junior shift awkwardly in his chair and down his vodka tonic.

"Alright, let's deal the shingles," he said, his tone all business.

I felt agitated for Jack, I felt sorry for Doctor Richards, and I felt a little queasy from that sketchy crab sandwich. I was wondering if any subject was safe, but I was resolute to lighten the mood. "So, Peter, how are the ladies on the *Gee Spot*? You've been over there quite a bit lately."

"They're real nice ladies." He smiled. "What you see is what you get," he added, and I wondered if mentally he had prefaced that sentence with "unlike Lisa..."

How right he would have been.

CHAPTER 8

I frantically reached my arms out, one after the other, and kicked my legs, but my efforts got me nowhere. I looked up to see the moon beaming down, the size of a dinner plate, on a vast expanse of water with no land in sight. I began to tire, and I felt the suffocating pressure of the water pushing me down. The water was dark. Black. If you've never seen black water, it's scary and the nightmare you're too old to believe in. It gives you the feeling that you'll sink for an eternity. I sputtered and fought against the water that was strangling me. In my last breath on the surface, I spotted the red light of a buoy in the distance. I felt myself sinking and then... I bolted upright, breathless, turned to my right, and saw the glow from the alarm clock illuminating the glass of water on my bedside table. I ran my hand through my hair and exhaled a deep, relieved breath. "I guess I'm up," I said.

It was still dark out, and I flicked on a light and shuffled across the passageway to my office and woke up my sleeping computer. At least one of us had gotten a decent rest. There was that email from my new client in Hamilton. He had itemized two work boats, a truckable barge, a generator, and a landing craft that he wanted me to sell for him. He said that he'd taken his marine coordinator with him on their latest project out of town and it'd be up to me to take pictures of the items and, in fact, he was giving me the exclusive rights to the listings. If only I could get there to take current photos and collect specifications. While I waited for morning to break, I read the news online, looking for updates on the robberies in town (there were none), and checking my horoscope (Geminis were in for an eventful week). I updated a few records in Salesforce, my CRM software, and got caught up on my financial statements. Then I found a station that had started playing Christmas music and I swiveled my hips to "Blue Christmas" and other bouncy tunes while I vacuumed the main level of my boat. Getting dressed, I rehearsed how to ask for a driving lesson or two. I mean, I had to learn to drive the truck at some point and I had a good idea who could teach me.

When I crossed the doorway into Aggie's, there *he* was. Seated at the counter on the middle red and chrome vinyl stool, wearing jeans and a blue and white checked shirt. On approach, I noticed the skin between the back of his ears and his sandy brown hair and the straight band of tanned skin above his collar, signs of a fresh haircut. He was spreading strawberry jam on his whole wheat toast and I took the stool next to him after waving my morning salute to the gang in the nook.

I smiled at the man beside me. "Hiya, Bugsy."

"Morning," he said and took a bite big enough to leave sugary red specks of jam in the corners of his mouth.

"Can you teach me how to drive stick?" I asked.

He instantly stopped chewing. Pausing, I presume, to wonder if he'd heard me correctly. He swallowed and looked at me with squinty-eyed surprise. "You don't know how to drive stick?"

"Not exactly. So, will you?"

"No." Bugsy shook his head vigorously without, it appears, having even for a moment considered the request before answering and then taking a sip of coffee.

"Why not?"

He swallowed the gulp. "Because I know you, and despite everything that has transpired, I still consider us friends."

"Come on. Please, pretty please. Pretty please with strawberry jam on top? You have a little right here, by the way," I said, touching the corner of my mouth to illustrate.

"No," he said and dabbed at the jam on his face

then licked his finger.

"Come on, Bugsy."

He looked at me flatly. The moniker still hadn't caught on.

"I mean, please Mr. Beedle, I'd be forever in your debt if you'd just show me how to drive Nat's truck."

"What's the urgency? It's been sitting for months," he said, taking another slurp of coffee.

"I have a big client in Hamilton and I need to get there." I batted my eyelashes at him.

"You have something in your eye?"

I smirked. "No," I huffed. Bugsy can't be won over by feminine wiles, but he's known to indulge in dessert from time to time. "Look, I might even bake you a pie," I said, keeping the language vague, no promises explicitly made.

Bugsy took another crunchy bite of toast. "What do *you* think?" he asked, looking up to survey Aggie who had just topped up our mugs.

Ags looked as though she were contemplating the response, for a little too long if you asked me. "I'd go for it, Bugsy," she said even though I know she's doubted my coordination skills since the intro to Zumba class she took me to, which I think we agree was a colossal mistake.

Bugsy took a sip of coffee and nodded as he swallowed. "I'm going to hate myself for this." He looked down at his watch. "Ok, I can show you at... fourteen hundred hours."

"Why can't you just say two o'clock like a

regular person? Nobody talks in hundreds of hours and thousands of seconds and—" I stopped myself when I saw the expression on his face had changed to one of annoyance.

"Young lady, you don't sound like someone who wants a favor." He smiled and batted *his* eyelashes at *me* this time.

"Ok, ok. Fourteen hundred hours. At the motor pool." I smiled back at him. He left with his to-go mug topped up and I tore a corner off the fritter Aggie had plated for me.

"I didn't want to say anything in front of Bugsy, and I know you hate it when I say this, but you look tired," Ags said lowly, looking a little concerned.

"I am," I said, intimating that there was something to it.

"What's going on?" She picked out a fritter and took a bite, fortifying herself and preparing for the details of my latest crisis.

"Do you ever, um, have recurring dreams?" I whispered. I didn't need the two cents from the guys in the nook.

"Not often, but my therapist says I'm not half bad at interpreting them. Lay it on me," she said just before taking another bite.

I downed a big sip of coffee. "Ok. Well, I've had this dream twice recently. I'm out in the water. Swimming, I mean, not on the boat, and it's nighttime. There's a moon and it's shining on the water but there's no land in sight and I can't touch the bottom. But there *is* a buoy off in the distance."

"Mmhmm? Go on." Ags narrowed her eyes and fixed them on me; I could see her wheels were turning.

"And my clothes are heavy with water and I'm panicking and…" I took a deep breath while I relived the feeling. "And I feel suffocated by the water and…"

She nodded. "Mmhmm," her tone different this time. Decisive.

"What 'Mmhmm'?"

"You want the short version or the long one?"

I rolled my eyes at her. "Just tell me."

"You're not gonna like it."

"Ags…"

"It's Bugsy."

I turned to look behind me to see if he was back in the store. He wasn't there and I swivelled back to face Ags. "Bugsy? What about him?"

"You don't want to rent Nat's boat to him because you feel it would suffocate you. You're so used to being single and dressing like a slob—"

"Ags!"

"I'm just kidding," she said. "About the dressing part. The rest is accurate, though." She took another bite of the fritter and sent me a satisfied smile. "Also, the deep water. You're afraid of falling into that bottomless, limitless pit of love," she said theatrically and got a silly dreamy look in her eyes.

I shook my head. "No way. That's not it."

Aggie shrugged. "That's my two cents."

"For your two cents, I owe you change," I said and looked up at the clock wondering how I could sneak in a nap before two and ensure a dreamless one at that.

***

"Ok, now the first thing we do when we get in a vehicle is...?"

I gave Bugsy a squinty-eyed skeptical look and wondered when he'd adopted the tone of a kindergarten teacher.

"Adjust the radio," I said confidently and reached for the dial.

"No, as the passenger, that's *my* job," he said, brushing my hand away from the dash and smiling, flashing those dimples he carried like a concealed weapon. The kind of heat-seeking missile that always makes my cheeks flush. "But, for now, we'll skip the tunes so you can concentrate."

"I can't concentrate *without* music," was my whiney kindergartner response.

"The way I hear it, you can't concentrate *with* music. I heard about that Zumba class."

I scowled toward the passenger seat and made a mental note to speak to Aggie *once again* about over-sharing. "Look, that class was for Zumba ninjas. I need the radio to..." I began to plead my case when I looked to see Bugsy lift the door handle as if to leave the vehicle. "Wait, wait. I'm sorry. Don't leave me."

"Are you going to take this seriously?"

"Well, not as seriously as you, but..."

Bugsy rolled his eyes. The way he did it gave me a twinge of regret for the countless times I'd done it to him. But what's done is done.

"Ok, are you comfortable?" he asked.

I bounced my tush up and down a few times on the baby blue upholstered bench seat. "Yes. For someone with no music, that is."

"That's two. One more and I'm going to let you sit here."

"Ok, I'm sorry."

"Now, dump out the coffee."

"Why? I'm tired. I *need* coffee."

"You'll understand in a minute."

"But—"

"No buts, just dump it or..." Bugsy motioned toward the door handle again.

"Geez, you are a little harsh, aren't you? I thought–"

"You thought what?"

"Nothing," I said and dumped the contents of my travel mug on the pavement. I guess I couldn't blame the man for being in a bad mood. I've never faced eviction, but I'm sure it's no treat to have that on your mind. Still, I thought he'd be a tad nicer to me considering I was mulling over the solution to his housing dilemma.

"Now you've got the three pedals. See them? Gas, brake, and clutch." He looked at me to gauge my level of understanding as if I had lost the ability to count.

"Hmmm."

"What now?" he asked.

"There are three pedals, but I've only got two feet, Bugsy." I looked over to see him in profile, closing his eyes, the corners of his mouth turned up slightly. Try as he might, he couldn't stifle that smile. A few idle threats later from Bugsy, the odd smart-ass remark from yours truly, and something like instructions from mission control at NASA, I got Nat's truck moving. First, slowly and jarringly, but the ride smoothed out along with the conversation.

"So, what's new?" I asked.

"Oh, not much, new dock going in at pier seven and I'm working on the laundry building."

I nodded as I concentrated on what little traffic there was and cringed at the grinding sounds I was sure the truck wasn't supposed to make. We talked about Jack's new girlfriend— Bugsy thought she seemed ok. We conjectured about Russ Shears' background or lack thereof— Bugsy wasn't bothered by it. We even discussed the *Gee Spot* gals—Gladys had put the moves on him and he politely turned her down.

"So, I uh, was at Aggie's the other night," I said.

"Oh yeah. Red light ahead," he warned me two blocks early. I could see him press his leg into the imaginary brake pedal on his side.

"I can see it," I sighed. "And she mentioned—"

"Lemme guess. She mentioned my—"

"Yeah, your dad. You want to talk about it?"

"Not much to say. He's evicting me. Trying to prove a point, I guess."

"And Ags said you want to move into Nat's boat." I looked across at him.

"Eyes on the road." He nodded at me. "That's just something she came up with. I couldn't ask you to..."

I pulled into the public parking lot on State Street. "Do you mind? I have to pop into the Hobby Mart to get a magnifying glass for my night school course."

"Sure," he said and stepped out of the truck, walked around the front, and met me on the sidewalk. "What is it you're taking again?"

"It's a communications analysis course. To-morrow night we're looking at handwriting."

"Does anyone still write by hand?" he asked, looking at me, his eyebrows raised.

"Just us throwbacks," I said while opening the door to the Hobby Mart. "Hey, if you don't mind me asking—" I began to say over my shoulder while I scouted the aisles.

"You know I'm an open book," he said.

"So, read me a page." I turned and smiled at him. "Why are you getting the boot?"

"Do you remember just why I got sent here?"

I picked up a magnifying glass and aimed it at my driving instructor who proceeded to make a ridiculous yet charming face. "You mean why you got exiled to the island of misfit toys?"

"Yeah," he said and, under magnification, the dimples he unleashed were startlingly huge.

I took my purchase to the counter. "Something about a land deal, right?"

"Exactly. So, it turns out the deal didn't go through because of me. The soil was bad and I couldn't live with myself if they put a kids rec center there. Heck, my boy might have even played there."

"I get it," I said and, even though Aggie had told me the story, I wanted Bugsy to tell me himself. It's something he should be proud of doing and I knew he wouldn't have told me unless I'd specifically asked.

"$10.27, please," the clerk said after making some noise with the cash register.

I dug out a twenty from my all-purpose red and navy canvas do-everything bag.

"And now your old man—your dad, I mean— is blaming you." I dropped the change in my bag along with the magnifying glass.

Bugsy opened the door for me. "Punishing me is more like it."

"Why doesn't he just fire you and put you out of your misery?"

"Because then he'd have to pay me out. Been there fifteen years and I've got a sweet severance package if he ever pulls the pin. Instead, I think he's just planning to make my life miserable."

"And I guess that's why you don't quit either."

"Yeah. Besides, other than dealing with him and my brother at the office, I kinda like my job. Thing is, I can't afford much in the way of rent. After paying child and spousal support, it doesn't leave me with a heck of a lot."

"I see." I nodded. "Well, I would have to run anything about the *Splendored Thing* past Trammer, of course."

"Oh, I get it," he said, and we were finally back at the truck in the parking lot. There was something about seeing it there, not at the marina and not with Nat walking beside me. Something about the emptiness of the *Splendored Thing*, something about the loss of my friend that washed over me like a wave. Something about the razorblades I felt in my throat that made me barely able to eke out my next words.

"Bugsy?" My voice faltered, my steps felt heavy.

"Yeah?"

"Would you mind driving me back to the marina?" I felt suddenly wan.

He looked at me. Somehow, he knew what I was going through. And when I climbed in the passenger side of the truck then watched him for a few minutes driving it with all the confidence and expertise of Nat, I couldn't hide my wistfulness.

He tried to overcome my sudden melancholy with a compliment. "You're actually a good driver. You know, I didn't think you would be, but..."

I cleared my throat and blinked away the tear I felt forming.

"Sorry. I guess you miss him a lot, huh?"

I nodded.

"You want another lesson sometime soon? I don't mind."

"Sure," I said and barely recognized the shakiness in my voice. When we returned to the marina, I went straight to the *Fortune Cookie*.

* * *

I was decompressing with Jack Junior, sitting on the stern of his boat, reminiscing about Nat and people watching when a couple aimed themselves down the dock toward us. I immediately recognized the woman as Lisa Claire—her petite and at the same time bulbus figure unmistakable.

"Who's that man with Lisa, Jack?"

"Him? Oh, he's-he's Lisa's son."

The man walking toward us coming down the dock with Lisa looked like a rough-around-the-edges type that was trying like the devil to smooth them out. He looked uncomfortable. Like he hadn't picked out his own clothes. Khaki pants with a hard crease in them and a blue button-down collared shirt. Even his gait was off, like he was just breaking in new shoes.

"Hi, sweetheart," Jack greeted Lisa and offered

his hand to her in assistance in boarding the boat.

"Hi, Jacky. You remember Roddy, don't you?" Lisa's 1950s starlet charade had resumed.

"Oh, sure, sure. Welcome aboard, Rod. Make yourself comfortable."

I smiled and cleared my throat ever so slightly, wondering if I'd rate an introduction, though it wasn't critical in my estimation.

Lisa's eyes flicked at me. "Oh, Alexandra, I didn't see you there."

"Hmm, must be my new diet," I said, hoping it sounded less snippy than I'd intended.

"Oh, uh sorry, kiddo. Where are my manners? Roddy Claire, this is Alex Michaels," Jack Junior finally said.

Roddy extended his hand. I noticed it was smallish for a man, and his fingernails were gnawed to the quick. He was small-framed for roughly 5'9" and didn't look trim so much as he looked deficient in iron and other vital nutritional requirements. He had dark features and deep-set eyes under heavy brows. Thin lips parted to reveal straight teeth, but I got the impression he didn't smile much. His nose looked slightly off center, like it'd been broken a time or two, and he had lines around his eyes and on his forehead. His dark brown hair looked an unnaturally uniform color as though it'd been dyed, and the sun glinted off the product that was keeping it in place. He reminded me of when you were in middle school and the new kid was introduced—he didn't look remotely like anyone else in the room and he certainly didn't look like he wanted to be there.

"How do you do?" I said. Heck, I can fake manners with the best of them.

"Hey! Would ya look at that! That a new purse, Lee?" Jack asked far too enthusiastically.

"Yes, honey. Roddy bought it for his mama," she said, and I really thought I'd have to stick my head over the side of the boat to be sick.

I raised my eyebrows and gave Lisa the once-over. She had the appearance of a proud mother to what I gathered was a pricey purse. Though I'm not a procurer myself, I was familiar with the gold emblem that dangled from the strap. Still looked like it paled in comparison with the practicality of my all-purpose red and blue tote bag with no special features but a rope drawstring. And, while we're on the subject, though I pride myself on my miserable grasp of brand names and conspicuous consumerism, I know a Rolex when I see one, and Roddy looked to be sporting a nice one.

Jack took the drink orders for the two and pulled out a chair for Lisa to sit at the table on the stern deck with us and Roddy took up the remaining chair beside me. I smiled politely as my eyes followed the watch curiously, when Roddy rested his hand on the arm of the chair. *What do you suppose it was? Real or fake as that horrible imitation crab Lisa'd served up on poker night?* My father had a real one that he left me. It sits on my desk as a reminder to make the most of each minute and, after many thoughtless hours of studying it during my fair share of daydreams, I'd learned the hallmarks of a Rolex and compared them to Roddy's arm candy in my mental checklist of telling real from fake. If only there was a checklist for bona fide people.

One. The second hand on Roddy's watch was smooth, not stuttering. Check.

Two. The little lens over the date looked as though it actually magnified it. Check.

Three. I leaned over and pretended to tie my shoelaces—all the better to spy on the quality of the winder. It looked as ornate as it ought to. Check?

The only other way I know to spot a real Rolex from a fake is by the heft of the watch —made with better materials than a fake, they tend to weigh significantly more. But I couldn't think of a way to ask Roddy to let me hold it. All things considered though, the watch checked out, but it seemed so incompatible with the man who wore it.

Jack emerged from the salon of his boat with a club soda for Lisa and a beer for her spawn. "Hard to believe he's her son, isn't it?" he said good and loud.

"Oh?" I asked, ready to play this game with Junior.

"Would ya believe she had him when she was *fifteen*?" He loud-whispered the age with such incredulity that he sounded like he actually believed that line.

"Oh?" I said again, not ready to burst his bubble.

"Owns his own company and he's just turned thirty," Jack said in a tone that led me to believe he took that as gospel.

"Oh?" I said again like a skipping record and smiled at Rod. Behind my aviator glasses, I rolled my eyes. If my past as a CFO had taught me two things, it was math and spotting a fraud. According to the little fairy tale Jack had been told, Lisa Claire was forty-five. Right. Maybe in dog years. Lisa was sixty-five if she was a day and her son had to be at least forty, though everything about him screamed fresh out of the package.

"Jack told Lisa that you sell boats. That true?" Roddy turned to ask me.

"Yes," I said in a tone perplexed by Roddy referring to his mother by her first name. "Well, I broker them. Are you in the market for one?"

"I'm in the market for a good deal on one. Something fast. The watch is real, by the way, in case you're wondering."

I nodded, taken aback for a moment by the brashness of the man. "Well, if you want to write down your contact information, I'd be happy to let you know if any screaming deals hit my desk," I said and looked around for the pad and pencil Jack Junior uses when he tests out his crossword answers before committing to putting them in his puzzles. I didn't care so much about Roddy's number or email address as I did about getting a sample of his handwriting to take to my night school class. Maybe it'd reveal the reason my Spidey senses were tingling.

"Look at her over there talking shop." Jack Junior nudged Lisa and pointed in my direction. "Hey, Rod, if you're looking for a boat, she's the best. Give him a card, kiddo."

I shook my head, pretending not to have any on me, which may have been true. I've yet to master the art of self-promotion.

"Come on, just give him a card. Hey, you know what, Rod, you can have one of mine," Junior said. My eyes followed him as he popped out of his chair and into the salon and took a card from a stack of business cards I recognized as mine—navy background with white lettering, anchor logo. "Here ya go, Rod," he said, handing him the card.

"Jack, why do you have a stack of my business cards?" I was intrigued and worried at the same time, wondering how diligently Jack Junior vets the folks to whom he hands out the card that includes my cell number.

"Oh, I took 'em during poker night one time at your place. You know, figured I'd help you drum up some business." He nodded to himself as he returned to his chair.

"I see." I gave him a raised eyebrow. "Well, I've got to be going," I said. "Nice to see you again, Lisa," I lied. "Nice to meet you, Rod," I lied again. "Going to the last night of the fair and I've got to get ready. Hagen'll be there, so I'll put in a little more effort," I said and sent a wink from the heart sailing toward Jack Junior.

❄ ❄ ❄

It's hard not to love a fall fair, isn't it? Even when it's known as Weener Fest, as in Halloweener Fest. Every year, Marysville's biggest fall event kicks off on Halloween and lasts for two weeks. The town council is not oblivious to the implications of such a risqué name, but anything that promotes unity and community is alright with them. They do, however, draw the line occasionally. For instance, although the haunted house at the Weener Fest is sponsored by Burcham's Petroleum, council refuses to allow them to call it the Gas Chamber. Good call.

I had been barking out my slogans in support of the puppy rescue and dog shelter to such great success—"Buy a t-shirt! Support a puppy!"—that we'd run out of shirts to sell.

"Do it doggy style" was the more interesting marketing line Aggie spouted as she held up identifying tags and an assortment of pet paraphernalia donated by Martin's Pet Store.

Weaving her way through the booths of candy floss and carnival games, I spotted Marcy Kennedy—local vet, head of the Chamber of Commerce, and the champion of the dog shelter.

"Ladies, how are sales going?" she asked.

"So far, about a thousand bucks and, let's see, we got three phone numbers," Aggie said, pulling the business cards from her rear pocket.

"*You* got three phone numbers," I clarified. "And we sold out of shirts."

"Great news on the shirts. Dance starts in five minutes, thought we'd come and relieve you," Marcy said, her youngest daughter in tow.

"Thanks, Marce. Gives us time to get ready," Aggie said, shook her head, and then looked down at herself disgustedly.

"What? I'm ready," I said, feeling quizzical.

"No, you're not," she protested.

"I am so." I looked down at my white blouse and skinny jeans and, just for the sake of making an adjustment, I tightened my ponytail. "Ok, *now* I'm ready."

"Girl, Officer Handsome's gonna take one look at you and—"

"Hagen. And he's used to seeing me look like... this," I said, for want of a better word.

"Girl, a man who looks like that and has money..."

"And who's taking you to the ball, Cinderella? Or dare I ask?"

"I'm going stag," she said.

"Oh, and where's what's his name? If that's really his name."

"Russ? He said he had an errand or something." She shrugged then ducked down and, like some professional quick-change artist, whipped off her dog rescue t-shirt in favor of a one-size-too-small plaid shirt she couldn't even close the top buttons of.

"Who'd you steal that from, some little kid?" I asked when she popped up and nearly popped out.

Ags looked beyond me over my shoulder. "Your date's here."

"He's not my *date*," I said, adding air quotes and hoping I wasn't slipping into a habit.

"Alex, ready to go?" Hagen asked, his voice raised over the sound checks in the distance, the feature band warming up.

When I turned to look at Hagen, I couldn't help but notice that he turned other heads as well. Twentysomethings to sixty-somethings were looking at him as if he were a sign that advertised half-price Burberry bags. He was dressed smartly in khakis and a white button-down oxford shirt with the sleeves rolled up. His forearms boasting a tan and that big silver diving watch of his. His jet-black hair parted to the side as perfectly as always. I had, for the longest time, tried to find something wrong with him, something that made him seem human. I'd finally landed on the fact that he had a screwed-up index finger, an injury from his college days where, of course, he was the quarterback of the winning football team.

"Sure. Yeah, let's go," I said. I tied my donation apron on Taryn, Marcy's daughter. "Now smile, tell the boys how much you like a boy who loves animals, and don't' give out your real phone number."

"And show a little cleavage if you can," Ags tossed over her shoulder as she left the booth.

"Don't listen to her," I heard Marcy whisper to her daughter. "Have fun," she shouted after us.

By the time we reached the stage area, the feature band had already begun to play. Out in the dance area, I spotted Sefton, Peter Muncie, and the ladies from the *Gee Spot* gyrating to a new take on an old song. Sefton looked as though he was single-handedly trying to bring back the Twist, while Peter Muncie twirled Gladys with one arm and Ginny with the other. Geraldine danced solo to the beat of her own drum.

"Hail, hail. The gang's all here," I heard a voice behind me say. It was Jack Junior and, when I turned, I noticed that, like Ags, he had come to the event stag—though I can't honestly say I was disappointed. Leaning on hay bales that served as cheap seating options, Jack was with Seacroft, Doctor Richards, Bugsy, and Johnny Fleet, and I felt myself smile with surprise when my eyes landed on lawyer Cary Tranmer. I wasn't aware he'd be coming for a visit. The last time he'd been at the marina was in late summer.

"Nice to see you again," I said.

"Pleasure's mine, my dear," he replied, and without skipping a beat, as the band transitioned into the next song, "Shall we?" he asked, motioning toward the dance floor such that it was—a big grassy area littered with errant bits of straw.

Without hesitation, I took his arm and his lead and, to the tune of a classic country music tale of woe, Tranmer floated across the dance floor and I tried to keep up. In his sixties, but moving more like a man half that age, Tranmer glided and cut an elegant figure amidst a volume of rustics moving indelicately. I felt classy just being in his arms. My eyes flitted over the sea of what, by comparison, looked like amateurs—Hagen had convinced Ags to take a turn on the floor, and the guys were enjoying the company of the Gee Spotters.

"How have you been?" he asked.

"Good."

"Been keeping an eye on Junior?"

"In as far as that's possible." I smiled. "Have you met his new girlfriend?"

"Junior has *a girlfriend*?"

"Yes, he does. I'm sure you'll meet her soon." I smiled. "How long are you planning to stay this time?"

"Oh, I don't know, until after Thanksgiving, I guess. I came to the dinner at the marina last time. It was good. Didn't see you at that one."

"Yeah, I had a thing," I said. My thing was called a pity party.

I ran my next sentence over in my head a few times before putting it out into the universe, briefly contemplating the karmic consequences. "Well, to avoid any awkwardness with sleeping arrangements and such on Jack's boat, do you want to stay on the *Splendored Thing*?"

"I thought for a minute you were going to invite me to sleep on your couch." He smiled. Tranmer's a smoothie. "But that's a good idea. I'll put my bags on Nat's boat."

Tranmer whirled me around the dance floor and, whether or not he planned it that way, he concluded our number exactly where we'd started just as the band played the last note of the song. Either he got lucky or he knows some secret dancing voodoo.

"Hey, save a dance for me," Hagen said once we'd all reconvened at our hay bale headquarters. "Would you like a drink?" he asked and motioned toward the very busy bar area.

"Ginger ale, if you please." And with that, Hagen's perfectly shiny, perfectly parted jet-black hair disappeared into the throngs. When he returned, his respite was short lived, and a buzz on his phone, like the bat signal, was his call to action. I held his drink while he took the call.

"Mmhmm... Mmhmm... Really? Ok... I'll be

there in fifteen, no, twenty minutes. I have to change," he said and returned the phone to the holster on his belt. "Sorry, I have to go. I owe you."

I nodded. "It's ok, I understand. I'll take a handwriting sample for my class." I smiled, hopeful that maybe his scrawl would reveal in him an imperfection or two I'd find irresistible.

"You'll get home ok?"

"Oh, sure, I'll thumb a ride."

Hagen cocked his head and gave me scolding eyes.

"I mean I'll get a ride with the gang."

"Ok," and with that he was off, practically galloping through the crowd.

Ags nudged me with that bony elbow of hers. "What's going on?"

I shrugged. "Work, I guess."

And so, I sat out the next two undanceable songs with Ags. Leaning on the bales of hay, people watching, and guessing how old Granny Fleet's boyfriend might be. The band struck up another ballad. I recognized the first few notes of "You were Always on my Mind" and watched as the gang seemed to naturally pair up with the Gee Spotters and Ags. I was left standing shoulder to shoulder with Bugsy.

It took me by complete surprise when he reached over and took my hand and, without a word, led me to the dance floor.

CHAPTER 9

"So, did you talk to Tranmer about Bugsy staying on the boat?" Ags asked.

"Not exactly. Last night didn't seem like the time. But I will," I said, sort of lying, sort of not. "He's staying on the boat for a bit. He didn't want to cramp Jack's style, what with Lisa around." Again, sort of lying sort of not, but I didn't want to get into a whole big thing about everyone's housing issues in the produce section of Mack's Foodland.

"Ok, cool. I think Bugsy has until the end of the month, though. Hey, what do you think Russ would like better? Chicken Kiev or Beef Wellington?"

"I think he'd be content with a hotdog." I smirked as I carried my basket around the impressively large produce section.

Ags peeked into my grocery basket. "Ugh, I can't believe you eat that stuff."

"What?" I asked, looking down at the contents of my basket and wondering just what she was judging so harshly—the kale or the whipped cream in a can—which by the way I feed my cat. I reached to squeeze the summit of a mountain of avocados and looked up to find Ags, but instead Lisa Claire caught my eye. Her unmistakably high teased and dyed hair made her easy to catch. She was perusing the cart of discounted vegetables. Little pink stickers are used to let the cashier know it's marked down 30%. She didn't see me, and I didn't let on that I'd seen her either. I strained my peripheral muscles to watch as she daintily peeled pink stickers off wilting heads of lettuce and bananas dying a slow brown death. I'd never seen anyone do that and wondered just what she was up to until my eyes followed her to the meat section. She leaned into the cooler and pulled out a few cuts of meat, and then she proceeded to nonchalantly pull a pink discount sticker from up her sleeve and smooth it onto the meat she placed in her mini cart. It was engrossing, to say the least, and I looked around, wondering if anyone else had seen her do it.

"Ready? I chose chicken," I heard from behind me.

"Hmmm?" Ags had jolted me from this episode of the *Lisa Show*. "Sure. Yeah, let's go." My words were quick.

"What's the matter? You look like you're

going to be sick."

"I might be. Let's check out," I said, and we made a beeline for the shortest check-out line. You can probably guess how that went.

"So? What gives?" Ags asked once we were outside near the cart return.

"I saw Lisa in there," I said, looking back toward the doors to the store.

"Lisa? Jack's booty call Lisa?"

"Something like that."

"Did she talk to you?"

"She didn't see me. But if I were stealing from the grocery store, I probably wouldn't wave to all my friends either."

"What friends?" Ags smirked. "And what do you mean *stealing*? You saw her stealing? She shove a roast down her pants?"

"Not quite. But there's no other word for it. She took the pink stickers off the old produce and put them on the meat she put in her cart."

"You're making that up."

"Ags, if I was going to make up a story, it'd be a lot more interesting than that."

"But—"

"Shhhhh," I said.

"What 'shhhh'?"

"There she is. Turn around," I said and whirred Ags by the arm so her back faced the sticker swapper. When we turned, Lisa was walking away from the store with a little cart.

"Hey," I said lowly, "you, uh, wanna follow

her?"

"No."

"Oh, come on, it'll be fun."

"No."

"Why not?"

"Alex, it's bad karma."

"Karma, shmarma. Look, Russ can wait for his dinner."

Ags pulled her phone from her back pocket and looked at the screen. "Ok, ten minutes."

"Ok, ten minutes... or so," I said. "She lives over in Brentwood Court. That's going to be a long walk with those groceries she's got," I said and hopped in Nat's truck. I'd been daring enough to take it out with a little moral support from my friend.

"Brentwood? Well, hoity toity. Isn't that where Officer Handsome lives?" Ags asked, buckling up.

"Hagen. Yeah."

As we moved down Main Street, I was surprised to see Lisa Claire make a left on Mergl. "Where the heck is she going?" I asked my partner.

"If she's going to Brentwood, she sure is taking the scenic route," Ags grumbled.

"Odd," I mumbled, transfixed by her movements.

I parked the truck at the corner of Mergl and Vine and we watched as Lisa walked into the driveway of the Vine Street Inn.

"The Vine?" Ags turned to me with a scrunched-up expression. "Seriously?"

I pulled up on the door handle of the truck.

"You're going to follow her?"

"Of course not. I'm going in the office. I just want to check this out. If she lied to Jack, I'll—"

"Cool your jets there, sista. What do you want *me* to do?"

"Just honk if you see her headed my way," I said and hoped that the horn actually worked.

"Ten-four. Be careful in there," Ags said and popped a few grapes from her grocery haul into her mouth.

Even in the brief time I'd lived in Marysville, I'd learned the reputation of the Vine Street Inn. It was somewhere between a cheap tourist motel and a flop house. It had changed hands recently and, while most people in town hoped the thing would be razed, so far the only change was that the grass had been cut. One of the last and most unfortunate examples of 1970s architecture was still intact, barely. When I looked up at the soffits at the entrance to the office, the aluminum flashing was stained grey from spider crap and maintenance put off too long. I cringed when I pulled on the door handle; an unidentified sticky residue was my reward for that lapse in judgement.

Unlike at Aggie's, where a ringing bell above the door cheerily greets you, upon entering the lobby of the Vine, one must duck with cat-like reflexes to dodge the amber-colored strips of sticky fly paper on each side of the lobby. They were being whirled around by the oscillating fan on the desk straight ahead. I felt the pull on a strand of the hair in my high ponytail and turned to see it waving goodbye to me amid the collection of dusty, decaying carcasses on the flytrap. To the right, there was a small stand of brochures and maps that looked like they hadn't been touched in ages. I even noticed a few pamphlets for places I was sure had closed down. Behind the paneled desk ahead, there was a man angled toward a television. He glanced up fleetingly. Maybe he thought I was a mirage or someone hopelessly lost who would just go away.

To the left of the entrance on the water-stained wall was what I shall loosely refer to as artwork. It was, however, like a train wreck, and I found that I simply couldn't look away. There he was, painted on velvet. Elvis. The king of rock and roll, and Jesus was standing beside him like his back-up singer. Each figure had a full-body halo. Elvis was clad in his black leather outfit from the '68 comeback special—my personal favorite Elvis era by the way—while JC was wearing a white smock with gold trim and over that he wore an orange robe with a lightning bolt emblazoned across it, a nod to Elvis' taking care of business schtick. I strained to look, but there was no signature in the bottom corner. Apparently, no one was fessing up to creating this monstrosity. There was, however, a little brass plaque attached to the frame. "The King and King of Kings." *Poetic in its own way.*

"What do you think of it?" asked the person suddenly beside me. I turned to see the man who had been behind the counter had abandoned whatever was on the tube. To be honest, he wasn't what I'd have expected to see there. He was a trim man, not quite six feet, wearing a light blue oxford button-down shirt and black jeans with a black leather belt. I'd peg him at sixty or so, and I'd bet he was the cleanest thing in the place. His grey hair was smartly parted to the side, he was tanned, smelled good, and the stubble on his cheeks looked intentionally trendy.

"Hmm?" I asked, still a little mesmerized by EP and JC.

"The picture. It's something, isn't it?"

"Oh, it's something," I said, smiling the phony smile I normally reserve for the new teller-in-training at the bank.

"You looking for a room?"

"Uh, no. I'm looking for a friend of mine. I think she's staying here, and I was wondering if you could tell me which room she's in."

"I can tell you if she's registered. What's the name?"

"Lisa Claire."

The man gave me a funny look before he met my eyes and answered without checking the

BUOY

reservation system... assuming there was one. "Oh, you're friends with Lee, huh? I think I just saw her walk up the promenade. She's got a shift coming up."

The promenade? I thought, briefly wondering how a dump like the Vine had a promenade, but more importantly... *a shift*? "Oh, is that today? Damn, I must have forgotten. What time does she get done?"

"Well, she's got to clean about a dozen rooms and do the laundry before she can go out with her gal pals," he said and shot me a wink. "If you stick around, though..." He looked me up and down as his words trailed off. "She sometimes brings in donuts."

"Oh, no thanks," I said, patting my stomach. "Gotta watch my figure."

"It's no trouble. She gets 'em from some other gig she's got at the bakery. You really a friend of hers?" He sounded skeptical.

"Oh yeah, we go way back. I guess I'll try her later," I said and, as I turned to leave, I was surprised when Aggie pulled on the door. She was supposed to be on getaway car detail.

"Hi. So, Lisa's got to work. We should come back later," I said to Ags with pleading eyes, pushing her toward the door, hoping she'd get my drift. She usually does.

"Hey!" the man called to us as we turned to leave.

"Yes?" we said in unison.

"Who should I say stopped by?"

As my eyes met with Aggie's, I froze. I hadn't expected to be asked the question for some reason.

Ags spoke up, "Oh yeah. My name is Zelda Fauntleroy and this is Euphegenia Coddlesworth," she said with all seriousness, and I still wonder to this day how she'd done it.

"Euphenia—" the man began to say.

"Euphegenia," Ags clarified while I stared at the floor and held my breath to keep from bursting out laughing.

"You, uh, sure you don't need a place to stay?"

"Who, us? No, no. Oh, hey, we'd love it if you didn't mention it to Lisa. We want to surprise her when we see her," Ags added and pushed herself out the door.

"Yeah, sure. You're coming back, right?"

I nodded, turned, and dodged the flypaper on my way out like a boxer bobbing and weaving before I hit my getaway stride.

"Thanks a lot, Zelda!" I said, once we were well on our way back to the truck.

"What? I was under pressure. You didn't want me to give our real names, did you? You said Jack Junior's head over heels for her, and if she finds out you're stalking her..."

"I'm not stalking her. *We're* stalking her, and you certainly could have come up with a better name for me than frigging Euphegenia!"

"Look, we're never going to see that guy

again," Ags said, plunking herself down in the passenger seat of the truck and pulling the door closed. "So? What'd you find out?" she asked.

"She works there. Housecleaning."

Ags nodded. "Technically, she works for the Maxi Maid company." Ags lobbed the fact at me like we were playing a verbal game of tennis.

"How do you know?"

"Because I saw her while you were in there and she came out with the Maxi Maid pink uniform. You know, with the big M in script on the left."

"Well, she's a busy gal. She also cleans the bakery," I said.

"How'd you figure that out?"

I flitted my eyes. "The new man in my life told me. And I wonder..."

"Wonder what?"

"Well, what do you think the odds are that she also cleans the pharmacy? I mean, just out of curiosity," I thought out loud and bit my lip.

"Alex." Ags said my name in an angry schoolteacher tone I rarely hear from her.

"What?"

"Don't you think that's a bit of a stretch?"

As my thoughts raced, I struggled to remember the driving lesson Bugsy had given me, and the truck lurched.

"Easy, woman," Ags griped. "So, you really think she robbed the bakery?"

"I didn't say that, did I?" I turned the truck

into the parking lot on State, parked, and rifled through my all-purpose bag. Something wasn't sitting right with me. Maybe it was the way the man from the Vine looked at me when I asked about Lisa or maybe I just wanted someone to confirm what Ags had seen.

"What are you doing?"

I found my phone and tapped it once to speak into the microphone. "Get me the number for Maxi Maid's head office."

The phone assistant responded, "Getting the number for Max Lawrence."

I looked at the phone incredulously and let out a heavy sigh and tapped it again, enunciating the next words with the precision of an ESL teacher. "Get me the number for Maxi Maid Cleaners head office."

"Getting the number for Maxi Maid Cleaners," came the voice from within the phone. Sometimes I swear she just likes playing games with me.

When the number came up, I hit the call button.

"What are you doing?" Ags asked.

I held up a finger for her to cool her jets.

"Maxi Maid, how may I direct your call?"

"Could I have the HR department, please?" I said and tapped the button to put the phone on speaker.

"One moment."

I was put on a brief hold and, instead of music,

we were treated to a recorded sales pitch for the company's services. "Are you too tired to clean at the end of a long day? Do your present commercial cleaners not leave everything spotless? Ready to treat your wife to a sparkling house? Then call Ma—"

"HR department, Nicole speaking," the voice interrupted the pitch.

"Hi, Nicole. How are you?"

"Um, fine," came a suspicious response. "Can I help you with something?"

"Yeah, I'm calling from AMM Credit Company and I'd like to do an employment check on one of your cleaners."

"Hang on, let me log into that part of the system."

"Thanks."

There was a brief pause. "Ok, would be nice if they integrated this system one day. It's not like we don't spend enough money on IT... Sorry about that. What's the name?"

"Let's see here," I said, pretending to be going over paperwork. "Lisa Claire, resides in Marysville if that helps."

"How do you spell that last name?"

"Charlie lima alpha indigo Romeo echo. Claire."

I heard some tapping on the end of the line. "Sorry, we have no one working for us by that name."

"Are you sure? It says right on her credit app

that she works for Maxi Maid."

"Yes, ma'am, I'm sure. As much as you think that every woman wants to list her career as that of cleaner of all things, I can assure you that we have no Lisa Claire currently employed. We also have no Princess Kate or duchesses on staff. Hard to imagine, isn't it?" Nicole said, and I wondered at what precise date she was going to go postal.

"Thank you, Nicole. Take care," I said and ended the call. I looked at Ags across the bench seat.

"What are you gonna do?" she asked.

"I have no idea."

CHAPTER 10

When Ags and I arrived back at the marina, Russ Shears—I'll stick with that name for now—was waiting for her, and Bugsy was with him.

"Now there's a couple of good lookin' guys," Ags said, and she got that dreamy high school girl smile on her face.

She was half-right, I'll give her that. As I lurched the truck into the parking spot I'd claimed as mine, I took a mental snapshot of Bugsy. The khaki work pants, navy blue t-shirt, and his caramel-colored locks whisked by the November wind. It left me in a bit of a daydream for a second myself.

"You coming?" Ags roused me from the open passenger side of the truck.

"Mmhmm." I cut the engine and we proceeded toward the two.

"Hey, Bugsy." Ags rubbed her neck theatrically, in my opinion, and nodded in my direction. "Somebody we know could use another driving lesson before she hits the highway."

Bugsy unleashed the dimples. "Any time."

"I'm not *that* bad of a driver, but there's some truth to what she's saying." I smiled, distantly. I'd felt a sick feeling forming in the pit of my stomach since the conversation I'd had with Nicole at Maxi Maid.

Ags disappeared into the store, giggling at something Russ had said under his breath, and I felt myself form a disgusted expression. I turned to the man beside me. "So?"

"So, what?" Bugsy's eyes narrowed at me.

"*So*, did you find out anything more about Russ?"

"You mean anything *incriminating*, don't you?"

"Potato, poh-tato," I said and flitted my eyes. "How's he like boat life?" I asked, looking in the direction of the *Summerwind*.

"Seems to be fine with it."

I smirked. Who wouldn't be fine with it?

Bugsy smiled at me. "What?"

I shrugged. "Just something I don't like about him."

"You mean other than the fact he calls you ma'am?"

"How did you know?"

"I hear things," he said and winked at me before we went our separate ways.

* * *

I took the scenic route back to my boat; my meagre bag of groceries didn't weigh me down nearly as much as what was on my mind. When I stopped off to see the gals on the *Gee Spot,* they were prepping for dinner—some exotic recipe they'd picked up in their travels—and they let me know that Sefton and Muncie were on the guest list. Making my way out of STD, I meandered toward the *Summerwind* and felt the overwhelming urge to snoop. It's a female thing and, while I readily admit I've been scolded and burned for being so nosy, thus far I've been too resilient to be deterred. I put my bag of groceries down and casually looked each way on the dock. Nobody coming and not much activity on the surrounding boats. I stood on the dock and leaned on the railing of the boat to peek into what I knew was the salon. Only thing was the blasted curtains were drawn and, due to Shears' occasional bouts of migraines, he'd insisted on having blackout curtains that were as opaque as a sheet of ten-gauge steel.

Nonchalantly, I moseyed down to the forward sleeping area and, after looking around for anyone spying on me spying on Russ, I tried to catch a glimpse through the crack between those curtains. The mesh of the screens on the window made seeing in difficult. *But not im-*

possible. I was startled for a moment when my phone, tucked inside my canvas bag, made a low vibrating sound, not loud enough for anyone but me to hear. Back to the order of snooping. Here's what I saw. A mess of clothes, for one thing. It looked as though the contents of Russ' duffel bag had exploded in the stateroom of the boat. The U of O shirts and the hoodie from Pike's machine shop were littered around the room. Scanning some more, as much as that was possible, I saw on the built-in bureau, typical guy things —change from his pockets, a few slips of paper, socks, and a book, though I couldn't make out the title. I squinted to make out the next item. Gloves, gardening gloves by the looks of them, and perched beside them a watch. *Hadn't Russ told us all that he'd sold his watch at the jewellery store up town?*

There was nothing else remarkable in the room except the fact that the bed was made. I only list this under remarkable items because A, Russ doesn't seem the type and B, I know for sure that I hadn't made my own bed that morning and shuddered at the notion that Russ outclassed me. I was pausing and considering what I'd seen when my phone went off again. I picked up my bag, rooted through it, and pulled it out. Two new text messages had arrived, both from a number I didn't recognize.

"Stop snooping" and "I mean it."

I looked from side to side down the dock

again, wondering who was watching me and from where. I picked up my bag of groceries and casually walked back to my boat, cognizant that *that* someone may still have their eyes on me.

* * *

Once inside my boat, I locked the stern door and peeked out a porthole. *Were they still watching*? I looked down at my guard dog/snoring throw pillow and wondered what Pepper'd do if a stranger *did* come on the boat and, while I was still in the mood to snoop, I continued. From the safety of home this time and on my computer. "Russ Shears" I typed into the search bar, and instantaneously the internet did the snooping for me. Beyond the Facebook profile I'd already seen, three LinkedIn profiles came up for Russ Shears, all in the UK. There was also a Russ Shears, dead artist, that came up. Nice pieces but not our man. And then there was an Instagram profile for a photographer of that name. Beautiful pictures. Of trees. None of the man himself. I had reached a dead end. For the time being anyway.

One thing led to another and, before I knew it, I found myself searching for results on Lisa Claire. Now, from the response I'd gotten from good ol' Nicole, I wondered if Lisa Claire was in fact her real name, or if Nicole was just having a moment. But with nothing else to go on, I asked my partner in sleuthing, Mr. Google, to give me some info. This was quite the rabbit hole. Do you know how many people are named Lisa Claire? A lot. Floral designer. Graphic designer. Lawyer. Nope. Nope. Nope. And the list went on. I added more criteria after each search result. Adding "California", "cleaner", and "Roddy" to narrow the results, tapping my hand on the top of my desk to some nothing of a tune as I scanned the results each time until results containing all the key words were zero. It seemed odd to me that a woman who liked to show off her pricey purses and Rolexed son didn't have a social media account. Eventually, one of my searches got me caught up in the world wide web of online recipes and Pinterest ideas and, before long, it was time to get ready for my night class.

* * *

"Anybody here?" I called out in Aggie's store. I was on the search for coffee to sip on my way to class, something to keep me alert since I was sleep deficient as of late. Looking across the aisles, I couldn't spot her adjusting the displays she so frequently changed up, and so I made my way behind the counter. I sized up the coffee pot, gave it a sniff—smelled fresh enough—and poured a cup to go. I was looking around at her counter, noting the interesting serving dishes pulled out already for the upcoming Thanksgiving feast. I went to the fridge, to scout for any leftover roast beef I could nibble on, and there it was on the door, staring me in the face like a lottery ticket. Well, it was beside the *actual* lottery ticket on the fridge, but there it was... a note. From Russ Shears. I looked toward the back room and heard nothing. I craned my neck to look outside and that's when I spotted Ags and Russ, looking up at the building then joking and laughing like they were in some high school romance musical.

Surely, Ags wouldn't miss the note for one night. I'd just slip it into my bag, take it to my course, and return it.

✻ ✻ ✻

"Aww, what a sweet note," my classmate Edna said as she looked over one of the handwriting samples I'd brought to night school. Unfortunately, it was the note from Russ to Ags and not one of the specimens I'd gathered from Hagen and Bugsy. Here's the note that Edna found so precious: "Hi Babe, Sorry I can't make it to the fair with you, something has come up. Xoxo R." Not exactly Lord Byron.

The course instructor, Mr. Hives, was at the front of the room talking as he scrawled on the chalkboard to illustrate his points. "Now, the way someone writes a lowercase O or A can be a decisive clue as to whether or not they are lying."

My ears perked up; he had my attention.

He chuckled. "Of course, there are secretive people." He seemed to be staring right at me and I glanced away. "And then there are downright liars." He didn't look at me that time, and I felt a little relief. It's not like we knew each other, but maybe he'd taken the time to analyse the registrations when everyone signed up for his class. At any rate, he went on. "So, a *secretive* person writes their O with a circle inside the O, and always on the righthand side. And a rule of thumb is that the larger this inner circle or loop is, the more secretive this person is, or the more secrets he or she has or keeps."

Heads nodded and craned at writing samples on desks. I looked down at the ones I'd brought. Russ Shears had this type of O in his writing and I circled the letters in pencil—I'd have to erase those marks before I returned the note to Ags. Hives must have been watching me because he approached my desk. "Yes, that's right, you've got the hang of it here." He was comically enthusiastic. Hives returned to the chalkboard and drew a few more samples. "Now, see these? Watch out for these people," he guffawed. He really seemed to be enjoying himself. "People who lie intentionally, rather than say by omission, write their O's in this way," he said, pointing to the board. "They'll *combine* interior loops or have *significantly* large inner loops like we see here."

There was a long drawn out "oh" from the corner of the room and Hives eagerly went on a mission to inspect.

"Ah, yes. You've got a good example here," he said to the pissed-off looking gentleman hovering over the note.

"Let's talk about T's now," he said. He went back to the front of the room, and used the dusty eraser to more or less remove the big fat lying O's from the chalkboard. In the chalky smear that remained, he printed something new. "See here? See how the bar on this T crosses very low on what we'll call the stem? This person fears failure and change. You might say they have low self-esteem," he said, and seemed pleased with himself. "Actually, that's a good way to remember it, isn't it? The lower the T, the lower the es-TEEM," he said, emphasizing the last syllable.

Hmm, memory tricks for the graphologist in all of us, I thought and looked down at my samples. One of the samples showed signs of this. It was on Bugsy's note where he'd written: "Alex, here is the handwriting sample you bothered me for." About what you'd expect from the man. I didn't need a handwriting course to tell me that Bugsy had low self-esteem; it did, however, reinforce what I had already gathered based on his familial relationships.

Over the course of the next two hours, Hives gave us insight into the hallmarks of other personality indicators. The variation in slanting from left to right—an indicator that the person has trouble making decisions and may be prone to mood swings. The loopiness of a T or D—an indicator of sensitivity or, at its extreme, para- noia. And then the stingers or hooks on letters— these people are looking for challenges and eas- ily become bored. "A good way of remembering this is associating the hook with fishing and *fish- ing for a challenge*," Hives said, another one of his handy memory tricks.

Edna's hand shot up in earnest. "Oh, Mr. Hives?"

"Yes, Edna."

"How about block letters? My husband writes everything in block letters," she said, and I won- dered if she should have disclosed that.

Hives went wide eyed. "Well..." He cleared his throat. "This is just generally speaking, mind you," he said, prefacing what must be something uncomfortable to come. I could hardly wait. "Block letters, in all caps that is, can be an indica- tion of someone who is not comfortable disclos- ing any information about themselves."

"Oh," Edna said lowly.

I cringed on her behalf.

Hives went on to address the class, come what may in Edna's marriage. "Furthermore, when the letters are not connected, this can show an un- willingness, or frankly an inability, to relate to people on an intimate or interpersonal level."

"Oh." Edna was at it again.

"Like a psychopath?" came a voice from the back of the class, and all heads turned to see a bespectacled and bookish looking young woman.

"That's not really my discipline, and I can't comment with any authority," Hives replied, no doubt acutely aware that Edna was feverishly taking notes.

"We studied psychopathy in my other class last night." The young woman adjusted her black rimmed glasses. "Next week's narcissism," she said, and I wondered what a hit she must be at parties.

"Thank you. Let's move on," Hives said, and I gave him sympathetic eyes.

A moment later, Edna nudged me and pointed to the last sample I'd brought. Hagen's. He'd left it on my door that afternoon. Written in block letters: "ALEX HAVE A GOOD TIME AT YOUR COURSE TONIGHT."

* * *

"Goodnight, Edna. See you next week," I said as I left classroom C210 of the Marysville College, and as I walked down the nearly empty hallways, I couldn't help but read into the writing samples I had. Of all three examples, how could Hagen's be so nefarious? I turned when I heard my name.

"Hey, Alex!"

It was Marcy Kennedy; she was jogging toward me from the end of the corridor.

"Hey, Marce, what are you doing here? Don't you have a full enough schedule already?" I asked the woman who didn't seem to have five minutes for herself.

"Oh, I'm taking a course on managing non-profits, just a three-week thing, once a week," she said. "Hey, you want a ride?"

"No thanks, Marce, it's not really on your way," I said. It's true, the marina's not on her way, but more importantly, every time I accept a ride from her, I'm invariably pulling white dog hair off my clothes for days. "Oh, by the way, I'm picking up more shirts for the shelter tomorrow. Randy said they're ready," I added before a little more small talk, and we eventually split off at the junction of C hall and the F wing, and I made my way out onto the street.

Turning the corner at Greenock, I headed down State passing the MMM Bakery and eyeing the brownies and vanilla squares in the window. The security camera at the front door made a faint humming sound, and the smell of fresh bread was being pumped out the exhaust fan on the side of the building. I looked across the street at the pharmacy and wondered what the link was—how is it they both broken into and in such rapid succession?

The street was quiet and dark. I looked up at the apartments above the stores. Lights were on, but I didn't see anyone spying on me and I tried to shake off the sudden feeling that I was being watched. I looked behind me just as a car turned the corner and then stopped at the traffic light. My imagination was getting the better of me. I shrugged and walked another block. The worrisome feeling returned when I heard a snapping sound, like a twig breaking, and I turned around again. No one on the sidewalk behind me. I let out a breath and picked up my pace. I wasn't going to win any speed-walking competitions, but I didn't feel like breaking into a full out run down the sidewalk in my jeans and with my canvas bag flapping behind me. I got to the corner of Main and Chapman. The light was red, and I was going straight—with no traffic in sight. I kept on walking. I heard a car door slam and then footsteps. Some of the streetlights on this stretch of Main were out thanks to the construction going on, the sidewalk torn up. I bounded through another red light. I was feeling tense and listened to my own heavy-breathing, suddenly too scared to look back to see what might be behind me.

"That's jaywalking, you know," I heard the loud voice. The familiar voice. The familiar smooth voice of Ben Hagen stopped me in my tracks, and I let out a sigh of relief.

"What are you doing here?" I asked.

"The question is, what are *you* doing here? Walking in the dark alone at night." He looked me up and down.

"Oh, well, I forgot they had the sidewalk torn up over here. I'm just on my way home from night school."

"I thought you might be. You shouldn't be walking alone, not with what's been going on." His voice was serious.

I couldn't argue with him, but I did wonder when or if I should bring up the revelation (such that it was) about his handwriting.

"How about I give you a ride? Just to make sure you get home alright. I'm parked just across the street," he said, nodding in that direction.

"Oh, so that was you behind me a couple blocks back?"

"No. What do you mean?" He furrowed his brow, more serious than before.

"Nothing. Must have just been my imagination."

CHAPTER 11

"Ready for another lesson?"

I had been nestled on the stern of my boat the next morning, taking in the sunshine and so engrossed in the Sue Grafton book I'd been reading, *T for Trespass*, that I hadn't heard Bugsy's footsteps coming down my dock. There he was in all his blue-shirt glory. I swear someone once told him that he looks good in blue and he never forgot it. It's true, though, he does. But he was offering and I needed to discuss with someone intelligent my suspicions about Lisa Claire and, by association, Roddy, and so with an offer like that, I smiled back enthusiastically and got to my feet.

"You seriously want to take me driving again?" I asked, giving him one last chance to back out.

"Yeah, sure. Why not? I like to live on the edge. Plus, I could use a change of scenery for a while. The dock at number seven is turning out to be more complicated than I thought it'd be."

"Fair enough." I rolled my eyes. "Got your crash helmet?" I asked, giggling as I snatched the keys to Nat's truck from the hook in the salon, closed the stern door, and then bounded up to the dock. As we passed Jack's boat, a pink flowered tablecloth flapped in the breeze, weighted down by a ceramic decoupaged turkey. I wrinkled up my nose and hoped my weak gag reflex wouldn't kick in.

I tucked myself in behind the wheel of Nat's truck and tried to remember the salient points of takeoff while I also sorted the slides of the PowerPoint in my head, the alliteratively entitled "Is Roddy a Rotter?" Ten minutes later, I had successfully managed to drive up the marina hill, stop for the train at the railroad tracks —after some worried sounds from my co-pilot, and we were on our way to do some parallel parking. Which I was dreading.

"Hey, Bugsy," I turned to him to say.

"Eyes on the road, and it's Beedle, remember?"

"Anyway. What do you think of Lisa and that Roddy guy?"

"Roddy, her son?"

"How many Roddies have you met recently? Of course, Roddy her son." I looked over at him.

"Eyes. Road," Bugsy ordered.

"Yes, boss."

"What do you mean, what do I think of him? As in, does he have a cute butt or something?"

"No. What I mean is, he's kind of... Well, he did..." My mental PowerPoint slides were suddenly out of order.

"Would you just spit it out?"

"Do you think he robbed the bakery and the pharmacy?"

"No."

Undeterred, I forged ahead. My slides were back in order. "Think about it. He comes from out of the blue just as the robberies start happening. He seems to have no means to support himself other than his mother, who let me tell ya, isn't what she seems, and yet he's buying her expensive purses, asking me about boats, and sporting a Rolex. A real one!"

"I thought Jack said he owns a company," Bugsy said, and I could see him on the lookout for a parking spot that would test both my skill and patience.

"Pfft! Anybody could say that. He didn't exactly brag about the details, and we all know that guys with successful companies can't keep their traps shut," I blustered. Been down that road with enough self-congratulatory businessmen to know that truth.

"Here's a good spot. Try parking here," Bugsy said, pointing a finger at an open parking space between two vehicles on State.

"Are you even listening to me?" My impatience was growing while inexplicably it looked like the parking spot was shrinking.

"Sadly, yes. You were talking about his watch and his company."

I paused to concentrate and got into position to pull off this feat of parallel parking I'd been assigned. My neck jerked and swivelled almost three hundred and sixty degrees. I put my arm on the bench seat, behind Bugsy, torquing my torso and working on my obliques at the same time. And, after two attempts, a little cursing, and a few encouraging words from the person seated next to me, we were parked. I let out a deep breath once the truck was in park and unclenched my fingers from the steering wheel. "That was rough. I need a smoothie. Want one?" I asked, hoisting my all-purpose bag. The jingling from somewhere near the bottom of it told me there had to be enough change in there for a couple drinks.

"Sounds good. Think they can spike mine?" Bugsy said, looking equally relieved that we had finally parked and happy when his feet hit the sidewalk.

"Wasn't that bad," I said.

"I'm glad you finally decided to stop for the train," he grumbled.

"Ok, so getting back to—"

"The watch," Bugsy added helpfully.

"Yeah. Where's a guy like him get a watch like that?"

"Maybe you should ask him."

"I'm serious," I scoffed.

"So am I. You think he just goes around robbing places to buy himself jewellery?"

"No. But his arrival in town seems awfully coincidental, and he just has that air about him. Kind of seedy. Well, you know what I mean."

"I know what you mean, but maybe he's just like that. Maybe he's shy or something."

"Or something," I mumbled and pulled on the door of the new juice place in town. A few minutes later, smoothies in hand, Bugsy and I opted for some window browsing as we sipped. Window displays had been silently converted over from Halloween to Thanksgiving meets Christmas. The windows of the hardware cum homeware store were divided into his, hers, and kids wish lists. The woman in your life apparently wants a buffalo checked toss cushion, a turquoise-colored stand mixer, and/or a pink drill. The man in your life is bucking for tools like the four-hundred-and-six-piece screwdriver set on display and the brats will settle for one of the many toys referencing the feature length animated commercial currently playing in movie theatres. While the composition of stores was about the same as always, it felt different. Jeff Thompson's Construction Company van was parked in front of the pharmacy, and it looked like bars were being unloaded to go up on the window.

"Hmph," I murmured. "So back to my theory," I said as we continued our stroll.

"Oh yes, Roddy. Look, he—"

"Hang on." I put my hand on Bugsy's forearm just as we reached Devon's Jewellers. I paused, looking for the heart-shaped diamond pendant I coveted each time I cruised past the store. When I looked in the window this time, it had been replaced by a silver locket and earrings as if they had sprouted among the mini pumpkin patch Mr. Devon had laid out.

"I'm not buying you anything here, so let's move along," Bugsy said, and walked a few steps ahead.

"I just want to see if it's been sold," I whined.

"If what's been sold?" he asked, the straw from the smoothie clenched in his front teeth.

"Oh, this diamond pendant I had my eye on," I said, the handle to the door already in my grip. I gave a smile to the burly security guard I'd never noticed before and, when I caught the eye of a salesman, I pointed to the window. "Excuse me, that diamond pendant you had there, is it—"

He nodded. "Gone."

I returned his nod. "Thanks." I turned on my heels and left the store. "Well, I'll have to put something else on my Christmas list for you to buy me. It's gone," I said to Bugsy as I hit the sidewalk again.

He flitted his eyes and we walked a few blocks on State, sipping and people watching. I debated telling him that Lisa had lied about her living arrangements, that she didn't reside in Brentwood Court but rather was holed up in the Vine. However, I figured Bugsy might be hypersensitive and find I was being too judgy about her economic status. *That* actually wasn't what bothered me. It was the lie. The outright lie and, in my experience, people who lie can rarely stop at just one. I've noticed that about myself when I'm on a streak. Before long, Bugsy looked at his watch and decided he ought to go back and tackle the dock at number seven, and I agreed that I should get to my errands as well, which included picking up more shirts for the puppy rescue.

* * *

I spotted Jack Junior reading the paper on the stern of his boat. Though I hadn't the heart to tell him Lisa had fibbed about her address, I did want to see how things were going between them. She seemed to make him happy, but if they were on the outs, I'd have no problem telling him what I'd discovered—that she lives at the Vine Street Inn, according to her uniform she works for Maxi Maid, and that she does so under a different name.

"Hey, want to go to Expose Yourself with me?" I asked.

"Uh-uh-uh, come again?" Jack blushed and then looked down at his lap.

"That's not what I meant. I mean do you want to go to the store Expose Yourself? You know, it's that place that does marketing stuff on Patterson. I need to pick up more shirts for the puppy rescue."

"Oh, thank goodness, because to be honest, kiddo, I haven't kept up with my man-scaping." Jack grimaced.

"Way too much information, Jack." I smiled. "I could really use a hand with the shirts if you have time."

"I've got hands and I've got time," he said. "You've mastered driving the truck?"

"Practically."

"And you and Bugsy are still friends?" Jack squinted up from his chair and shielded his eyes from the sun behind me.

"So far. Now come on, we're burnin' daylight, handsome," I said, and with that invitation, Jack bounded from his chair, tucked his book inside the salon of his boat and practically danced toward me on the dock.

In no time at all, we were cruising down Main Street and I was prying about his love life. "So, no Lisa today?"

"Nah, she's shopping or something," he muttered.

Or something. "I see. So, how's that Lisa thing going?"

"She's so great. She likes you a lot too," Jack said, and I marveled at the ease with which he lied.

"Sorry I haven't spent much time getting to know her. Tell me, is she divorced or did her husband pass?"

"Died. Heart attack, poor bastard."

I nodded. "Oh, that's tough. What does she do for work?" I asked as I shifted gears clumsily and cringed.

"Easy, kiddo," Jack said and reached out for the dashboard to steady himself. "Her husband left her quite a bit of money, you know. You know the kind of guy, really took care of her and the boy."

"I see," I said, not really seeing anything but that she'd told him another lie. I figured since we were on a roll, I'd try to suss out another one. "Have you been to her place? What's it like?"

Jack cleared his throat and I looked over to see him shaking his head. "Nah, she's having some renovations done to her master bedroom, so she's sleeping in one of the guest rooms. Doesn't want me to see the place in a mess."

"Oh, I see," I looked out at the road ahead and rolled my eyes. It appeared as though Lisa had an answer for everything.

"Hey, why don't you and she have some girl time tonight after the game? I told her it'd mean a lot to me if she came. Tranmer's hosting on the *Splendored Thing*. Told her I'd like her to meet him, you know, since he's one of the guys. Hey, if you want to come to dinner, you can. Lee popped in this morning and dropped off some steaks, there's plenty enough to go around."

"Mmhmm," I said, not expressly agreeing to any quality time with Lisa. "Here it is," and I put on my blinker to turn into Expose Yourself. It's a good-sized place for Marysville. They do printing on site of every imaginable medium—banners, shirts, flags, even pens and stationary. You want to put your name on it, you bring it there. I had a stash of business cards printed there last year after I'd fully committed to the business. It's the sort of place that leaves me a little nervous though. There's no cashier station per se, but instead a number of desks with creative-looking types pumping out logos and, ironically for a company that specializes in signage, you're not sure who does what or where you find what you've come to pick up.

Jack and I stopped at the first occupied desk inside the door, entrusting our future there to a young lady with purple streaks in her hair and cat eye glasses. She was wearing denim overalls and a tie-dyed bandeau shirt underneath.

"Hi there, I'm here to pick up some shirts for the Kennedy Puppy Rescue and Dog Shelter," I said and tried not to stare at the creative genius with the giant nose ring.

"Pickups are over there," she said in an Australian accent I couldn't tell was real or not as she pointed.

I glanced at Jack Junior who was by this point

staring with utter bemusement at the girl. How is it that the older generation seems to get away with so many things including prolonged, impolite gawking? "Thanks," I said, smiling and lightly shoving Jack Junior toward the back of the store and out of his stupor.

We were waiting at our designated station when I heard it. Actually, it was the second time I heard the calling out when I realized it was directed at me. "Euphegenia!" came the voice, and I turned to of course see one of only two people who *knew* me by that name. The man from the Vine Street Inn. He was coming at me, winding his way through carousels of windbreakers and t-shirts.

"Eupha-what?" Jack Junior contorted his face and asked lowly.

"I'll tell you later, just play along," I whispered.

"Hi!" the man addressed me and then looked at Jack with disappointed eyes. "Where's Zelda?"

"Oh, she's around." I smiled. "I'm so sorry. I didn't catch your name the other day."

"Zane... Wilcox," he stumbled over his reply.

I nodded slowly, thoughtfully. It sounded as fake as the name by which he knew me. "Zane, this is—"

"Dirk Gable," Jack said, dropping his voice several octaves and extending a vigorous handshake to the man. "How are ya?" Junior asked, smiling with all his teeth and reminding me of a used car salesman.

I felt my mouth go slightly agape. Never a good look. When I asked Jack Junior to play along, I didn't mean for him to make up a ridiculous porn name.

"Fancy meeting you here, of all places," Zane said, and he looked around the shop and I wondered why he thought I didn't belong there.

"Yes, fancy..." My words drifted off and I looked down to the white shopping bag in his hand.

He hoisted it slightly. "Oh, just picking up something."

"Yeah, us too," I said.

"Shirts for the dog rescue in town, we're big animal lovers," Jack boasted heartily, and seemed to take some pleasure in the charade he continued.

"Oh, that's nice. Do you have a dog?" Zane cocked his head and found my eyes.

"Oh, she's got the most beautiful black lab," Jack boasted. Through mental telepathy I was telling him to shut the hell up, but he wasn't picking up on my vibes.

Zane looked down at his watch. "Well, nice seeing you again. Nice meeting you, Dirk. Hey, you'll have to stop by and visit the painting again." He winked at me, reveling in the private joke we apparently shared.

I smiled. "For sure."

"Bye now," Jack said, waving him off and gunning for him again with all his teeth.

I exhaled a deep sigh then glared at Junior. "Dirk Gable?"

Jack shrugged. "Why not? So, what was all that about?"

"It's a long story. Just someone Ags and I met and didn't think we'd ever see again, so she gave him a couple phony names."

"Oh. Like the broad who gave Peter the bogus number, huh?"

"Something like that."

Jack Junior's brow furrowed. "He looks familiar. Can't place him," he said and shook his head as if that would put the pieces into place.

* * *

"I can't help but think I know that guy," Jack said a few times in the twenty minutes it took us to drop the dog shelter shirts off at Marcy Kennedy's vet practice and get to the parking lot on State Street. Above us, the police chopper buzzed around, and I imagined Hagen doing exercises out in the bay. The stuff of nightmares. Speaking of bad dreams, there she was, straight ahead of us. Lisa was in the Juice Box. Marysville's latest answer to healthy food choices which was quickly becoming my favorite spot— I was on my second visit that day alone.

"Lee! Hey, Lee!" Jack walked up behind Lisa and put his hands on her shoulders.

"Oh... hi, Jack." She seemed to fumble her words when she turned to see me with him, her voice slightly different from the breathy, sultry tone I'd known her by.

"How are ya, honey?" he asked and kissed her on the cheek.

"Good, Jacky. I'm... just surprised to see you," she said and, with each word, her voice shifted to the one she uses when she puts on that vamp act of hers.

"Oh, I was helping the kid with an errand. What, uh, what are you getting? Let's see..." Jack said, looking at the menu board in vain. Without his glasses, he'd never be able to see that far.

"Here's your strawberry banana, ma'am," the man behind the counter said as if on cue, and Lisa clutched the plastic cup with her tanned hand, bejeweled and adorned with bright red talons.

"Oh, that sounds good, Lee," he said, and to the man behind the counter, "I'll take one of those too."

I smiled. Jack frequently does this little routine when he can't make out the menu. "Pineapple kale," I said once the waiter had gotten around to me. He gave me a look like he recognized me from earlier along with the kind of expression where he might be thinking I'd exceeded the daily recommendation of kale.

"So, do you want to go back to the boat, Lee? Nice day for a cruise," Jack said, and I could see the hope in his eyes and hear it in his voice.

Lee or Lisa or whatever her name is looked down at her watch. "I can't, Jack. I've got so much to do today," she said, and by that I wondered if that included a little fluffing and folding at the Vine.

"But you're coming tonight to dinner and poker, right? It's-it's-it's gonna be on the boat Tranmer's staying on. I told you about him, right?" I attributed Jack's stammer to Lisa's coolness. There was no smile, no enthusiasm to match his, just ambivalent eyes looking back at him.

"Sure, honey," she said.

The words were a tonic to Junior and he smiled gratefully and, in an old school move, before she left the store, he tucked Lisa's hair behind her ear. And as he whispered some sweet nothing to her, I couldn't keep my eyes off those *somethings*. Her earrings.

"Those are nice earrings she has on. Did you get them for her?" I asked after Lisa sauntered and swayed out the door.

"Who, me? No. Say, I didn't even notice them."

I nodded and smiled. I *had* noticed them. It was hard not to. They used to sit right next to *my* diamond pendant in the window of Devon's Jewellers.

❋ ❋ ❋

The last time Lisa and Jack Junior hosted poker, I'd brought my vodka lemonade coolers. They were received like the low-brow drink they are. But do you think I'd learned my lesson? Nope. So, I packed up another four pack and away I went, bopping to the dock to where the *Splendored Thing* was tied. I had barely left my boat when Ags appeared, strutting toward me at a purposeful gait.

"Hey, sista," I greeted her.

"Hey, girl." She smiled and tossed her hair back. "Where you off to?"

"Poker. On Nat's boat," I said, and while I looked at her, she tossed her hair again. "Are you alright?"

She gave me a frustrated look and unnaturally elongated her neck, doing her best giraffe impression, and that's when I noticed it. Smack dab on Aggie's neck. *My* pendant. The one from Devon's window. I looked from the heart shape, outlined in diamonds, up to Aggie's bright smile.

"Well, would you look at that." I was stupefied. "Where did you—"

"Russ. Isn't it gorgeous?" Her smile was bigger than I'd ever seen and she got that weird dreamy look in her eyes.

"Yes, it is." I had always thought so when I admired it in the store window. I really was at a loss for words, at least on the subject of the pendant, and I let my eyes drift over to the *Splendored Thing*. "I love it, but you know, I have to go." I hoisted the coolers. "We'll talk later, ok?" I said, noticing the gang was filing onto the boat nearby, Tranmer meeting them with a tray of drinks as they boarded.

"Yeah, let's chat later. I can hardly wait to tell you what he said when he gave it to me." Her voice lilted and I restrained myself from scrunching up my nose.

I did miserably at poker that night. It wasn't because Ags had the diamond pendant and I didn't, or that Lisa had the matching earrings. I just couldn't for the life of me figure out how those deadbeats Russ and Lisa could afford them. The only saving grace of the evening was that Lisa didn't show up.

CHAPTER 12

The pins and needles in my feet were sending shots up my legs like bolts of lightning. I struggled to move. I willed myself, knowing I had to kick. It was either that or sink. I heard the whir of engines and I frantically looked in every direction through the darkness, but I couldn't see a boat. After that, all I heard was the lapping of water on my ears. My arms were cold and heavy, my hair drenched, my clothes thick and weighted down with water, making each stroke a struggle. I was alone in black water again. A red flashing beacon barely visible, the lights of shore a distant memory. I screamed out. "Whyyyyyyyy!" I opened my eyes. I was in my bed, the sheets were on the floor, Pepper put his paw on my shoulder, and I let out a deep sigh.

With not a chance in hell of getting back to sleep, I spent the pre-dawn hours in my office at the computer. I printed out a few spec sheets to take with me on my upcoming trip to Hamilton where I'd promised to collect information on the items Jack Albright wanted me to list while he was out of town. Once those were prepared, coffee in hand, I watched the sun come up while I made my latest to-do list. Number-one priority, if I was venturing out of town, was to get an oil change for Nat's truck.

As it turned out, when I mentioned to Junior over coffee in Aggie's that morning that I wanted to get the truck serviced, he immediately sprang into problem-solving mode and called his friend Rick who runs the Chevy dealership in town and who is also a vintage truck fanatic. Jack's beguiling ways and connections finagled me an appointment for two hours later.

I humored the dealer's fawning over the truck and knew that it would be in good hands when I settled into the waiting area with *T for Trespass* and a complementary cappuccino. The odd announcement over the PA became less annoying the more I waited and the more engrossed I became in my reading. I couldn't ignore them altogether though. "Service, line five," the receptionist would say or "Parts on one," she said another time. But when I heard "Roddy to bay four," my ears perked up. Roddy?

I stopped reading, turned down the corner of the page, stuffed the book in my canvas bag and went in search of bay four. I wandered to the service desk and nonchalantly looked beyond the service advisor and into the garage, visible through a massive window. While I made small talk with Linda, the lady who takes the appointments and makes out the invoices—I found out she's from Oklahoma, has four cats, and is a fan of the Star Wars series—I caught a glimpse of the action in bay four and, wouldn't you know it, there was *our* Roddy. Washing a car. Oh sure, he was in coveralls and had swapped out those uncomfortable loafers for work shoes, but it was him. I don't think he saw me though. I finally settled up with Linda and drove back to the marina, wondering what the deal was and adding the latest factoid about Roddy to an ever expanding list of lies.

* * *

I'm coming over. I looked down at my phone and read it again. Three little words, coming from the same number that had told me to stop snooping the day I'd been peeking into the windows of the *Summerwind.*

I didn't answer the text—what could I say? I went to the stern porthole and looked out, then I dialled Aggie's number. No answer. I paced. I didn't have a getaway plan, and if this guy, Russ or Roddy or whoever it was, was watching me, they'd know if I made a run for it. I dialled Ags again. "Call me, will you just call me."

I walked down the passageway of my boat to

the galley in search of a weapon and pulled a big carving knife from the drawer. "That ought to do it," I said, and by the time I'd returned to the corridor I could hear footsteps on the deck. I exhaled a deep breath. There came a banging on the door. *Oh crap,* I thought. Then I wondered, *What kind of a serial killer knocks anyway?*

Knife in my right hand and hidden behind my back, I opened the door to find Bugsy, and I felt my body relax. "Thank God, it's you."

He smiled. "I get that a lot, if you can believe it."

"I can't."

"Can I come in?"

"Of course," I said and looked behind him to see if the serial killer was on his way. Nope.

"You looking for someone?"

"No. Was it you that texted me?"

"Yeah," he said into my confused eyes. "Oh, that's right, I didn't give you my new number yet."

"You got a new number?"

"Yeah, along with getting the boot from the cottage, they pulled the plug on my phone. That is, if it had a plug, which of course..."

I nodded. "Yeah, I get it."

"Head office was either going to start charging me for my personal usage or told me I could get my own phone and charge them, so I figured, rather than have them look at the numbers I dial, which is what got me into this mess to begin with, I'll just get a new phone and—"

"And a new number." I nodded. "I guess you saw me the other day around the *Summerwind*."

"Snooping. Hey, I was just teasing. Happened to see you peeking in the windows, just didn't want you to get caught. You do have a nasty habit of snooping, though."

"Thanks for looking out for me. Hey, you know Russ gave Ags my pendant."

"Your what? Oh, that thing from the jewellery store?"

"Yep."

"Hmph," Bugsy said.

"Hmph is right. Where do you suppose he got the money for that?"

"Not from robbing the bakery and pharmacy."

"You're pretty sure of that," I said, and Bugsy looked back at me with tired eyes. The kind of tired eyes that told me something was on his mind. "Anyway, what's up?"

"Can we talk for a minute?"

I braced myself. Nothing good ever followed those words. *Your mother has gone to sort herself out.* She never came back, by the way. Or *your husband was in a car accident,* and you know how that turned out. Or *sweetie, I'm sick.* You can't blame me for dreading serious conversations now, can you?

"I'm kind of busy."

"You don't look busy," he said eyeing me, looking for signs of this busyness I claimed.

"Looks can be deceiving," I said, pulling the carving knife from behind my back and placing it on my desk.

"You cooking or something?" Bugsy tilted his head so his nose was in the air, trying to catch the scent.

"No," I said and smirked down at the knife.

"Well, I just want to know if... if I've offended you in some way."

"What do you mean?" I scrunched up my face to ask. It's usually *me* doing the offending, not him. "Please, sit down," I said, and he took a seat beside me on the grey tufted sofa in my salon. He stretched his arm out across the back of the couch and looked comfortable.

"The boat. Nat's boat." He looked across at me. "Have you spoken to Tranmer about it yet?"

I looked at my hands and picked at my fingernails, then finally I found the courage to find his eyes. "You, uh, you think I'm scared, don't you?"

"Maybe... Am I scary?"

"No..." I said and shook my head. I let my eyes drift down to the opening in the collar of his blue and white plaid shirt. I could see curls of blonde hair, and I picked up the faint scent of the soap he used.

"Well, what then? Is it Hagen?"

I let out a sigh. "No..." How could I tell him that I hadn't had so much as a real date in the three years since my husband died on his way home from the fishing trip to Canada? I'd either sound like a nun or a nut. Or a nutty nun. How could I look into those blue eyes and tell him I really *was* scared? Scared of having him for a neighbour, scared of messing up something that hadn't even started yet, and scared of what was underneath that superficial layer of sarcastic comments and jabs we shared? Like the dark water Hagen was plunging into, I was scared of what was below the surface. That maybe I wasn't good enough or maybe even that I didn't really like him so much. So, I lied.

"I'm sorry, but I've rented it to Tranmer."

"You did?" Bugsy was surprised.

"Well, he needs a place to stay when he's visiting, and he thinks he may buy it and he is one of Nat's closest friends." As soon as I was done explaining, I thought how, if I had been listening to me, there's no way I'd have believed me.

"Oh, oh I see. Well, that's different. That makes sense."

"I... I just didn't want anyone's feelings to get hurt. I know you and Ags practically had it all sorted out, but Tranmer—"

"Oh, you don't have to explain. I get it," Bugsy said, looking quite disappointed.

"Besides, I don't want to see the endless parade of nubile young bodies leaving your boat."

"What?"

"Yep."

"Where'd you come up with this idea?"

I shrugged.

"Listen you, while I appreciate the sentiment and you think I'm that desirable—"

"I don't remember those words passing my lips."

He winked at me. "They were inferred."

"No, they weren't! They may have been implied, don't you know the difference? Hey, do you want to come to the market with Jack and me? We're getting a few things for Aggie's dinner."

"Thanks, but I can't. I've really got to finish my work on the laundry building. I might be living in it one day." He chuckled. "You have fun." He smiled and the dimples came out again to make my day.

* * *

I had a mission to complete, and I don't mind telling you that it was good to have a distraction even if it was just going to the Marysville farmers market and procuring some fancy items for the soiree Ags was throwing. You see, once a week, the local organic farmers and folks who specialize in artisan items including fancy chutneys and cheeses gather together to sell their wares. This week's event was touted as one not to miss with samples from hard cider distilleries and the local wineries permitted to attend. When the gang and I clamored out of Jack Junior's SUV, we broke off in separate directions.

Sefton and Muncie headed to the booze tasting area, Seacroft and Tranmer went in search of items for the upcoming dinner, and Jack Junior, Stephen Richards, and I hit the cheese and chutney aisles looking for samples that, in aggregate, would constitute a late lunch. And while the market seemed to stretch out forever, it quickly became apparent what a small town Marysville is.

"Dirk! Diiiirk! Euphegenia!"

I froze when I heard the words and my head snapped towards Junior. He had just popped a cube of smoked jalapeno gouda into his trap, and I was mentally preparing to give him the Heimlich manoeuvre. We exchanged horrified looks and, in synchronized fashion, we turned toward Doctor Richards who sported a handsome but perplexed expression.

"Dirk! Euphegenia!" the voice called again, louder this time.

Zane was nearly upon us. I eyed the closest exit path, clogged with seniors and dogs.

"I'll give you twenty bucks if you play along," I mumbled quickly to Doctor Richards, who didn't have time to respond before Zane was directly in front of us.

"Why, I didn't think I'd be seeing you so soon. Dirk, how are ya?" The man from the Vine held out a hand toward Jack Junior.

"Oh, fine, just fine. Uh-uh-uh, Zane, isn't it?" Jack's tanned face was suddenly blanched.

"That's right." Zane nodded and looked toward our third, Richards.

"Uh, Zane, this is—" Jack began to say and, to this day, I long to know what fanciful name he would have come up with for the good doctor.

Doctor Richards glanced down toward the corner of the bill I'd poked into his jeans pocket. "Jackson. Andrew Jackson, nice to meet you."

I looked at the ground and rolled my eyes. *Doctor Richards needs to work on his creativity.*

"Imagine seeing you here." I smiled at Zane and nodded curiously at the fancy nutmeg in his hand.

"Oh, this? I put it on my oatmeal. They say it's a superfood, whatever that means." He shrugged.

"What are *you* cooking up, Andrew?" Zane asked Doctor Richards, a spice jar in his hand as well.

I stepped on Richard's size twelve Blundstone boot. "*Andrew*, what *are* you going to make with the saffron you have there?"

"Oh, right," Richards got himself back on script. "Well, I'm planning to whip up some saffron rice and chicken for the little lady here. It's an aphrodisiac, you know," he said, put his arm around my shoulder, and pulled me close.

"Oh." Zane's voice went flat.

"Yeah, she's a good eater," Doctor Richards went on, nodding smugly. "But she's worth it."

I hung my head and clenched my jaw. How I ever got mixed up with these crazies, I'll never know.

"I see. So, you're an item," Zane said.

"An item? Who, them?" Jack got that mischievous twinkle in his eye that always worries me. "Why, some nights I have to turn the volume up on the TV just to drown out the sound of these two."

"Ok, that's enough. You ready to go, *dear*?" I asked through a stiff smile toward Doctor Richards. "Nice seeing you again, Zane," I said and tugged at the shirt sleeves of the comedians as I led them away.

Two booths past the lady who specializes in red pepper jelly, Richards spoke up. "So, what was that all about?"

"It's a game we play with that guy. We gave him fake names the last time we saw him so now we have to keep it up," Jack explained, something I really couldn't since the genesis of the whole thing involved me doing recon on Lisa. "Guess you're stuck with Andrew Jackson." Junior chuckled before he stopped to sample some mango chutney on a gluten-free cheddar cracker.

Eventually, we rounded up the rest of our gang. Muncie and Sefton were tipsy from the tastings, Tranmer could have opened his own cheese store with what he'd bought, and Seacroft was loaded down with chutneys and crackers. If, for some reason, the car broke down on the way back to the marina, we'd be able to subsist for weeks. We stopped at the organic farmers on the outskirts of town and picked up the turkey and prime rib Aggie had ordered and, before long, we were back on home turf. Trouble is, someone else had been there too. You know how you can tell someone has been in your space? That's how it was. I could smell cologne when I stepped into the salon of my boat.

CHAPTER 13

I t was not an offensive cologne, but since my spritz testing with Jack, I had been sensitive to scents of all kinds. This one seemed familiar. Like I'd encountered it once or twice maybe in the past week or two.

"Pepper! Pepps!" I shouted out – one of the butchers at the market had sent me home with a bone for my dog, he was sure to be over the moon about it. Normally when I come home, and particularly when he smells food, he bounds up from wherever he's been sleeping and his swooshing hairy tail greets me almost immediately. Not so this time. I took tentative steps further into my boat, which seemed strangely quiet. George was also nowhere in sight. On my way through the main deck, I peeked into my bedroom. No comatose cat or dog lying on the king-sized bed, nor in the en suite bath and nothing to indicate that anyone else had been there except the trace of cologne.

The office/salon area was also devoid of animal companions. My desk looked undisturbed. Computer still in sleep mode like I always leave it. I took the narrow steps down to the galley and flicked on the lights. From the steps, I scanned the U-shaped layout from starboard to port. The table and bench seat, the sink area, the pantry, fridge, prep area, and broom closet. I made that kissing noise, known the world over for attracting cats and dogs. I made the noise again and took the last couple of steep steps down into the galley and, somewhere mixed in with my ridiculous smooching sounds, I heard a faint meow coming from the port side of the galley. I smooched the air again and tracked the meowing response. I opened every cupboard George could have trapped himself into, looked under the stainless-steel prep counter, and finally unlatched the broom closet. There he was, sitting in the red mopping bucket I should use more often.

"Meeeeow," he cried at me, and his yellow eyes glinted in the light.

"Oh, baby," I said and scooped him out of the bucket. I put him on the galley floor to make sure he wasn't injured and could walk alright. He seemed fine once he'd taken a few steps, but then again who wouldn't be a little slow to move after being cramped up in a bucket like that.

I closed the closet door and secured the catch. Then I opened it. Then I pulled on the latch which sits at about three feet off the floor. Weird. In the two years or so I've lived on the boat, not once had George trapped himself in the broom closet. Not once had I ever come to that closet to find it unlatched. "Where's your brother?" I asked him.

I called out Pepper's name again. Nothing. I opened the heavy door to the engine room and called his name. Silence. George and I scrambled to the main level, and his incessant meowing and the broom closet trauma earned him the can of salmon I plunked down on the floor for him. I went out through the stern door and stood on the deck and yelled, "Pepper!" My mind raced. Were it not for the gnawing feeling that someone had been on my boat and George's curious hiding spot, I'd have been more relaxed. Enough people in town and the marina know Pepper to know where he belongs, and if he had gotten out somehow, they would return him or let me know. But this was different. Someone had been there, and they had messed with my family.

From the stern deck, I proceeded to the starboard side stairs, climbed one set and then the other to the wheelhouse so I could retrieve my good set of binoculars. I unlocked the door and, to my relief, astonishment, and curiosity, I found my dog. He looked at me with lethargic eyes from the bunk of the wheelhouse and in what seemed like a move that consumed all of his energy, he hopped down from said bunk.

In the corner of the room there was a puddle of vomit. I kissed the top of his head and hugged him.

The next thing I knew, I heard footsteps coming up the rungs of the ladder that led to the wheelhouse. My heart caught in my throat, and I looked around for a weapon. Why is it there's never one when you really need one? I put on my best scowl and braced myself to do some serious cursing when Doctor Richards popped his head into the open doorway.

"Hey, I heard you calling your dog," he said and looked down at the listless animal leaning into my lap. "Everything ok?" he asked in a tone that knew that everything was *clearly* not ok.

I let out a sigh of relief at the sight of him. Even though he'd teased me earlier, a friendlier face I couldn't have asked for, and at over six feet and in good shape, I knew he had a better chance of carrying Pepper to my truck than I had.

"What's going on?" His voice was serious, his look concerned and a bit demanding at the same time.

I was skimpy with the details since, frankly, I didn't know many of them for sure, except that my dog had been sick. My guess is that he'd been drugged or poisoned, though I didn't tell Richards that. All he had to know was that I wanted to get my hundred-plus-pound dog into a truck and get him to the vet.

* * *

"He'll be ok," Marcy Kennedy said as she patted Pepper on the head. She'd done an exam, taken his temperature, felt him up, and checked his eyes and mouth. "He probably just got into something he shouldn't have, but he's a good boy. Yes, you are." Her baby-talk voice and gentle hand elicited some serious tail thumping on the exam room table and I breathed a sigh of relief. "You have any new foods or cleaners on board lately?" she asked as she made a note on the paper on her clipboard.

"No," I said, slowly trying to recall. I'm not overly adventurous with new cuisine, and I'm not that voracious a housekeeper to warrant buying the latest new and improved cleansers. Besides that, I was still somewhat sure that Pepper hadn't gotten into whatever it was on his own.

When we exited to the waiting room, I was surprised to see Doctor Richards seated figure four—resting one leg horizontally over the knee of the other leg—and reading *Dog Business*, a magazine devoted to entrepreneurs in the canine field and not a periodical about the kind of dog business I have to stoop and scoop on Pepper's rounds. He looked up from the magazine anxiously.

"Oh, hi, you didn't have to—"

"Is he ok?" Richards cut in, asking in earnest. He'd first met Pepper when Nat took him to his doctor's appointments with him.

"He'll be fine," Marcy said. "Remember lots of water, and here are the antibiotics, and he'll be good as new. Won't you, baby?" She puckered her lips at him and rubbed his head.

"Thanks, Marce," I said, clipping the leash to Pepper's collar before Richards and I walked the patient to the parking lot where I saw Richards had parked his car beside my truck. He helped Pepper into the passenger side of the truck and closed the door.

"You sure everything's ok?" he spoke to me through the half rolled down window.

"Mmhmm. Thanks for your help," I said and smiled.

He nodded and lingered and looked like he was waiting for more.

"Well, I've got to get some work done back at the ranch," I said, avoiding eye contact and starting the truck, wishing he'd have left before me so he wouldn't see my amateur driving skills.

"Ok." He nodded. He was curt. Curt like he knew there was more to the story, curt like he didn't like that I wasn't telling him, or curt like he didn't believe me.

Later that day, as I sat at my desk, clearing emails and transferring salient contents to Salesforce, I looked across at Pepper, curled up with his sometimes archenemy, sometimes bestie George. Pepper was snoring and George didn't seem to mind. I began to wonder if it was all in my head—the cologne, George finding his way into the broom closet, Pepper being sick in the wheelhouse. How had he trapped himself in there? Had I left the interior door open to the wheelhouse? But what could have jarred the boat enough to shut it? Say it did happen, for the sake of argument—what was in there that Pepper could have gotten into? The brass polish I use on the wheel? I was just about to go up to the wheelhouse to see if that's what it was when my eye caught it, or the absence of *it* I should say, and, in an instant, the self-doubt and maybes dissolved. My father's Rolex was missing from my desk. Someone had *definitely* been on my boat.

* * *

I sat down at my desk chair and cried. And then I got mad. And then I threw my coffee mug against the heavy stern door. And, finally, I picked up the pieces. Like I always do. "Sorry," I said to the concerned-looking duo on the couch. I walked around the boat, trying to somehow save the memory of the cologne. What was left of the scent remained vaguely familiar. Someone had been on my boat, violated my space, probably drugged my dog, trapped my cat in a closet, and I was mad as hell. But that's the thing with being mad as hell. What are you supposed to do about it? Phone a friend? As I picked up the pieces—of the mug, that is—I thought about who to call. Since my first suspect was Russ, there was no way I could talk to Ags about this. She'd tell him and, if it was him, he'd leave town and I'd never see my father's watch again, or find out where he'd pawned it. Jack Junior? With suspect number two on my list being Roddy Claire, I couldn't go to Jack for the same reason I couldn't go to Ags. Stephen Richards? I got the distinct impression he already thought I was nuts, and he had no trouble voicing his opinion about me, *to me*, and if I told him who I thought took my watch, he'd think I was on another witch hunt. Bugsy? Yes! Bugsy would have the security cam footage and he could help me.

I dialed Bugsy's new number. He didn't pick up. Now, this is not altogether unusual for him. If he's in the middle of something important or speaking with someone, he refuses to answer his phone, which I have to respect. Unless it's me that's doing the calling; then it's downright annoying. I headed out to the stern deck of my boat, locked the door tight, and made my way down the dock toward Aggie's. I struck out there, but Ags did tell me that she thought the Bugster was still working on the new laundry building and, I headed off in that direction.

"Anybody home?" I called out as I entered the laundry facility that was the latest feature in our landscape.

"Under here!"

"Under where?" I called out.

Bugsy came from around an interior corner of the building, wiping his hands with a rag and looking smug. "Made you say underwear." He smiled.

I winced up at him. "You been smelling paint fumes all day or did you just turn five?"

"What may I do for you, Miss Michaels?" Bugsy smiled.

"Did you notice anyone around my boat today?"

"Well, no. But I've been working over here for most of the day. Why do you ask?"

"Someone was on my boat."

"You sure?"

"Of course, I'm sure!" I insisted. I hate being asked if I'm sure about things. "Sorry. Look, whoever was on there, I think they gave my dog something and stole something from me."

Bugsy's smile flattened immediately. "What'd they give Pepper?"

"I don't know. We just got back from the vet. Marcy says he got into something, but there's no way he could have locked himself in the wheelhouse. Someone put him there while they went through my place."

"Did you call Hagen?"

"No."

"Why not?"

"Because I think there was only one thing stolen and I have a good idea who did it, I just need to prove it. You have that security camera app on your new phone?"

Bugsy shut his eyes, exhaled deeply, and looked dejected. "Dammit, I knew there was something I hadn't done."

"Oh," I said and tried not to look as devastated as I felt.

"Hey, don't worry, we can still review the footage. Command central is in the back office at Aggie's."

I pulled a face.

"What?"

"It's just that the person I think was on my boat is—"

"Russ?" Bugsy's voice was cold now, severe.

I nodded, too angry to say the name myself.

"Well, let's go find out. We'll look at the footage and, if it's him, I'll..." he said and threw the rag in his hand to the top of his toolbox carelessly.

I looked up into his concerned blue eyes. "You'll what?"

"I'll kill him."

* * *

I'm not sure who between us would win a speed walking competition, but I was impressed with the zeal with which Bugsy headed with me to Aggie's. On the way, I relayed to him how I'd found Pepper and George in improbable locations within my boat, how I noticed the faint smell of cologne, and how I planned to dismember Russ if he was the culprit.

"Hey, girl," Ags greeted me as soon as I entered her store. She was seated behind the counter, applying gold paint to a mini pumpkin. A little arts and crafts time.

"Hi." I nodded, seething and trying not to let it show.

"Hey, Aggie," Bugsy said. "We've just got to get something in the office," he said calmly.

"Ok." Ags didn't seem to care and Bugsy led me to the room in the back of the store.

The back room is roughly a ten-by-ten space and is one of those multipurpose marvels. In it you find filing cabinets, a safe, a bunch of computer looking thing-a-majigs, a bookcase of office supplies, and extra framed prints for the walls Ags switches out as the seasons change. Bugsy sat at a desk behind a computer. "Come here," he said, beckoning me to his side. He leaned back and pulled up a stool for me to perch.

"Let's see." He used the mouse to click on the icon for the security cameras. In the username box, he typed the letters B-u-g-s-y, and below them a password that appeared all in asterisks.

"Hold the phone!" My head snapped toward

him. "Your login is Bugsy? Seriously? You gripe at me for calling you that and—"

"I was thinking you wouldn't notice," he grumbled as his eyes studied the next screen.

"Well, think again." I shook my head.

"Look, I picked the most improbable login, cut me some slack."

"So, what's your password?"

"Alex, I'm not telling you my password."

"Is it A-l-e-x? Is it, huh?"

Bugsy ignored me and clicked on some screens and menus that meant something to him. "Ok, so let me pick this afternoon one to five pm as a range."

"Sounds good." I nodded and watched, waiting impatiently to see the dirty rat that'd been on my boat. I picked nervously at my fingernails.

"Do you have to do that?" he asked, throwing me a shady look that made me stop what I was doing. "Ok. Hang on a sec," he said, and I saw his eyes narrow. "Ok, here we go," he went on, and with that, video from East Camera Two was playing on the monitor. Bugsy put the footage on fast forward and I saw myself leave my dock walking at cartoon fast speed. The time clock on the feed told us that I left at 13:05. Nothing happened for a bit and then the screen went black save for the following sentence that popped up in red in a text box. *Your video experienced technical difficulties, Error 1442.*

"What's that?" I nudged him.

"I don't know," he said and fast forwarded through a black screen until the footage resumed at 16:12.

"Where's the rest of it?" I urged him.

"Hang on," he said. He clicked a few links until he got to the page entitled "Troubleshooting". On that page, he typed in "Error 1442". The results of this query came up as follows: "This error denotes a technical difficulty. Please check your electrical connection".

We exchanged simultaneous puzzled expressions.

"Aggie!" Bugsy yelled out.

Ags came to the door almost immediately; she was probably eavesdropping now that I think about it. "What's going on, you two?" she asked, leaning in the doorway.

Bugsy squinted at her. "Was there a power failure in here today?"

"Yeah, how'd you know?"

"Why didn't you come get me?" he asked.

Ags looked embarrassed and uncomfortable. "Well, Russ was putting up the Christmas lights and I guess the breaker flipped. We didn't catch it until later."

"Oh? Like *a lot* later?" I asked, a little testy.

"Well, he thought one of the bulbs was out on the lights, so he tested them for, oh man, it seemed like forever, until he came in here and noticed the power was out in this room. That's when he figured the breaker popped."

Bugsy gave me a consoling look. "I'm sorry," he said as soon as Ags left the room.

I was speechless. I left Aggie's, asking anyone and everyone if they'd seen anyone near or on my boat. No one had and, over the course of the evening, I resigned myself to the notion that I'd never see my father's watch again. I also drove to the hardware store and invested in the most expensive padlocks I could find.

CHAPTER 14

Somewhere along the way, in some useless, overpriced corporate team building I'd been asked to take part in, I'd learned the six stages of anger. The graphic on the presenter's childish slide showed a bus and its voyage to what looked like Armageddon. Starts in Bothered Town—that's where I was when I first met Russ Shears with the vibe he gave off. Further down the road we get to Mild Irritation Ville. This is the place where you know you are right and you can't help but show it. I got to this point round about the time Bugsy determined Russ was legit enough to stay on the *Summerwind* and I thought with all my eye rolling I'd end up with vertigo. Next stop Annoyed City. Here, you don't give a hang what other people think of your opinions; that was me at the poker night Russ crashed, sitting there across from him, sizing him up and letting go with that involuntary tick he evoked. Port Indignation follows shortly after this stop on the anger bus. I felt, though didn't admit it, a little indignant when Doctor Richards admonished me for my anti-Russ sentiment shortly after said poker fiasco. All of this gets your blood boiling and you reach Frustration Falls. This here is where things get messy and you take out your feelings on inanimate objects, like the mug I smashed on the stern door. Rewarding for the half second it was in mid air, but then came the clean up. Last stop the Hamlet of Hostility. This is where the driver can either take the fork in the road to Rage (a lonely place where the food tastes bad) or Recovery (a less lonely place where they serve fritters and excellent coffee). My eyes flicked past my rifle and I headed off to Aggie's for a little Recovery.

"How would you like an all expenses paid trip to Hamilton?" I asked Ags just after the bell above the door in her store announced my arrival. Hearing it again was like hearing an old friend and, still smarting from my previous day's trauma, I needed all the friends I could get.

"Hmmm, you make it sound so inviting, but I'm going to have to pass," she said, poised at the counter, one hand on a hip, the other on the coffee carafe.

"Oh, come on. A nice visit to a little industrial marina town. We'll have lunch at the docks."

"Again, you really put a spin on things, but I've got a meeting this morning."

"A meeting?"

"New distributor," Ags said, pouring.

"Where are the guys?" I asked, noting the unusual emptiness in the nook.

"Let's see, Jack left town with his honey today. Said they were going antiquing."

I laughed.

"What?" she asked.

"Oh nothing, just at that age, can't they just call it 'us-ing'?"

"Oh, bad. That's a very bad dad joke, you know. You might have to stop hanging around the gang," she said.

"How about the rest of them? Where do you suppose they are?"

"I saw the *Gee Spot* leave early this morning. Maybe they went for a ride on the boat while it's still here."

I nodded and sipped my coffee. "Hmmm."

"What's up?"

"I need to go to Hamilton to see those boats and things to list, but you remember, Nat told me to never go alone," I said and sipped.

Ags nodded. "How about the doc?"

"I think he might be mad at me, I'm not sure why. Could be one of a thousand reasons, I guess." I smirked. "Pike!" I said as if in a eureka moment. Surely, he could be persuaded to go and see some new boats.

"Sorry, but I made him a to-go cup a while ago. He had to fix an engine somewhere out of town."

"Dammit! How about Bugsy? Have you seen

him?"

"I have."

"Oh good, where is he? He's not at his cottage."

"Went to see his kid today," she said, almost as frustrated as I was.

I let out a heavy sigh. I wanted to get this listing work done. I knew I'd have people interested in what Albright had to sell.

"You can borrow Russ if you want," she said and gave me the side eye while she wiped down a chrome sugar dispenser.

"Mmm." *Rage or recovery? Rage or recovery?* My mind kept going back to that ridiculous presentation. On the one hand, rage would feel temporarily rewarding, that is until I became a permanent resident of the Marysville jail. At least I'd get to see more of Hagen. Recovery would mean borrowing Russ for the day. What is it they say, keep your friends close and your enemies closer? Perhaps if I took him with me (and possibly water boarded him) he'd tell me where my watch was. I was having this debate with myself when, as if on cue, Russ appeared from the back room.

"Alex can borrow you, right?" she asked him before I'd even had a chance to decide.

"Sure, what's up?" he said all too willingly.

I paused, wondering for a moment how to get out of this, but as the saying goes (I know a lot of them in case you hadn't noticed), when you're going through hell, keep going. So, I did. "I'm going out of town to do some listings and I usually take someone to...you know..."

"Sure, I'll go. What do you need me to do?"

I must admit I found his agreeableness worrisome. Was Russ planning to drop me off out on some remote highway and steal my truck? Was he hoping I'd give him a ride clear of town? Or was this just his way of making amends for a litany of undisclosed crimes? "Do? Oh, nothing. Just look as if you *could* do something if I needed you to." I smirked.

"Oh, trust me girl, he can look anyway you want him to." Ags smiled a look of fond remembrance and my stomach turned a little.

"Too much information." I smirked back at her. By that time, Russ was beside her in an outfit from his tight jeans and University of Ohio t-shirt collection. His hair was gelled to within an inch of its life and the shadow on his face was well beyond five o'clock.

When Ags noticed the tag on his t-shirt sticking out from the neckline, she adjusted it like a doting mother. "Oh, by the way babe, I hope you like Elvis. Alex can't even take a trip to the grocery store without the king," she sent a playful warning in Russ' direction.

"Not a fan," he said flatly, shrugging.

You know that feeling when you're pretty sure your heart has stopped? That's how I felt at that moment. I fluttered my eyelids briefly to process the sacrilege in the air, and my gaze drifted up to Ags. She looked back at me, her eyes big as saucers. She knows how seriously I take my Elvis and I was one foot back on the rage bus.

"So, when do you want to leave?" Russ asked, jarring me from my homicidal thoughts.

"What?" My thoughts went to my missing watch and what may be my only hope of seeing it again. "Oh, in an hour or so," I said.

"Sounds good."

I nodded and walked my empty coffee mug toward Russ, still wary of his latest character flaw —poor taste in music— and with the sole purpose of detecting whether his scent matched the one I'd smelled on my boat the day before. I couldn't tell for sure but thought hard about it as I walked back to my boat to prepare for my trip to Hamilton with him. The paperwork was a no brainer. The real preparation was in psyching myself up for an hour ride each way with the guy who *may* have robbed the places in town, stole my father's watch, drugged my dog, or all of the above. And as if all of that weren't enough, he didn't dig the king.

* * *

Russ Shears may have been a lot of things, but obtuse he was not. We were twenty minutes out of Marysville when he broke the frigid air between us.

"You don't like me much, do you?"

And the award for being perceptive goes to... "I just don't know you, that's all," was the diplomatic response I opted to give.

"Well, if you have questions for me, go ahead and ask."

"Ok," I said and noticed the road sign ahead indicated seventy miles to Hamilton. "Let's start with the most pressing subject on my mind. Were you on my boat yesterday?"

"No. Someone was on your boat?"

"Yes, someone was on my boat, drugged my dog, locked my cat in the broom closet, and stole my father's Rolex from my desk."

"Alex, it wasn't me. I'd never do something like that. You're like a sister to Aggie. I swear on my grandpa's life."

"Mmhmm, while we're on the subject... are you really Robert Shears' grandson? I mean, you can tell me. I won't spill the beans if you just disappear quietly."

"I *am* Robert Shears' grandson. I swear."

"Then why no ID? What's the *real* reason, and no phone when you showed up?"

"You wanna know the real reason?" He sighed. "I guess we've got time." He paused. "The real reason isn't very flattering. I'm a screw up. I've always been one. I've got this addiction problem," he said.

"Oh," I said lowly.

"Probably not what you're thinking, though.

It's gambling. See, where I was last was Vegas, and I could do no wrong with the dice. Then things went south."

"South of Vegas? Must have been toasty," I muttered, and Russ let out a chuckle.

"You *are* funny, you know that?" He continued. "So, anyway, I got into some trouble and had to borrow some funds from a private lender, shall we say."

"Well, you didn't *have* to," I rationalized unhelpfully.

"I took ten grand and turned it into twenty-five that night," he said proudly, looking out at the highway ahead.

"And then?"

"And then I switched to cards, but the cards didn't come."

"You mean you–"

"I *mean* the cards didn't come. I lost twenty."

"Twenty of the twenty-five?"

"Twenty of the twenty—I had bought myself a few new things."

"Like?"

"Like what does it matter to you?"

"I was just wondering what a geography grad with a gambling problem buys himself."

"Women."

"Oh."

"Yeah." He shook his head.

"So, you couldn't go to your parents?"

"I'm not a trust fund kid like you, my dad

owns a hardware store for Christ's sake."

"You don't know me very well, Russ. So, where did you find him?"

"Who?"

"The loan shark."

"Through a so-called friend of mine. In the back of some Italian restaurant."

"What's the interest rate?" I looked over and asked.

"Why?"

"I used to be in finance, I'm just curious."

"Twenty-five per hundred per week."

"What! Are you nuts? You jumped at *that* rate?"

"I had no choice, and I've been trying to make the money back since. They took my phone, my ID, my car—"

"And you didn't drive a rental car to Marysville, right?"

"Yeah, that was a lie. I hitched a ride on a truck."

"So, you told us poker wasn't your game. Why's that?"

"No, what I said was that *it wasn't for me.* I could have cleaned you all out that night, taken all your money, but you're friends with my gramps and I just couldn't do it."

I nodded. Is this what they call honor among thieves? "So, you've given up gambling?"

"Hell no, that'd be like asking you to give up coffee and apple fritters." He smiled. "I've been hitting a few out-of-town games when I'm not helping Aggie."

"Is that how you could afford the necklace you gave her? I love that necklace, you know."

"Actually, I won it in a poker game the other night, here in town."

"Really? The guy you won it from, was his name Roddy? About forty years old, your size, anemic looking?"

Russ shook his head. "No, older guy. David something."

I flitted my eyes. I don't know any David's except Sefton. "You, uh, don't know who robbed the bakery, do you? Or the pharmacy?"

He shook his head. "You mean did I do it? No, that's not my style."

"So how about your watch? I thought you said you sold it to the store in town."

"I did. Then after I'd made some money at a game, I bought it back. My gramps gave me that watch when I graduated high school. I even graduated with honors, if you can believe it."

"Wow. That's a lot of information. I'm sorry I didn't ask sooner."

"It's ok. It *is* a lot," he said. "Actually, I'm kinda glad to tell it to someone."

By the time we got to Hamilton, I won't say that Russ Shears and I were friends, but we were no longer enemies. I had told him a few of my own hard luck stories—not as hard luck as his, of course.

* * *

Now, you can probably guess that commercial marine businesses aren't often, or *ever,* located in the fancy parts of town between, say, Starbucks and the nail salon. You're more apt to find them beside a welding shop or a fish processing plant. As Russ guided me to our destination via the app on my phone, I laughed as I watched his eyes widen. This wasn't the gritty city life he was familiar with. We were in actual grit, the kind that gets under your fingernails. I had just turned down Harbor Drive and headed into the chain-link enclosure of Jack Albright's when we pulled up onto a chaotic scene. Albright and his crew were supposed to have been out of town. Instead, workers were moving hastily, cranes and excavators were on the go, and I spotted the police and a couple trucks from the Coast Guard. I looked to my right at Russ who was wider eyed than before.

"Let's see what's going on," I said. The truck in park, I stepped down and into an oily puddle, and when Russ met me on my side of the vehicle, we headed toward an older man who was giving orders. When he noticed us, he issued a speculative expression.

"Hi, there," I said. "What's going on?"

"Hi. You from the paper or something?" he asked.

"No, I'm from Marysville. I'm a boat broker, Alex Michaels. Mr. Albright invited me to come list some of his things."

The man shook his head, lifted his cap, and rubbed his forehead with his massive hand tanned and stained with grease. "I'm sorry, I forgot to let you know. I'm Jack Albright," he said, extending handshakes to Russ and me.

"So, what happened?" I asked, giving the man consoling but inquisitive eyes.

"Fire on one, she's sunk. Took the barge down with her. The other's still floating, barely. They're pumping her out."

"Any idea what happened?"

He shook his head. "I keep my stuff in great shape," he said, and when he looked at me, I thought I saw a tear in his eye. "Can't understand it. Coast Guard'll let me know," he went on, looking at the ground and shaking his head. Something caught his eye and he shifted into boss mode. "Michael, get in a boat and move that other barge, we're takin' her out!" he yelled to his worker.

"I'm so sorry," I said. "You've got your hands full, so we're going to get out of your way," I said, hitching my thumb toward the truck.

"If you need anything, if we can help in any way, don't hesitate to ask, ok? You know how to reach her," Russ said to the man, his look sincere and, even though there's nothing Russ could do for him and would certainly never see him again, it was the fact that he'd said it, that he wanted Albright to know that someone cared, that got to me.

The man nodded and made a stoic expression. "Thank you," he said and, in no time, we were on our way back. Even though we took the identical route back to Marysville, it seemed different. With the humanity I'd seen Russ display toward Jack Albright, and the way he unabashedly disclosed his faults and failures to me, I saw him through a new lens and, by the time I'd parked the truck back in the Marysville marina, I was ready to bid Russ a pleasant rest of the day and really mean it.

CHAPTER 15

"Bye, hon," Lisa Claire called out and waved to me from the stern deck of the *Fortune Cookie* as she and Jack Junior motored out of the marina early the next morning. I could see him through the window into the wheelhouse, sitting at the helm and wearing the awful hat she'd bought him. You know the type, white cotton captain's hat, black brim, black and gold insignia on it, the kind of hat no captain really wears unless doing so offers the prospect of getting laid. They were off for a day of fishing and bonding with little grown-up Roddy who simply nodded at me as I waved back politely from the stern deck of the *Alex M.*, where I was stretching before my morning jog.

Once the boat passed, I rolled my eyes at Pepper, who was watching me from his chair. I swear he rolled his too. I put on my favorite hat, pulled my ponytail out the back of it, tapped my ear buds in, and before long my feet were pounding to the beat of Don Henley smashing on the drums for the Eagles. Ironically, the song was "Witchy Woman". Up the hill from the marina and to Main Street and then State, I tried to clear my head of nagging thoughts. And, when Elvis came on with "Suspicious Minds", I nearly skipped through, but it's Elvis after all and nobody skips an Elvis song, do they?

When I crossed over the intersection of Main and Vine, I looked left down the street toward the Vine Street Inn and wondered if or when Lisa would ever divulge that she was not living on the tony side of town as she'd said, but rather in the two steps up from a flop house Vine. I just couldn't get her and Roddy off my mind. When Bonnie Tyler's "Holding Out for a Hero" came on, I spotted hunky Officer Hagen. He was walking on the opposite side of State Street, his trim, tall figure in his dark blue uniform and jet-black hair cut an unmistakable figure. I whistled at him in cat call fashion and, when he turned to spot the culprit, his look of agitation instantly changed to one of amusement. His bright white smile flashed against his tanned complexion. I sped up my pace in case he was watching, but thoughts of him didn't distract me. For long. By the time I was on the return part of my circuit, my mind was racing faster than my feet. At the intersection of Main and Mergl, I turned down Vine toward the inn.

The parking lot was mostly empty save for a few vehicles with out-of-state plates. Folks looking for something cheap and cheerful on their way to somewhere else. Well, at least they got half of what they were after. From where I stood—I won't say skulked—behind a tree, I could see that Zane was inside the gate, sunning himself by what passed as a pool and chatting to what I assumed were guests. From where I stood, I *still* won't say skulked, behind a tree, I spotted the upper row of rooms. 214 had to be there. I recalled the room number with ease courtesy of a memory trick that'd make Mr. Hives himself proud. 214 was the squadron number from what came to be known as Black Sheep Squadron. Making the association between Lisa and Black Sheep seemed natural.

The Vine Street Inn is an L-shaped place. The office and the doors to two levels of rooms face Vine Street and the balconies to the rooms either face the Glass Half Full winery to one side or an empty field behind the water treatment plant. A car passed me and I pretended to stretch my hamstring. I proceeded closer to the Vine. What harm could come from a little peeking in the window of Lisa's room? I walked through the parking lot like I was staying there and quietly took the stairs two at a time. I turned down the volume on my ear buds so I could hear if anyone called out to me. At the top of the stairs, there was a helpful directional arrow. Rooms 200 to

220 to the right.

I walked past 214 slowly. The curtains were open on the big window that faced the street. For the benefit of anyone looking, I pretended to check my reflection. Then I walked back and tried the door. Now, you have to understand that the Vine has not been marred by modern conveniences such as key cards, and I also hadn't spotted any security cameras. These features tend to keep the nightly room rates low and, besides that, the Vine caters to folks who probably don't have much to steal and don't want to be seen anyway. I took a bobby pin out of my hair and, just on a lark, put it in the lock that had to have been vintage 70s. A jiggle here, a look over my shoulder there, and voila, the lock gave way. Trust me, I was just as surprised as you.

Now, even if I had doubted my little memory trick that this was Lisa's room, once inside the suite, my olfactory senses confirmed it. Through the musty air being pumped out noisily via the dusty air conditioner fins moving ancient thick polyester curtains, I could smell Lisa's perfume —a musky blend of spicy scents mixed with cleaner. I closed the door quickly and quietly behind me. To my immediate right was what we'll call the kitchenette—a microwave that looked like it could have been one of the first produced and a scratched stainless-steel bar sink set into a four-foot span of countertop with chipped edges. It looked like it was once off-white but now resembled something in the greige family. There was a particle board cabinet beneath it, along with a tiny fridge that sounded like it was just clinging to life. On top of the counter were Lisa's go-to grocery staples. Store brand potato chips, those tri-color wafer cookies I didn't think they made anymore, and a box of pinot noir.

The bed was straight ahead and, for a housekeeper, I'd expected it to be made, but it wasn't. Maybe she's like those accountants who don't like to do their own taxes. Anyway, there was nothing remarkable about the bed. Built on a particle board platform, there was nothing to see under it. Which is fine, because I didn't know what I was looking for other than an indication that Lisa and/or Roddy were somehow tied to the robberies. A stash of money, powdered sugar from the bakery break-in, just something that would confirm my suspicions.

When I pulled the string to turn on the closet light, I found it stuffed to overflowing with trendy looking outfits... for a twenty-year-old. However, Lisa was pushing sixty-five and the off the shoulder and spaghetti strap numbers in the closet had passed their expiration date as far as she should be concerned. There was also her pink Maxi Maid uniform—the color of a certain liquid antacid. Looking down, there was a jumble of painfully cheap high heels and one pair of athletic shoes.

I poked my head into the second room of the suite where the sofa bed was opened. Another bed unmade. On the chair near it was draped the shirt I'd seen Roddy wearing the only other time I'd seen him. I remembered it because it looked so ill-fitting. I nosed around the closet space he shared with the extra pillows and blankets and opened a couple bureau drawers. Nothing remarkable. I did note that he'd managed to score a hoodie from Pike's machine shop, but Pike gave those out to everyone.

Between the two bedrooms, there was a Jack and Jill bathroom. Worn vinyl flooring and faded in some places, and cracked turquoise wall tiles topped with a row of black tiles about two thirds up the wall. The vanity looked as though it may have been part of the last renovation, which would put it around circa 1980. It had two cream-colored clamshell-shaped sinks set into a marble top that looked to have rust stains on it. The origin of which I couldn't imagine, but the saving grace of the vanity was that it was large. From the looks of things, Lisa had commandeered three quarters of it and left Roddy with a measly space for his razor and toothbrush and a little kit bag.

Looking at the display of items on the vanity, I flitted my eyes. I could have built most of a new person out of what was on the counter. Hair pieces, fake nails, a box of eyelashes, and a knee brace were highlights amidst the mountain of lotions, potions, creams, and wipes. On the shower rod, she was drying two pairs of Spanx. It made me cringe to wonder what Jack Junior might see if she ever went au natural.

On my way out of the room, I looked under the vanity. I spied a grocery bag tucked behind the sink trap, wrestled it out, and untied the knot made with the handles. Translucent amber prescription bottles. I took one out and examined the label. I couldn't correctly pronounce the name of the contents if you paid me, but the prescription in my hand was made out to Reg King and had come from the Marysville pharmacy. Probably just as well that Reg hadn't picked this one up since side effects listed on the bottle included constipation and diarrhea. I guess they offset each other. But that didn't change the fact that Roddy Claire had Reg King's prescriptions. I cursed myself for not taking my phone on my jog, or I'd have taken photos, but my stop into the Vine was more impromptu than planned.

I leaned in the doorway between the two bedrooms and bit on the end of my right index finger as I surveyed the rest of the space. I dismissed the idea of looking for any loot in a wall safe since the room didn't seem to be equipped with one. At least the owners of the Vine knew their clientele. The pill bottles were one thing, but I needed more. Roddy could easily deny or dump those bottles.

Now, I don't mean to toot my own horn, but sometimes a horn is worth tooting, and my particular horn or talent, as it were, is that I'm pretty good at finding things, a skill that had yet to let me down. Not when I needed to find Nat's boat key in Bugsy's cottage and not when I found that needle in a haystack at the fair when I was a kid.

The desk. My last chance to find proof. Of something. I sauntered over and let my fingers trip over a scattering of papers. Pay stubs from Maxi Maid, take-out menus with a few items asterisked, the free magazine that they give out at the real estate office and... what's this? I flipped open the Hilroy spiral bound notebook. "MMM Bakery 0511, Stokes Pharmacy 9119, Devon's Jewellers 1124, Roberts Auto Sales 1589, Marysville Library ...." And the list went on for about eight rows. I read it again, trying to make sense of the numbers. They certainly had nothing to do with the phone numbers of the places. I'd called the MMM Bakery enough to know their last four digits were 2253–it spells CAKE, by the way. What then? Too many digits to be dates, not addresses either. *Security codes?*

The next page in the notebook was a list of dates with notes beside them. *Nov 1, 3 hrs MMM* was scrawled in cursive. And so, the list went on and on. This had to be Lisa Claire's work log book, and my bet was that she had all the security codes for the places she cleaned, including the two that had been broken into. By the way, her handwriting had those super-loopy vowels Hives told us to watch out for. I ripped a page out of the back of the book and jotted down the numbers. I also jotted down the name Reg King, the person for whom those prescriptions were meant. Just for kicks, I pulled on the center drawer of the cheap plywood desk. It stuck but finally gave way after a lot of persuading, jiggling, and pushing the drawer bottom from the underside. Something was jamming it, and when I finally got it open, it only opened enough for me to get my wrist in and rummage around blindly. With the tips of my fingers, I felt something smooth and metallic and slid my wrist in as far as I could until the pinching pain was unbearable. I drew the item to the front of the drawer with the middle and ring fingers of my left hand like the claw game at the arcade, and when I looked down at my find, I could hardly believe my eyes. I flipped it over to look for the engraving, and there it was. "Capt. J.M." on the reverse of my father's Rolex.

"Oh my God!" I growled and clasped it onto my wrist.

When I heard conversation outside the door, my heart got pumping hard and slowed when the voices moved along. Probably just a newly registered guest extolling the virtues of the place. *Look, honey, there's actually a roof and windows.* I stood behind the door for a minute, waiting for the voices to leave earshot, and I made my hasty exit as covertly as I'd made my entrance, priding myself on remembering to depress the door lock before I closed the door behind me. I had being sneaky down pat. Or so I thought.

* * *

Fueled by adrenaline and a desire to get the heck back home and mull over my fruitful visit to the Vine, I am sure I broke a personal record for best time on my run. Each footfall was charged with a blend of energy and curiosity. I held my right arm close to my side as I ran to keep my father's Rolex, too big for my wrist, from sliding off. I tapped the pocket of my running shorts a few times to ensure the paper I'd tucked in there was still with me. How much proof would Hagen need and how much would he chastise me for having obtained it in the manner I had?

I had showered, re-dressed, tucked the page from Lisa's notebook into my jeans, and was about to lay out my findings to Ags over lemonade at the table and chair set in front of her place when, from the corner of my eye, I spotted a police cruiser coming down the marina hill. Hmph. *Hagen stops in for coffee all the time*, I told myself, yet I couldn't keep my mind from wondering if it really was a mere coincidence.

"What's the matter?" Ags looked across the table and asked me intently.

"What?"

"You just went white as a sheet. Are you alright?"

I nodded and felt my chest heave out the deep breath I didn't even know I'd been holding. What was I worried about? He couldn't possibly know what I'd done, and even if he did, how could he be angry about it? I was practically doing his job for him. And yet, as lug soles crunched on the gravel toward us, I could feel my leg tremble nervously under the table. I tried to decipher the tone of his steps. They weren't hasty, but at the same time they weren't relaxed.

"Oh, hi!" I said cheerily, noticing my voice was a little higher than usual while I forced a nervous smile. *Don't look guilty,* I told myself.

Ags looked up at him. "Hi, there."

Hagen smiled weakly at Ags and slid me a steely expression, then he pulled out the chair between us, put his hat on the table, and took a seat. "Ladies. How are you both?"

"Oh, fine." I added a nod. "Ags, how about you, are you fine too?" I locked eyes with her, letting her know something was up and that I'd explain later.

She nodded slowly, acknowledging my signal. "Fine. Yes, I'm fine. If there was one word to describe me today, it sure would be fine."

"How are you?" I asked Hagen and hoped that

he wouldn't notice my leg still shaking uncontrollably under the table.

"Honestly, I've been better," he said, turning his gaze from Aggie's face to mine, where it lingered until I shifted my attention to the top of the table, counting the scratches in the woven aluminum.

"Rough day?" Ags asked, trying to thaw the frosty air that had descended upon us like a cold front.

"You might say that," Hagen replied. And while I felt he was looking at me, I couldn't lift my eyes to meet his. "See, I was out making the rounds. Actually, I was a little tired, a little cranky today." He folded his arms in front of his chest as he leaned back in the chair.

"Oh, well, it happens," Ags said.

"Didn't get much sleep since I've been studying when I'm not at work." He cleared his throat. "And then my boss texted me a picture."

"Oh?" Ags asked, her voice laced with intrigue.

"Really?" I said, and my voice trickled up again to that surprised-sounding octave.

Hagen looked from Aggie to me and I averted my gaze again.

"Yeah, see, one of the guys at the station told the lieutenant that I knew the woman in this photo that'd been circulating. In fact, he told him that I knew her quite well."

Ags looked from Hagen to me and found me

biting my bottom lip.

Hagen cocked his head and looked off into the distance. "See, the funny thing is, she was photographed after she'd trespassed and broken into a hotel room."

I flitted my eyes. *The Vine Street Inn could scarcely be called a hotel. It barely qualifies as a hovel.*

"You don't say?" Ags broke the pregnant pause, and I think I saw the corners of her mouth turn up.

Hagen was about to launch into something when the front door of Aggie's place opened and Bugsy emerged with a bottle of juice. We all exchanged cordial nods and half smiles. Hagen waited until Bugsy was out of earshot before he pivoted his body toward me. I looked up from the table, a little chagrined to see his jaw tighten. If he wasn't in such a mood, it would have been sexy as hell. He paused for a moment, perhaps to consider what to say, as if he hadn't rehearsed it a few times already. I know I would have.

"Why?" was all he said.

"That's a great question. How much time do you have?"

"This isn't funny, Alex. You broke into the Vine."

"You did?" Ags was incredulous, though I don't know why. She'd been a party to my breaking and entering before, and if she'd been around earlier, I would have enlisted her to keep watch for me. One could argue that it was partially her fault that I'd been spotted.

"The owner took a picture of you with his phone. Did you know that?"

I took a sip of lemonade, stalling. "Can't blame him." I took another sip, figuring it might be my last taste of lemonade for a while.

"Told the desk sergeant your name was..." Hagen produced his notebook from his chest pocket and flipped up a few pages. "Euphegenia Coddlesworth."

I choked on the lemonade as it went down.

"Oh my." Ags began to rub her forehead.

"Are you ok? Seriously?" he asked me.

"Define ok."

"I mean, have you experienced a massive head injury recently?" Hagen shook his head. "You know I'm supposed to find you and bring you in."

"What? For breaking into *that dump*? Don't you even want to know what I found?"

Hagen put his hat on and pushed his chair back, then his hand went to his belt from where he drew his handcuffs.

Jack Junior, who had probably been watching the entire time, came out to the steps of Aggie's store carrying a snack pack of peanuts. "Hey, you two. Uh-uh, what's going on here? Can't you save the handcuffs for alone time?"

"Jack," Hagen nodded. "I'm afraid this is business. I've got to take her in."

"What'd you do this time, kiddo?" Jack called

out.

"Oh, he's arresting me for —"

"Alex, you have the right to remain silent. Why don't you try exercising it?" Hagen said, the cuffs dangling in his hand.

"Ben, come on. You don't *have* to," I protested.

Hagen was suddenly official. "Turn around, please."

When I did turn, I saw the gaggle from the *Gee Spot* speed-walking toward us. I overheard Gladys ask Ginny if her hair looked alright. Looked fine to me, and in no time, they had front row seats to an episode of *Cops*.

"See, I told you he likes it rough." Gladys smiled and elbowed Ginny.

Ginny nodded. "I knew it that day in the park when he was putting on that show."

"Ladies," Hagen said by way of greeting, and when I looked back at him, he was blushing. "And that wasn't a *show*, that was a primer in self-defence. Now—"

"I was arrested once," Geraldine's words cut over the sound of Hagen's explanation, and with that the attention was suddenly off me. "Remember when I let those rabbits loose from the lab in Chicago?"

"Oh, yeah, that's right." Gladys guffawed. "Didn't y'all—"

"Most certainly did," she answered Glady's question that had apparently only been asked telepathically. After twenty years of friendship,

I guess that's possible. She shook her head. "Added assaulting an officer to it just because I kicked him."

"Geraldine, you kicked that boy in the nuts. Didn't he talk with a falsetto for about a year and a half?" Gladys asked in her typical twang.

"True. Don't kick this one in the nuts, honey," Geraldine offered by way of legal advice.

I heard Hagen's heavy sigh from behind me. "Ladies, if you please, I'm just going to—"

Gladys inched closer to me. "Bet he has nice ones, don't he?" she asked in a voice louder than a whisper.

"Now's a good time to exercise that right to remain silent, Michaels," Hagen said loudly as he clinked the bracelets on me.

Truth be told, I had no idea what his naughty bits looked like and, while Jack and Hagen had a brief exchange and Geraldine reveled in the sisterhood of being jailbirds with me, I hadn't noticed Bugsy coming back our way until it was too late.

"Thanks, Geraldine. Um, Hagen, can we hurry this up please?" I raised my voice. If there is one thing I didn't need to hear, it was Bugsy telling me "I told you so". For some reason, he consistently condemned my snooping. The closer he got, the more I felt myself get red. "Ok, Hagen, I'm ready. Jack, can you lock up my boat and feed my zoo?"

"Sure, kiddo."

"Hang on a sec," Hagen said as he babbled something into his radio.

I walked toward the cruiser sideways, angling my cuffed hands behind me and out of Bugsy's line of sight, but it was too late. He could hardly contain his smile, and his dimples looked like they had grown bigger. "This how you're getting dates these days, Hagen?" he asked on approach.

"Just doing my job, Bugsy."

"Beedle," Bugsy corrected him.

"Whatever," Hagen replied.

"What's going on, Junior?" Bugsy asked.

"Takin' the kid," Jack Junior said and popped a few peanuts into his mouth like he was at a ball game.

"You didn't," Bugsy said, and when I glanced up from the ground, he had issued me a look that was a masterful cross between gloating and disappointment.

CHAPTER 16

"Don't you even want to know what I found?" I asked Hagen as he drove us out of the marina.

"No."

"But—"

"No."

"Well, for starters, I found the watch they stole from me!"

"Which watch? Who?"

"My father's Rolex. And Jack's girlfriend and her rotten kid."

"And let me guess, you took it back."

"Damn right I did! I think I want to press charges. Can I do that when I'm at the station?"

Hagen gave me disapproving eyes then put them back on the road. "So, you want to press charges for them taking your father's watch that you then broke into a hotel room to steal? How did you know who had it?"

"I didn't. I got lucky. I also found a list of—"

Hagen pulled the car over to an empty parking spot on State Street, put it in park, and turned his body to face me. He'd been kind enough to let me ride in the front seat. "Do you realize that you could have been hurt? What if they'd come back to their hotel room and caught you?"

"I didn't steal anything. Look—"

"No, *you* look. Just because you have a feeling about somebody doesn't mean you go off half cocked and conduct your own investigation."

"The woman who is staying in that room is dating Jack Junior and she's a liar. I just needed to see the extent of it for myself."

"You sure that's why?"

"Yes... What are you getting at?"

"You sure you just don't want to lose Jack?"

"Lose Jack?"

"Or see him happy?"

I was speechless; of course I want to see him happy.

"You're not the only one with theories, Michaels. You surround yourself with Jack and his gang, you get companionship, and they pose no threat to your status as single. Maybe you don't want them to find relationships either."

"You've been watching too much *Dr. Phil*. So, do you want to know what I found in the Vine or not?"

Hagen let out a sigh. He knows how adept I

am at changing the subject, especially when it gets into icky emotional territory. "Well, since you're not going to remain silent, tell me."

"When I was in the Vine, I made a list. It's in my back pocket. Right cheek. Alarm codes I think—the bakery, the pharmacy, Devon's, et cetera."

"Devon's?" Hagen's voice and his eyes lit up.

"Yeah, why?" I looked at Hagen's intrigued expression. "Why is *that* so interesting?"

"May I?" he asked.

I giggled. "I'd be disappointed if you didn't."

Hagen shook his head at my impertinence then unbuckled my seatbelt and motioned for me to raise my derriere while he put his hand in the back pocket of my jeans. I'd like to say that it lingered there for a few seconds longer than it should have, but it didn't. Hagen was all business, took the paper and unfolded it.

"Ok, what's it mean? Who's Reg King?" he asked.

"I have no clue. Maybe King is their real last name. Her name isn't Lisa Claire. Her employer told me that much."

He smirked across at me. "I don't even want to know how you got *that* information."

"Why are you so interested that Devon's is on that list?" I studied his reaction.

"Can I keep this?" he asked, folding the paper he'd plucked from my pocket.

"If you tell me why you're so worked up about

Devon's."

Hagen let out a deep breath. "I can't."

"Devon's, huh? Devon's, Devon's, Devon's." I repeated the word as though it were a mantra and as if the answer would magically come to me and, when I looked at Hagen, he was beginning to look worried that I'd guess what it was he couldn't tell me.

"Devon's. Hmmm." I thought about the demeanor of the sales clerk the day I'd popped in to ask about the pendant, about the security guard I'd never noticed before. "Devon's was robbed, wasn't it?" I asked and watched as Hagen's eyes darted away from the hold they had on mine. "I'm right! I know I'm right!" I said, jubilant as a kid on the last day of school. "Tell me I'm right, just—"

Hagen pounded both fists on the steering wheel. "Dammit," he scoffed. "Alex, I swear if you tell anyone..."

"What?"

"I'll be blamed and I won't get that transfer to the marine unit."

I weighed my options—either I spilled the beans and Hagen would never speak to me again or I didn't and he'd get assigned to the marine unit and be eaten by a sea monster. Each one had its drawbacks, that's for sure. "So, why wasn't this on the news?"

"Keeping it hush hush. The chief has a strategy. Alex—" He turned to face me, and his green eyes were soft this time.

"I won't tell anyone. I promise." I smiled at him and, when he reached across me to get my seat belt fastened, I picked up the scent of the soap he'd used that day.

"I still have to take you in. Don't mention the watch while you're there."

* * *

Aggie picked me up at the jail. I'm sure in my lifetime this is not the last time I'll say those words. I was charged with trespassing. Again, I'm sure in my lifetime I'll have to repeat that sentence at some point. On the ride back to the marina, I explained to her what I'd found in room 214 of the Vine, and we swore that until we had more information, we wouldn't tell Jack or any of the gang unless we were confronted. I had to be one hundred percent sure before I became the reason Jack got his heart broken. And so, in an effort to dodge prying questions, we came up with a cover story for my arrest. It had to do with failing to register the truck I'd been driving.

I decided my best bet was to lay low and not answer too many questions regarding the ridiculous story. Ags was good enough to make me a sandwich before she went on her date, and I was perfectly ready to hibernate on my boat for the night. It was a pleasantly cool November night, the moon was almost full, the stars were plenty, and the bugs were few, and so with the stern door of my boat open, I sat on the grey tufted sofa in the salon, soaking in the night air and reading. That is to say, keeping out of trouble. At the end of the chapter, I folded back the top of the page and picked up the oversized cup of green tea I'd made ten pages earlier, hugging it with both hands. I looked down at my dog and my cat curled up together on a swath of faux sheepskin. With the exception of having been in jail that day, all things considered, it felt like I was having a bucolic little moment from a Hallmark movie. All was peaceful in the world. Until it wasn't.

A clang somewhere off in the near distance broke the calmness of the night and caught my attention. I pulled the binoculars from the top of my desk and proceeded to scan the marina for movement. I really ought to be head of the neighborhood watch, don't you think? I tapped on the button to illuminate my view and strained my eyes—something darker than the night was moving around outside of Aggie's place and I couldn't tell if it was of the four or two-legged persuasion. But I knew two things for sure; she was out for the evening and the next day was garbage pickup day and it wouldn't kill me to put her garbage cans in the shed at the back of her place. It'd save me helping her pick up gunky wrappers from expired food she'd thrown out if the critters got into it.

"Be back in a sec," I said in the direction of the comatose twosome on the floor, and I hopped out onto the deck to do my good deed for the night. Thing is, the closer I got to Ags' place, the less I was convinced there was a trash panda messing with her garbage bin and more convinced I was that it was something of the human variety. The rash of burglaries was making us all a little paranoid, but when I heard someone stifle their cough, I knew for certain there was a person behind the store.

I leaned against the siding on the front of the store. I could see the lights on in Bugsy's cottage and, recalling Hagen's chastising me for being impetuous, I texted Bugsy's new number. "Are you there?"

I waited for an interminable amount of time, which in truth, was probably no more than thirty seconds. No response. *Dammit.*

Flashes of memories from Hagen's self defence/wrestling class in the park flickered in my mind. What was it he said? *If all else fails, go for the groin.* What else did he say? What were my other options? Why the heck did I have to make contact with someone's groin, anyway? My blood was pumping so hard I could feel my earlobes throbbing as I made my way around the side of the building and peeked at the back.

There was someone. On a ladder. He went up the rungs in clangs until he was near the top of the ladder, just below Aggie's bedroom window. *Not on my watch, buddy!* He took a rung down and then another, and I knew that If I was going to catch him off guard, I had to do it quickly, before he got to the bottom of the ladder and took off. In my head I counted down from three, took a deep breath, and rushed the side of the ladder. My feet dug into the gravel with every step. The ladder scraped along the siding of the building until it clanged down. I thudded down with it, landing on the hard aluminum rungs, hitting my chin on one rung with such force that I swear it rattled all the teeth in my head. The ladder wasn't resting on the ground, though. Somehow, I'd managed to trap part of the prowler under the cold aluminum frame.

"What the hell are you doing?" the agitated voice blustered nasally.

"Listen, dirtbag, you're busted," I said in my most menacing voice, the one I use when I want to sound taller.

Next there was a distinctly exasperated sigh. "Alex Marie Michaels. You drive me absolutely crazy," came the pained words of Bugsy and, from the sounds of things, he was getting a cold.

"What are *you* doing here?" I asked as I pushed myself up from the rungs I'd landed on. One of them had really smarted.

"The question is, what are *you* doing here? Haven't we talked about your little heroics before?"

"I'm not the one skulking around Aggie's place in the dark, am I?"

"Sure you are," he said and pushed the ladder off himself.

"Well, so are you!"

"I wasn't skulking, I was replacing the light in the motion detector up there," he carped.

There was a long pause between us. "Oh," I said, and looked up at the building.

Bugsy put his hand on my leg to push himself up. "Here, help an old guy up. Are you ok?" he asked.

"Me? Oh sure," I said, lying. I knew I was in for a fresh bruise or two, but nothing I couldn't handle, and I helped Bugsy to his feet. "Sorry, are you ok?"

"Yeah," he said and, against the dark of the night, I saw him arch his back. "What are you doing here anyway?" he asked, swiping the pea gravel from his jeans.

"Well, I saw some movement. Why didn't you answer your phone? I texted you."

"Probably because I was putting up this lad—"

Bugsy's words were cut like a knife with the sound of the shrill alarm that came from inside Aggie's.

"Don't move!" he said and ran around to the front of the store. I watched as he flicked on the inside lights and I pulled out my phone from my back pocket and dialled 911.

"911, what's your emergency?" I could just

barely make out the words of the operator over the shrill, incessant mechanical sound of the alarm.

"Break in. We need the police," I shouted.

"There's a break in where you are?"

"Yes."

"Are you calling from within the structure?"

"No, I'm outside. My, um, friend has gone in to catch the guy," I said and stood on my tiptoes to try to see into the glass of the back door. "You better hurry. Is Hagen on duty?"

"What's the address?"

"Aggie's place at the Marysville Marina. Please hurry."

"We have a unit nearby."

"Thanks." I disconnected and shifted nervously from one foot to the other and wondered what to do with myself when, out of the back door, a figure crashed and knocked me ass over teakettle into the steel garbage bins. It just wasn't my night. Hadn't been my day either, come to think of it. I looked up to see Bugsy run out the back door, the glow from the inside of the store backlighting his figure. "That way." I pointed toward the pavilion behind the store and Bugsy gave chase.

* * *

Ten minutes later, red and blue lights were strobing in Aggie's parking lot and a pack of curious onlookers had assembled. Among them, the couple that bickered the whole of the previous weekend, Sefton, Peter Muncie, Stephen Richards, Seacroft, Jack Junior, and Cary Tranmer. Apparently, they keep the police scanner on at the VFW hall and the gang wasted little time in getting back to the marina.

Lights from one of the cruisers were angled toward the back of the store and shone on the ladder on the ground. I had considered hiding from the police so I wouldn't have to explain my second run-in with them in the same day, but Bugsy talked me out of it.

After a few preliminary questions from everyone's favorite officer, Ben Hagen, he got to the nitty gritty. "So, what's with the ladder?"

"*That* ladder?" I asked.

Hagen looked from me to Bugsy and back to me. "Yes, *that* ladder," he said, and he was ornery already.

"Oh, well that has nothing to do with the break in," I said.

"Humor me," he said with no humor whatsoever.

I looked at Bugsy and sighed. "Well, if you must know–"

"That's why I'm asking," Ben cut in.

I smirked, surprised at his impatience. "I was just about to tell you, but if you're going to be like that about it…" I shook my head and pulled my hoodie closer, wincing at the tenderness on my side.

"I was on the ladder," Bugsy spoke up.

"*You*?" Hagen asked, his voice up in tone and volume.

"Yes, the light in the motion detector wasn't working and I was replacing it."

"So, when the guy came out the back door, he knocked down the ladder?" Hagen asked.

"Yes," I said. Lying. It's so much easier in the dark.

"No," Bugsy sighed. "Nancy Drew here came and knocked me off the ladder."

"Is *that* true?" Hagen turned and asked me, shining his flashlight in my face.

I put up my hand to block it. "Maybe. Yes. Now that I think about it, that's the way it happened." I nodded and looked agitated as if to add credibility—like that ship hadn't already sailed.

"And why would you have done that?"

"Well, I... I didn't know it was Bugsy."

"Mr. Beedle," Bugsy corrected me.

I chuckled. "Yeah, right. You see, it's simple. I saw some action over this way and thought it might be an animal in Aggie's garbage, but then I saw someone on a ladder and–"

"And you took it upon yourself to try to catch him? How'd that work out for you? Didn't we just have a conversation about jumping head first into situations?" Hagen looked at his watch. "Wasn't that, oh, less than six hours ago?"

I was pretty sure that was a rhetorical question, though he looked at me with expectation in his eyes.

Hagen was still humorless. "Then what happened?"

"Then? Well—"

"You mean after she pinned me with the ladder and called me a dirtbag, or before?" Bugsy interjected.

Hagen sighed and tapped his pencil on his notepad.

"Why aren't you looking for the guy in the field?" I asked, trying to change the direction of the inquisition.

"That guy's gotta be ten miles away by now." Hagen sighed. "You have a description of him?"

"Well, one thing's for sure, he's a fast runner," Bugsy grumbled.

"Said the slow runner," I muttered.

"Look, I'll have you know I was on the track and field team in my day."

"For the one-room schoolhouse?" I asked, smiling.

Hagen unhitched his handcuffs from his belt and, having had a brief encounter with them already that day, I wasn't looking forward to wearing them again.

"What, uh, what are you doing?" My smile dissolved as I looked from the glint of the cuffs to Hagen's humorless expression.

"You two are about an inch away from obstructing justice," he said. "And furthermore–"

"The lady who owns the store just got here," another officer approached Hagen to say.

"Tabarnac." Ags sighed when she got closer to Bugsy and I. "What happened?" She searched my eyes.

"Sorry, Ags, we couldn't catch him," I said.

She looked at Hagen. "Can I go in?"

"Sure."

"Can I go with her, you know, moral support and all?" I smiled at him.

"Alright, but I'll have to talk to you later," Hagen said and turned to Bugsy. "Ok, so give me details. Straight this time, Beedle."

As I turned to walk with Ags, the pain in my side sharpened, I winced, and my hand shot to hold my side.

"You ok?" she asked, looking over at me.

"Yeah, I'll tell you all the gory details inside," I said a little breathlessly.

"Ma'am, do you need an ambulance?" a young officer approached me on the steps into Aggie's place.

I sucked in through clenched teeth—he was about to find out that today was not his day. "First of all, I'm not a ma'am, I'm a miss, and I do *not* need nor do I want an ambulance. Thank you for asking, though!" The young officer looked petrified and backed away.

I strained up the steps into Aggie's store. I don't know what I'd been expecting, maybe for it to be ransacked, but it didn't look much different than usual. Ags ran to the back part of the building toward the little office she hated spending time in, and I slowly made my way to one of the red and chrome seats at the counter.

Russ Shears bounded up the stairs and into the store. "What happened?" His eyes were big. Angry mixed with concerned.

I couldn't help but look at him critically. He was wearing the hoodie from Pike's machine shop and, I swear, so was the guy who knocked me over. I didn't like where my mind was headed. "There was a break in."

"Your leg's bleeding," he said, and when I looked at my jeans there it was—an expanding blood stain on my best pair of ripped jeans. I looked away. I'm not so good with blood.

Ags emerged from the back office, her hands lifted out at her sides, an exasperated look on her face. "Took the safe," she grumbled and shook her head. She perked up a bit when she saw Russ.

"How 'bout I make some coffee, babe," he said, already poised at the machine. "And you should probably see a doctor about that." He nodded in my direction.

Copy that, Sherlock.

The young officer from earlier poked his head into the door. "Ma'am, I mean Miss... I know you didn't want an ambulance, but this man says he's —"

I rolled my eyes and thought about changing

my name from Alex to Ma'am, but all I could envision was the mountain of paperwork that'd require. "I told you—"

"Hi." Doctor Richards took the door handle from the officer and entered the store. He looked casual in a heathered grey shawl collared sweater, faded jeans, and short brown suede boots. I looked at him wondering why I never managed to look as good as he does for such impromptu get-togethers.

I waved off the young officer. "It's ok."

While Russ made sympathetic noises to Ags in the kitchenette, throwing in an embrace for good measure, Doctor Richards took a seat on the chrome stool beside me. "You're hurt," he said, looking down at the wound on my thigh.

"It's nothing. I'm fine," I said and winced to let out a breath.

"You don't sound fine. Hop up here," he said and patted the Formica countertop, now a makeshift exam table.

"It's just a scratch." I moaned a little breathily and gingerly eased my butt onto the counter.

"I'll be the judge of that. What else is going on?"

"Hmm?" I asked, wrapping my right arm around my middle and putting pressure on my left side.

"There, what happened?"

"Oh, I crashed into a ladder," I said and took a sip of the coffee Russ Shears had placed beside me.

"Thanks," I said over my shoulder to him.

"You *what*?" Ags squawked and put a first aid kit on the counter.

"Thank you," Richards said and opened the box, looking at the contents like a kid at Christmas. He selected from it the tiniest pair of scissors I'd ever seen. They looked ridiculous in his massive hand but some how he used them to enlarge the hole in the thigh of my jeans. He wet a cotton pad with something from a bottle that turned out to be liquid fire, at least that's what it felt like when he dabbed it on my skin. I tried to pull my leg away, but Richards kept a firm grip on me; he must know the type. He pulled the backing off a few bandages and smoothed them on my leg while I recounted the play by play of the intruder to Ags and sipped on the not-half-bad coffee Russ had made.

I tried to turn to make a point to Ags in the kitchen and couldn't. I sucked in air through clenched teeth as my side smarted, worse than before. It felt like my ribs were going to poke through my vital organs at any moment. Doctor Richards looked up at me from the stool in front of me. His blue-grey eyes were intense, and I found myself suddenly unable to maintain eye contact.

"Let me take a look."

"What?"

"You may have cracked a rib. Just let me take a

look."

"At *me*?"

"You want to see my credentials?" Richards stood and took a hold of the zipper on my hoodie. "May I?"

I nodded and he unzipped.

I felt my cheeks flush again and I looked around Aggie's store at anything that would hold my gaze, a re-jigged aisle, a knot in the wooden floor, just anything to divert my attention from the fact that Doctor Richards had slipped his hands up the inside of my shirt to feel my ribs.

"Take a breath," he said.

I sucked in a sharp shallow breath.

"Oh my," Aggie said from the direction of the kitchen. I heard her turn around and scurry toward the office.

"Starting to swell there."

"Swell," I said murmured and resisted the urge to pass out or throw up.

* * *

Findings concluded outdoors, Hagen trudged up the steps into Aggie's, his head bent as he read from his notepad. "Beedle says the guy was wearing a hoodie with a big logo on it. That sound right to you? Might have been the one for Pike's place," he said and finally glanced up to see me being tended to by the doc. "Hey, I didn't know he hurt you."

"He didn't. Doctor Richards just wanted to feel her up." Ags cackled from somewhere in the back.

I cut her some slack and ignored the comment. Her place had just been robbed and if that doesn't merit you a pass, I don't know what does. "The hoodie, huh? Well, that narrows it down to most of the fishermen and half the strippers in town." I smirked.

"You'll be ok, no gymnastics for a while though, and let me know if it gives you any trouble," Richards said and zipped up my jacket like I was that one kid in kindergarten who couldn't quite manage.

"Thank you," I said and eased down from the counter that normally hosted my coffee and fritter and not my behind.

Richards re-assembled the first aid kit and handed it to Aggie and, seeing the practicality of not contaminating the crime scene, crammed the used cotton pads and backing from the bandages into his hand. My eyes followed him as he quietly excused himself from the store, but not before exchanging cursory nods with Hagen.

"Well, that guy's gonna be some kinda disappointed when he sees my measly savings," Ags muttered, putting the first aid kit up on a shelf in the kitchenette.

"Was it just money in the safe?" Hagen asked, taking notes.

"That's right," she said toward Hagen who moved quickly to the back-door frame to examine the damage.

"How much?" I whispered.

"About five grand. Oh, and a—" She motioned with her index finger and thumb in the shape of a gun.

"You had a *gun*?" I whispered.

She shook her head. "Carlos," she whispered back.

Ahh, Carlos. The on again, off again professional soccer player who'd been deported last month.

"Who had a gun?" Hagen called out from the back door.

"Who what?" I asked, wondering when Hagen had acquired super hearing.

"I heard the two of you."

"Oh."

"There's a gun missing?" Hagen asked.

I nodded and gave Ags a contrite expression for of all things being a loud whisperer.

"Your gun, Aggie?" Hagen asked.

"No. I was just hanging onto it for safe keeping. In the safe."

"What kind of gun was it?"

"I dunno, a black one. It had some silver on the handle. Family heirloom, I think. Belongs to Carlos."

Hagen cocked his head at her. "You know, by law you have to report that within five days."

"Didn't I just do that?" she smiled coyly. Even in her desperate hours, she manages more charm than a bevy of debutantes at a cotillion.

Hagen smirked. "Noted. Alex, can I see you for a minute?" he asked and, when I locked eyes with Ags, she looked at me like I was going to the electric chair.

I walked with Hagen to the sunglass carousel. I didn't have the stomach to check out the view and just assumed I looked as awful as usual. "I'm sorry," I volunteered before the chastising I was sure was coming.

"For what?" Hagen asked, and when my eyes flicked up at him, he looked quizzical.

"I don't know. Didn't you call me over here to bawl me out?"

"No," he said and held my gaze. "I wanted to tell you that the owner of the Vine doesn't want to press charges."

I felt my nose wrinkle. "He doesn't?"

"Nope."

"Really?"

"Don't ask me why."

The night turned into morning and, in its early hours, we all went back to the safety of our homes. I offered Ags my couch, but she opted to stay in her apartment above the store. Russ volunteered to be her sleepover security guard. While Hagen wrapped up police business, Bugsy walked me to my boat where another restless night awaited me.

CHAPTER 17

The more I tried to sleep, the more awake I felt. I threw the covers off me in a huff, walked across the corridor to my office, and sat behind my computer wondering what search words would give me the answers to all the questions I had. *Where was Mr. Google with the snappy results when you needed them? Who was breaking into the places in town? Where had Russ been tonight? What's the real story behind Lisa and Roddy? Why didn't the owner of the Vine want to press charges?* He didn't owe me or know me. And while I got the impression he kind of liked me, I have an inherent distrust of people *that* magnanimously forgiving.

I typed "Zane Wilcox Marysville" into the search bar, although I had my doubts that was the real name of the man from the Vine. Nothing important popped up. I drummed my fingers on the desktop, they paradiddled in step with my thoughts. The only thing I knew, or assumed about the man, was that he may own the Vine Street Inn. With that fragment of knowledge in hand, I ventured onto the California Property Records website where I proceeded to type in the address for the dump. The owner came back as D.E. Enterprises, and through searching "D.E. Enterprises", I learned that the sole director of D.E. Enterprises is David Earle. David Earle turned out to be nobody, at least nobody I could find who looked remotely like the guy from the Vine. After that little dead end, I managed to get a bit of sleep, no thanks to the pain in my side and thoughts of Doctor Richards' warm hands.

With the light of day that morning, so too came the rain. In fact, rain was forecast for the whole day. It kind of summed up how we were all feeling. I think someone years ago coined the term *pathetic fallacy* for this kind of thing when the weather sympathizes with the prevailing mood. The mood of the Marysville PD had to be agitation–still stumped by the break ins at least as far as the public was concerned; Jack was in the dumps because Lisa hadn't been to the marina in days; and Aggie was going to have to explain to Carlos that his dead father's gun had been stolen from her place. Yes, it was the kind of rainy day that made me want to pull the covers over my head and shut my phone off, but then I wouldn't have seen the message from Jack Junior later that day.

Are you home?

I read the message over and over again, reading volumes into the three words he'd tapped. Wondering if he just wanted to make sure I was around so he could scold me for breaking into Lisa's room, wondering if our friendship was irreparably damaged. Finally, I responded with a curt reply. *Yes.*

Can you come over please? he texted me back almost immediately.

Sure, I typed out. I know I could have picked up the phone. Texting seems so cowardly, but I'm nobody's role model.

I changed out of my sweats and into jeans, a sweater, and a yellow rain slicker, runners, and pulled the hood up before I pushed myself out the stern door of my boat into the pouring rain and headed to the *Fortune Cookie.* When I got to Jack's boat, letting myself in, he turned to look at me. He didn't look mad at me as much as he looked apoplectic with whatever situation he was wrestling.

"Hi." I was sheepish mixed with curious.

Jack paced to the sideboard. He was fidgety and skipped the greetings. "Here, kid, have some coffee. Want a cookie to go with it? Lisa made them. They're pretty good."

"Thanks," I said, taking a coffee and oatmeal type cookie and wondering when he was going to start yelling at me.

"They're questioning Lisa and Roddy. Can ya-can ya-can ya believe it? Can't you tell your boy

Hagen to back off?"

"Oh?" I asked innocently, now keenly aware that Jack was still in the dark about my scavenger hunt at the Vine.

"About the robberies, ya know." Jack shook his head.

I nodded.

"Kid, I'm just sick about it. What if they..." His voice trailed off and wavered.

I felt something in the pit of my stomach slowly rising, past my aching ribs, past my heart that was breaking for him, and up my throat until it came out. "Jack, how much do you really know about Lisa?"

He looked up at me from the sofa and, suddenly, he looked older, frail, sensitive. "What do you mean? Look, kid, I know you don't like her —"

"I didn't say that."

"But-but-but I can tell," he said, his stammering back.

"Jack, how much do you *really* know about her?" I asked, shrugging off the implication that I didn't like her for no good reason.

"I know she makes me smile," Jack Junior said and just like that he looked lost in dreamy memories. He snapped out of his near stupor and pulled up the cookie he'd been dunking only to find half of it had been claimed by the coffee in his cup. "How do ya like that?" He looked into the cup, sneered, and looked back at me, his eyes narrow and inquisitive.

I plodded on. There was no turning back. "You don't think that she's...?"

"She's *what*?"

"That she's a little phony?"

"You think she's phony? You have some woman's institution thing going on or something?"

"Something," I said, smiling at Jack's choice of words. I put my cup on the sideboard. I'd never been a fan of decaf anyway. "Jack, she's not what she seems." There, I said it.

"What do you mean?"

"I mean I think she's broke, she's living at the Vine, she's a cleaner, and I don't think her name is even Lisa Claire."

"Oh, I know that. Well, I knew most of that."

"You *did*?"

"Yeah." He nodded and took a sip of his decaf and oatmeal cookie concoction then made a dissatisfied face.

"Doesn't it bother you that she lied?"

"Years ago, it might have," Jack said and got up to pour himself a coffee he didn't have to chew.

"Jack, I just want the best for you. And I think–"

Jack ran his hand through his hair, rubbed the back of his neck, and looked at me. "You know, kiddo, one day you're going to look around and your ass is going to be sagging and you're going to have wrinkles and you're going to wish there was someone around to brighten your day. Even if they're not rich, even if they work as a cleaner. Someday just having a warm body there is going to be enough. But I'm not like Sefton and Muncie, after those *Gee Spot* ladies. They've always been like that. A girl in every port, but not me. When I met my Jeanie, it was 'til death do us part, and that's how it went. And now Lisa—"

I rolled my eyes. I'm about as far from elitist as one could get, but I don't cotton to liars, whoever they may be.

"Don't do that! Don't roll your eyes. You're not me. You don't know what it's like to wake up in the morning and my bones are creaking and my head hurts and I've stubbed my toe because I had to get up and go to the bathroom for the seventh time that night and all I want is someone to shine a little light in my direction. You don't know. You're young. You're healthy. You're not going to your friends' funerals every other week."

"Jack, I—"

"No, no just think for a minute what it must be like. Do you want to be like me in thirty or forty years? Dragging your ass out of bed just so people won't think you're depressed? Putting on a clean shirt even though nobody is there to give a damn? No, kid, it's not all roses when you get older." Jack shook his head and took a sip.

I swallowed hard and stared at the carpeting, feeling ashamed that I hadn't considered Jack's feelings more. To me, he'd always been "smilin' Jack Junior"—quick with a joke, loaded with charisma, and blessed with a twinkle in his eye. It had never occurred to me that the light could go out.

"When I see her, I feel good. She's like... like a beacon. Like one of those buoys out there," he said, pointing to the bay. "I found her when I needed her."

His buoy. My dream. Was my recurring nightmare really about Lisa? Was it really about love? I shook my head. "I'm sorry."

"Well, it's-it's-it's alright. But if it's all the same to you, kid, my lumbago is acting up and I've got to lie down," he said, eyes averted.

"I'll just, uh, see myself out. I'm sorry." I left the *Fortune Cookie* feeling like a heel. Out in the teeming rain, I pulled my hood up and listened to the patter of the drops on my jacket and headed toward the lights that were on in Aggie's. My own personal beacon whether she likes it or not.

"Why so glum chum?" Ags asked as I crossed the threshold, my spirits as soggy as the rest of me.

"Oh, I just came from Jack's."

"What did he do? Tell you again about his dog that died?"

"No, he gave me a lecture on love," I said, making my way to the counter.

"Oh, well, I'd guess he's an expert. Want a fritter?"

"How old is it?" I said, plunking myself down with a whoosh.

"Just this morning. Split it with ya."

"Sure, why not."

"So, what happened on your ride to Hamilton with Russ?" Ags finally asked the question that must have been plaguing her.

"What do you mean?"

"You... you're being far too understanding and nice to him."

"No, I'm not."

"Girl, you are too, and it's not like you one bit."

I shrugged. "Ags, do you think it's better to have someone to love, even if it's not perfect? And they aren't exactly to your taste?"

"You're asking me? How should I know? I haven't found my main course. I'm still working on the sample platter concept," she said, smiled at me, and then we devoured the fritter.

* * *

Class that evening was sort of a greatest hits version. Mr. Hives, clearly in his element, enthusiastically discussed highlights from all our previous classes with fresh examples. Students could ask questions on any topic relating to what had been covered thus far. A few had questions for the bookish young lady taking the course on personality disorders. This progressed into a tangent about the veracity of the news industry, which struck a nerve with another classmate, the editor from the *Marysville Herald*. And *this* got my wheels turning, and I made a note to stop by the college library on my way out to see if David Earle would pop up in any of the newspaper databases on site.

And so, while Julia North, the student librarian, scrambled around the college library, impatiently tidying, waiting for me, I logged in and typed the name David Earle into the search bar of the local newspaper archive program. This is a handy little system where you can type in a name and a list of results will pop up with the name and the date of the article and most times the title of the article. However, since the program had required some element of manual entry by prison inmates, the degree of accuracy and completeness of the results could be called into question. But it was a source. And so, with a keen awareness that I was the only thing standing between Julia and her date with Frank the Tank Hubbard—the quarterback—I scanned the results. No direct hits for David Earle, but there were a few for Earle Davidson. I hit Print All and, within moments, the printer beside me was whirring and spitting out pages. By the time the printer beeped to let me know it had finished its job, Julia was standing beside me with a ring of keys in her hand and a Marysville College canvas bag on her arm. She picked up the pages off the printer, handed them to me, and I stuffed them into my own all-purpose canvas bag.

"Thanks, Julia. Have fun tonight," I said as I headed out the door of the library to find Frank the Tank lingering on the bench in the hallway. I suppose dating Julia was as close to being scholarly as he was comfortable.

By the time I'd reached the end of the hall, I could hear Julia locking the library door and giggling to her beau. "Do you need a ride, Alex? It's raining," she hollered at me.

"Oh, no thanks, I brought the truck. Thanks again, Julia," I called down the hall and, before long, I was dashing through puddles to the vintage truck I'd been using. I squinted through the dimness of the lights in the parking lot to read the papers that'd been printed off.

The first Earle Davidson article was an obituary. That particular Earle Davidson died in his eighty-fifth year back in 1973. Wrong dude. I placed it at the back of the pile and continued reading. The next article was a birth announcement. "To Earle and Melanie Davidson born today a son, Michael." That article was about thirty years old. *Hmm.* I flipped down the top left corner of that page as something that may be relevant and placed it at the back of the sheaf of papers. I wasn't expecting what I saw next. Page after page, one article after the other, beginning with the one entitled "Earle Davidson Convicted of Aggravated Burglary." Seven articles covered the arrest, trial, conviction, and sentencing. There were even a few pictures and, though they were grainy black and white, I could tell this was in fact the same man I met at the Vine Street Inn, the man I knew as Zane Wilcox. Same nose and deep-set eyes. I immediately locked my truck door and got moving. The wipers eerily squeaked across the windshield and, as I passed the turn for Vine Street, I wondered how many people knew the checkered past of the local inn-keeper.

CHAPTER 18

I pulled into the marina, found the parking spot I'd claimed as mine for the time being, and cut the motor. The rain pelted down through the dark of the night and, for a moment, I squinted out through the truck windows nervously as if implausibly, Earle Davidson was watching me. With no end to the rain in sight, I grabbed my canvas bag from the passenger side, hopped out of the truck, locked it, and dashed toward my dock. On the way to the *Alex M.,* I spotted lights aboard the *Splendored Thing* and made a detour to pop in and see Cary Tranmer. Maybe he'd have some recollection of Earle and his newsworthy past. By the time I got to the stern door of the boat, Tranmer had it propped open and was waiting for me.

"Wild night out there. Come on in," he said, squinting into the rain that was coming down sideways.

"Thanks." I shook the drops from my soaked

hands as I stepped into the salon. My eyes drifted around the space, remembering the times Nat and I spent watching movies and philosophizing, testing out new recipes and shooting the breeze. As I stood in the entrance by the hooks that still held Nat's windbreaker, I picked up the faint smell of his cologne. It's funny, it wasn't hard to see Cary Tranmer enjoying the space— they were life-long friends—but had it been anyone else, I'm not sure I would have felt the same.

"Martini? I'm just mixing one for myself."

"No, no thanks."

He nodded. "Have a seat. How are you tonight?"

"Good. Thanks," I said and shrugged out of my raincoat, hung it on the brass hook by the door, and sank into one of the down-filled sofa cushions. "Hey, I wonder if I could jog your memory."

"Be the most jogging I've done in a while, unfortunately, but shoot." Tranmer smiled and landed on the cushion beside me.

"Earle Davidson," I said, looking into his eyes, waiting for a reaction.

"What about him?" Cary's eyes narrowed and he took a sip of his cocktail.

"You remember the name?"

"Oh, sure, I remember that one," Tranmer said, placing the glass on the teak side table. "He knocked over the banks in Hamilton and Evanston and– Hey, why do you want to know about him?"

"Just curious. His name came up today."

He raised his eyebrows, a little surprised. "Yeah, I think he might have died in prison. That was an interesting case. Glad I wasn't involved."

"The case was here?"

"No, not really. Funny, though, there's a connection. Matt Martin from the MMM Bakery, I remember he was the jury foreman. Lived in Hamilton at the time."

"Really?" I said, connecting the dots.

"And, uh, Brooke Rain. He was also on that jury," he said, and for a guy who wasn't really involved in the case, he seemed to recall some pretty important details.

"Brooke Rain?" Still relatively new to town, the name didn't ring a bell.

"Yeah, his kid owns Stokes Pharmacy."

"Oh?" More dots connected.

"Yeah, I think the sentence was twenty years or so, but like I said, I heard he had a heart attack in prison. Something like that anyway."

I nodded and looked across at Tranmer. The light in his eyes told me how much he enjoyed talking shop.

"If I'm not mistaken..." Tranmer pinched his eyes tight to try to remember the next detail. "Someone ratted him out, someone close to him." He shook his head. "Can't remember who, or if it ever came out. Where did his name come up again?"

"Oh, I saw it in an old newspaper clipping."

"You know what's funny..." Tranmer looked vacantly at the glass in his hand.

"What's that?"

"That Albright guy... You went to see about listing his stuff, right?"

"Yeah?"

"Albright married Earle Davidson's wife after she divorced him when he went to prison," Tranmer said and took a sip. He smiled, looking pleased to be back on track remembering details.

"You don't say." My eyes ping ponged around the room.

"Sure you don't want a drink, kiddo? Warm you up on a night like this."

I nodded. "Actually, I will take one after all."

❈ ❈ ❈

I spent the next hour or so piecing things together and wondering what to do with the jigsaw puzzle once it was done. I'd already felt like the girl who cried wolf, what with my suspicions about Lisa and Russ—suspicions that were valid in their own right but not the big news like I thought I had about Earle Davidson. I paced, I talked things over with Pepper and George, I drafted yet another PowerPoint in my head about the subject and wondered how I could relay my findings to Hagen without looking like a Nancy Drew wannabe. Slide one—Zane Wilcox, aka David Earle, aka Earle Davidson served time for robbing banks. Slide two—that same Earle Davidson buys the Vine Street Inn and not long afterward the bakery, pharmacy, and jewellery store are robbed. There's an asterisk on this slide; the bakery and pharmacy are tied to the jury that convicted Earle. Slide three—Russ Shears wins in a poker game from a guy matching Earle's description, the heart pendant probably taken in the jewellery store robbery. Slide four—the header on this slide is Questions. In bullet points, they included: Are Lisa and Roddy involved with the robberies? Is that why they didn't press charges against me? Was Davidson responsible for what happened to Jack Albright's boats?

I'm not sure how, but I finally fell asleep.

✳ ✳ ✳

"Aggie's dinner" written in red and circled for extra impact stood out on the calendar in the galley of my boat. The boat calendar, another giveaway thanks to Pike Murray, and while we're on the subject of his promotional products, if he were only more discriminating about who he gave his hoodies to, it'd be much easier to narrow down who the papers were calling the 'Bayside Burglar'. That hoodie had been spotted at no fewer than two of four places that had been broken into. While I figured Earle Davidson was involved, I still wasn't convinced that Roddy and/or his mommy dearest were not. I pondered that and other mysteries of life as I went about the business of baking. I'd let Ags know I'd be making the two pies that morning—apple and cherry—and that I'd be over after they'd cooled. I was in the midst of pie prep when, as typically happens to me, a visitor stopped by.

"Hello!" I heard a voice shouting up on the main deck of my boat.

I went from the prep area in the galley to the narrow set of stairs that led to the main level. From the second rung up, I could see Doctor Richards standing in the stern doorway.

"Down here," I said and turned back to face the mess I had created. In the time it'd take him to get down there, I could neither clean nor hide my mess. I usually opt to store messes in the oven when I have an unexpected visitor, but seeing as how it was on preheat, this wasn't going to work for me. Best I could do was wipe the flour from my fingers.

Doctor Richards caught my eye as he descended the stairs. "Do you mind?" He motioned toward the galley and I nodded that it was alright for him to step into my laboratory.

"Sure, what's up?"

He took the last rungs down. "Jack Junior asked if I'd, uh, check on you."

"Oh?" I said curiously. The way he said the words made it sound like he wouldn't have been there save for the request.

"How are you feeling?" he asked flatly, his bed-side manner nowhere in sight.

"Right as rain." I smiled, figuring one of us ought to.

"How are the ribs?"

"A little sore," I lilted.

Richards flitted his eyes and looked down at my jeans. "And the cut? You change the dressing?" he asked in a gruff manner still not like him.

"Yes. I changed the dressing."

"Good," he said and turned to go up the stairs to leave.

"Hey, hey wait a minute," I said and reached out to grab him by the forearm, the material of his shirt my only purchase. He turned and looked at me, his blue-grey eyes flashing. His greying hair had been tossed by the wind, but it still fell into a place that looked good. I think that's a guy thing. "Are you alright? You don't seem yourself."

"Right as rain."

"People who say that are usually lying." I shot him a crooked smile, trying to break the ice that had suddenly formed between us. "So, how are you really?"

Richards searched with his eyes for the words he wanted, as if they were written somewhere up and to the left. When he found them, he looked at me again. "You're perceptive, you know that?"

"Do you want to tell me what's wrong? You seem mad. Are you mad at *me*?" I asked, my tone surprisingly incredulous although I should just naturally assume that someone somewhere is mad at me at any given time.

Richards leaned against the stainless-steel prep counter opposite me and crossed his arms in front of his chest. His gaze floated from the deck to my eyes, fixed on him with intrigue. "I wish you'd be more careful."

"*Me*?"

"Yes, *you*. Whatever *really* landed you in jail, the thing at Aggie's, and I know there's something else you're not telling. You just... "

"What? I just *what*? I don't think? I don't care? I don't what?"

Richards heaved a sigh and sported an exasperated look. "You don't realize..."

I looked at him, waiting for him to finish his thought.

He continued after a pause. "That you're important to people here."

I couldn't help but roll my eyes. Why, every time Richards and I spoke one on one, did I feel completely admonished by the man? I didn't really need him to tell me this. I knew what he was getting at. Jack Junior and I had become as inextricably connected as Laurel and Hardy, Butch Cassidy and the Sundance kid. Sure, we had our ups and downs, but what family doesn't?

And the gang, I guess they'd gotten used to me too. I nodded and told myself I'd try to use a bit more forethought in the future, and I'll admit I'd been on a bit of a reckless streak.

"Ok," I said.

"Ok." Richards nodded once and turned to go up the steps.

When he left the galley, I made an immature facial gesture and returned to the task at hand. He could see himself out. I popped my head into the fridge for more chilled butter and, when I closed the door and turned back to the stainless-steel counter, there he was again, so close that my hands pressed against the chest of his dark red cotton shirt. The fabric soft and crisp at the same time. My breath caught in my throat and, when I looked into his eyes, he placed one hand on each side of my face. I took a step back, feeling the coolness of the stainless-steel fridge against me. He leaned down so close that I couldn't tell if the breath between us was mine or his. He kissed me hard, then he turned and went up the galley stairs without a word.

When I heard the stern door close, I stuck my head in the freezer to cool down.

* * *

Even after the pies and I had cooled, I was still wondering what kind of wormhole I'd dropped into or parallel universe I was suddenly occupying that Doctor Richards would plant one right on me in the galley of my boat. I walked my two works of art to Aggie's place, pausing just inside the entrance, ready to scold the first person I saw for not getting the door for me and my full hands—but there was no one in sight. No Aggie and no gang gathered in the nook to critique the omnipresent twenty-four-hour news channel. I glanced toward the TV and, while the sound was muted, the message was clear. They were playing the tail end of a video from a location I'd been to recently. The words below it read "Sabotage Suspected in Hamilton Boat Sinking", and I was reminded of the connection to Earle Davidson that Tranmer had mentioned the night before. Jack Albright had married Earle's ex-wife. That deserves a new slide in the PowerPoint deck.

"What the hell happened between you and Doctor Richards?" Ags appeared from the back of the store and barked at me before I'd even had a chance to lay the pies on the counter.

"What are you talking about?" I asked, wondering if Ags was just fishing or if Stephen Richards had a penchant to kiss and tell.

"He said he won't be coming to dinner later." She crossed her arms in front and looked at me impatiently.

"And you just automatically assume it has something to do with *me*?"

"Well, I happened to be looking out the window when he came from the direction of your boat. Then he came in here and said he couldn't make it for dinner."

"Ags, trust me, *I* did nothing to the man." I let out a huff.

"Why'd you say it like that?" she said, pouring me a coffee topped up with Irish cream.

"Like what?"

"As if there's something you're not telling me." She eyed me while she screwed the top on the bottle.

"Ags..." I shook my head and took a sip and felt my face flush with heat.

"I knew it," she said and raised her eyebrows at me devilishly.

I called her bluff. "You don't know anything."

"He's got the hots for you, doesn't he?"

"No."

"Your neck is turning red. I know you're lying when your neck starts turning red and blotchy."

I lowered my chin to hide my tell.

"Psyche! That, my friend, was called a fake out and you just played into it," she said, raising her arms victoriously.

I shook my head at her. "Ok, he kissed me. That's it."

"Did you kiss him back?"

I looked around to see who might be listening. If there's one thing I can't stand, it's being fodder for gossip. "Yes, I kissed him back," I said just above a whisper, and I took a seat at the counter.

"And how was it?"

"Amazing. Ok, it was amazing," I conceded.

"Hmph, then I wonder why he cancelled on dinner."

"Ags, I have no idea," I said, and I turned to see who the bell above the door was announcing. It was Tranmer, and he was toting a wicker basket loaded with goodies from the farmer's market.

"Hello, ladies. I come bearing gifts," he said with a smile for each of us.

"Whatcha got there?" Ags asked and peeked anxiously into the basket Tranmer handed her.

"Just a few things for the dinner, or pre-dinner, or whatever you want to do with them," he said.

Together, Ags and I oohed and aahed over the cheeses and meats and jars of olives and fancy spiced pickles. "Coffee?" she asked him as she took the basket to the kitchen area.

"Sorry, can't. I'm going for a run. I really need to get back in shape," said the man in his sixties who could run circles around any other guy in the marina or, likely, the town. "Hey." He turned to me.

"Yes?" I asked, taking a sip. I looked back to the kitchenette to see Ags sorting through the goodies.

"I had the strangest conversation this morning with Bugsy."

"That in itself doesn't surprise me," I kidded.

"Yeah," Tranmer went on. "He asked me if

I needed any more boxes for packing up Nat's things. Said he was going to get some for himself and wouldn't mind picking up a few more for me."

"Oh," I said lowly and, looking back toward the kitchenette, Ags was in full eavesdropping mode. Personally, I hadn't expected Bugsy to bring up the topic of Nat's boat with Tranmer. "And, uh, what did you say?"

"I told him he must be confused and that I was only staying once in a while." Tranmer pulled his right foot up behind him to stretch his hamstring.

"I see." I nodded. "And what did he say?"

"He apologized for the misunderstanding, said he had to work on something, and walked off," Tranmer said, stretching the other leg now.

"Oh," I said. Why did Bugsy have to be so damn mature? The least he could have done is come swear at me or call me a liar.

"You think we should rent it out? You know, to someone we know? Someone we can trust? It's a shame to let her just sit there," Tranmer said. By now, he'd moved on to stretching his arms.

I looked back toward Ags who was in full stop now, not even pretending to mind her own business. "I think maybe we should talk about this later," I said sheepishly.

"Cool beans. I'll be here a few more days, but for now I'm off. Later, ladies," he said, and I watched him jog out of Aggie's store, his dark hair bouncing and behaving like mine never has and with legs I'd kill for.

I turned back toward my friend the coffee cup and took a sip. There was silence in the store for, oh, I'd say a solid ten seconds before there came an eruption from the kitchen area.

"You mind explaining that?"

I looked up from the countertop to see Ags, hands on hips and angling for a fight.

"Oh, Tranmer? What about him? Nice legs, huh?"

"You know damn well what I'm getting at, girl." She sighed. "Why'd you lie to Bugsy about renting the boat to Tranmer?"

"I don't know," I said, and that was the truth.

Aggie's behind began to make sounds, and she pulled her phone from her back pocket. From her reaction to the message on the screen, it wasn't good news.

"What's the matter? Who is it?"

"Guess."

"Ags, I can't. I'm mentally drained."

"Bugsy. Now *he's* not coming to dinner." She tapped something into the phone.

"What? Why not?"

"I just asked him that, but you know it has to be because of the big fat lie you told him about Tranmer and the boat." She stared at the screen and shook her head disgustedly.

"Ags, it wasn't a big fat lie. It was a *little skinny*

lie. Tranmer *is* staying on the boat and I certainly would have offered him the option to rent it... if I'd gotten around to it."

"Yeah, still. Lie." Ags smirked at me. "No answer," she said, motioning with her phone before she tucked it back into her pocket.

I let out a sigh that made me feel physically deflated. So far, two dinner invitees had declined based on my being there, and I wasn't feeling good about it. But Ags and I plodded on. By late afternoon, the long plastic and metal tables Ags pulled out twice a year were disguised by black and white buffalo check tablecloths, mini white and gold pumpkins, and hurricane lanterns with candles resting on layers of clear glass beads. The counter nearby had been transformed into a buffet draped in tan linen. A large boat-shaped serving dish already contained the Hawaiian dinner rolls from MMM's, and other unique and nautically inspired pieces were laid out as placeholders for gravy, roasted and mashed potatoes, turkey and roast beef, Caesar salad, cranberry sauce, and there was an enormous, tempting charcuterie board covered in plastic wrap, courtesy of Tranmer's contributions. Plates and pumpkins and cutlery wrapped in napkins and tied with blue and white striped ribbon were also laid out. By late afternoon, we were due for a rest, and with the sun sinking low, it wouldn't be long before guests began to arrive.

"Hey, Jack," Ags said, and when I turned to

look toward the door, there was Jack Junior peeking in sheepishly.

"Hi, Junior," I said. Although Jack and I tend to make up quickly, he still didn't look thrilled to see me.

He opened the door with trepidation. "Hi, kiddo," he said meekly in my direction.

"What's new, Jack?" I asked, searching for but not finding the light in his eyes.

He took off his fishing cap and wrenched it in his hand. "I, uh, I don't think I'm going to make it to dinner tonight, Aggie."

"What? Why the hell not?" Aggie was clearly getting agitated. Having planned a feast for twenty, at the rate things were going, there'd be enough leftovers to feed a small army.

Jack glanced at me with apologetic eyes and then looked at Ags. "See, Lee said she just wouldn't feel comfortable—"

"With me here," I said, finishing his sentence.

Jack's face got red. "I think she just needs a little time. You know, we talked and she knows that you know she put on that façade and she's-she's-she's just embarrassed, that's all."

I nodded.

Ags bit her bottom lip..

"Sorry, kid. Sorry, Aggie, I, uh, I'll see you later," he said, and even the tone of the bell above the door suddenly sounded melancholy.

I glanced at Ags with a penitent expression. "Hey, at least the *Gee Spot* ladies are still here.

They'll be coming for sure."

"Yeah, but that's just Gladys and Ginny. Remember, Geraldine brings her own food and drinks wherever she goes," Ags said, rolling her eyes.

"Oh yeah, that's right. I keep forgetting she was at Jonestown. Well, I can't really blame her for that."

She smirked. "Anyone else you piss off?"

"Probably. Look, Ags, I'll stay home. Let Richards, Jack, and Bugsy know I'm not coming and–"

"No way! Somebody's got to be here to help me pack up all the leftovers."

"Well, the least I could do is take care packages to them, TV dinner style, you know," I said and felt the buzzing of my phone in my bag. I took it out and looked at the screen. "Johnny Fleet."

"Alex, I swear if Johnny, his gran, and her boyfriend cancel—"

"Easy, sista, he just wants me to come over. Listen, I'm sorry about the others—"

My words were cut like a knife by the sound of the smoke alarm in the kitchen.

"Oh my God, the pumpkin pie!" Ags sprinted away and I headed out the door to see what Johnny Fleet needed.

CHAPTER 19

As I walked down the steps of Aggie's store, I re-read the text message. "Hey come 2 the bait stand." It was followed by a smiley face emoji, and nothing about the message looked like it had come from Johnny except the number that sent it.

Texting Traits and Techno Truths had been the alliterative lesson title of night one of the communications analysis course I'd been taking at the college. Mr. Hives, the oh-so-enthusiastic head of our class was open in his condemnation of texting, a medium he fell just short of calling the devil's work. Iterating that if the medium was indeed still the message, the message was that it's ok to be emotionless, curt, and impersonal. And no, emojis and gifs are not substitutes for inflection, feeling, or genuine emotion. However, Hives' crusade would seem to be an uphill battle with Americans sending six billion texts a day, and that number is growing.

The funny thing was, though, in the two years I'd known him, Johnny Fleet hadn't once texted me. I looked at my screen again, perplexed by the message itself. First of all, Johnny has this weird affliction they call manners. If he *had* suddenly taken up texting, I know he'd still throw in a "please" and "thank you". Second, Johnny doesn't seem like the kind of kid who would be cutesy enough to use the number two instead of the word "to", or the type to put a smiley face in his message. Finally, I had never heard Johnny Fleet refer to his operations as "the bait stand". Not once.

His new-to-him truck was parked in the driveway. I pushed open the front door of the store, expecting to see him, but he wasn't at the counter. "Hey! Since when did you start texting?" I shouted. "Hey, Johnny!" I bellowed and waited for an answer. I looked out the front window toward his new boat and, seeing no one aboard, I proceeded behind the counter toward the back room. As soon as I pushed open the door, I found Johnny. Sitting in the corner by the refrigerator. He was bound by ropes and had a rag stuffed in his mouth. The pleading expression he gave with his eyes registered a moment too late, and Earle Davidson yanked me by my arm into the room and slammed the door. My breath caught in my throat and my heart began to thump rapidly. I looked down at Johnny—no blood and he didn't look like anything was hurting but his pride. He looked back at me with remorse. I looked at Earle. And his gun—likely the one Aggie'd been holding for Carlos.

"Nice to see you again." Earle's expression oozed anger and confidence at the same time. "What was your name again? Euphegenia? What's that, Latin for nosy bitch?" He smiled at his own comment he must have found clever.

I smirked. "I've been called worse."

"Well, Blondie, you and I are going to go for a little boat ride."

"What's the occasion, Zane? Or should I say Earle?"

"Oh, I think you know. In fact, I think you know more than you're letting on. Just figured I'd get to you before you spill your guts to that cop who brought Lisa in. The one hangs around you," he said, and his eyes bored through me. "Lives in Brentwood Court."

Earle had been busy spying on me, Hagen, and who knows how many others. "Look, I'm really not as much fun as you probably think, so why don't you just take the boat and go?"

"You may not be fun, but I hear you're worth a pile of money and somebody's gonna pay to get you back."

"You don't know me very well. Nobody'll care if I'm gone. They'll probably have a parade," I said, trying to win over Earle with my cynicism and self-deprecation. He didn't fall for it.

"Move," he barked, and with the gun in his

hand he motioned me toward the door. "Wait a second," he said, and I froze while he proceeded to cold cock Johnny Fleet.

I flinched and sucked in through clenched teeth and, when I looked down to see Johnny, I was relieved when I saw his fingers move and, as Earle shoved me through the doorway, I prayed that Johnny would be ok.

Earle and I proceeded toward the *Fleet's In*, Johnny's baby, the new name freshly applied by Armstrong Signs just two days earlier. With our steps nearly knitted together, Earle pressed the barrel of the gun into my side and I slowed my gait, hoping that someone would notice what was going on. "Start the boat," Earle grumbled, handing me the key, and I complied while he quickly untied the bow and stern lines and then hopped aboard.

"Ok, get us out of here, nice and easy," he said.

I nodded, the gun pointed at me tending to make me agreeable, and we motored out between the piers, at a casual pace so as not to arouse suspicion. I looked over my shoulder back at Aggie's place and, a minute later when her Christmas lights flicked on and they outlined the profile of the store in white, my hopes flicked off.

Once we were out of the piers, Earle used the gun in his hand to point to the passenger seat he wanted me to take, like he was some usher at a play for Mafioso. "Give me your cell phone," he barked over the sound of the twin Yamahas, his palm up, his tone demanding.

"I don't have it. It's in my bag and my bag's in Johnny's place," I said, but he patted me down anyway. "Hey, watch it!" I gave him angry eyes for the way his hand lingered on my behind, and he chuckled until the boat thudded against a wave and he resumed his place at the controls.

"Where are we going?" I asked, looking across at him while I rubbed my arms with my hands. The chill of the night was already upon us.

"Haven't decided yet." His face was hardened by concentration.

"What if we don't have enough gas to get there?"

"What if you shut up?" he groused.

"I'm just saying, maybe you should slow down so we don't burn all our gas so quickly," I said, looking through the dark expanse ahead of us. A shiver ran down my back as I felt some spray when we thudded down on a wave.

Earle cut back on the throttle a little. "You, uh, you're not half bad, ya know."

Hmm, another glowing endorsement.

"Maybe when we get where we're going, you'll be a little nicer to me."

"I doubt it," I was quick to say.

"Smart too," Earle flitted his eyes at me.

"Oh, not that smart, trust me."

"You figured out who I am, didn't take long either." He looked at me with almost a congratulatory expression.

"How did you know that I figured it out?"

"That little program at the college library? I built a code into it that lets me know every time someone hits on my name." He smirked proudly. "You can learn anything in prison."

I shook my head. I can't even set the alarm on my phone and the guy across from me is coding. "So, tell me this. I get that you robbed the bakery and pharmacy because you wanted to get back at the jury for putting you away, right? But the jewellery store? And Aggie's?"

"I needed some things to fence. The jewellery store was good for that, and I knocked over your friend's place for lying to me with those fake names."

I smirked. The worst I'd ever done to someone for lying to me was rat them out to the IRS.

"And you drugged my dog..."

"Well, duh. What do you think the nutmeg was for, my oatmeal? You bought that *superfood* garbage?"

"So, instead of going to jail for robbery, you think kidnapping is going to get you off scot free?"

"I've already done my time for those jobs. Did ya know I had nothing to do with those bank jobs way back?" He looked at me. "Hey, I saw that."

"What?"

"That eye-rolling thing—that's a nasty habit."

"I know, I need a twelve-step program. Look, Earle, everyone ever accused of anything always says they didn't do it."

"But I didn't. My ex-friend threw me under the bus. You know his old lady."

"I know lots of old ladies, Earle."

"The one and only Lisa."

"Lisa Claire? She was married to your friend?"

"Lisa King. Claire's her middle name and she was married to my *ex*-friend. The both of 'em pointed the finger at me. And I lose twenty years of my life, and my relationship with my kid."

"Michael?"

Earle turned his scowl on me. "How'd you know that?"

"I'm nosy, like you said."

"Anyway, all the money's spent and her old man croaks and she comes looking to me for sympathy. Says it was all his idea to lie to the cops. So, I'm a soft-hearted guy—"

"No kidding."

"Anyway, I give her this place to live at the dump I bought. The Vine. So I can keep an eye on her, mess with her life for a change."

"And you just happen to get the security codes to a few places you can knock over, plant the goods in their room, and frame Roddy for it."

"They had it comin'. Nobody gave me a fair shake. I spent twenty years in the pen while they lived high on the hog with the money her old man stole. She gets to watch her kid grow up.

What a loser."

"That why you tried to frame him?"

"Why not? The best way to hurt his mother is to get him sent to jail."

I nodded.

He rubbed the stubble on his chin. Maybe growing a beard was going to be part of a future disguise. "Didn't count on a goody two shoes like you, though."

"I'm far from that."

I scanned the lights on the shoreline. "Look, Earle, there's a cove over there. Just take me in and drop me off and I'll get a ride back to the marina. You don't even have to take me all the way into shore."

"No. I'm not going back to prison."

"What? You think I'd rat you out? I can keep a secret, and I'm really a pain in the ass. You don't want to hang around with me."

"You'll do for a while. Are you really a screamer or was that thing with *Andrew Jackson* a lie?"

"Andrew? Oh, look, that's Doctor Richards. He's a good guy, he was just playing along."

"Well, you and I are going to *play along* for a while too," he said and put his hand on the gun that was tucked into his waistband as if to remind me it was there. Like I could have forgotten.

I sat with my knees tense, and I felt ready to spring from the cushion any moment like I'd go through the roof of the cabin. My eyes darted around the boat like a pin ball machine. I had to find a way out of this. Damn me anyway. Why couldn't I have kyboshed Johnny's desire to buy this boat?

The further we got from shore, the more I felt my stomach churn. Would I ever see my friends again? I looked up to the radio affixed to the ceiling of the boat. It was directly over Earle's head. Even if I did get on the radio and call for help, it'd be a long time coming. That idea was out. I looked around for another way out and, there, in the glow of the dash of controls, I spotted the kill switch. If I could just pull it and cut the power, we'd at least stop moving farther from home.

I needed to create a distraction. Seducing Earle was out—that was a given—and so I thought to rely on annoying the piss out of him. The build up was swift but subtle. I shrugged my shoulders and rubbed my arms with my hands, shrinking myself into a pathetic, sniffling mess. Heavy on the sniffling. A constant, urging, agitating sniffling that would drive any man crazy. Earle glared at me. It was working. I replied with a sheepish expression and got to my feet.

"What are you doing?"

I reached over the console. "I need a Kleenex—cut me some slack, it's getting cold out" I looked down into his eyes to say. I put my hand on his shoulder and steadied myself, planting my legs like trees. I let my hand appear to move clumsily over the dash and, in the process, I pulled out a tissue and then removed the kill switch. The engines died almost immediately and the boat coasted a few feet before the only forward movement was caused by the waves. The only sounds were the thudding of the hull followed by Earle's expletive outburst.

"What'd you do?"

"Got a Kleenex, what do you think I did?"

"You cut the engine! Fix it!"

"You're gonna need this," I said, waving the kill switch I'd palmed in my Kleenex.

Earle grasped my arm and squeezed it hard until, in the face of unbearable pain, I let the kill switch fall, swallowed in the darkness of the floor of the boat.

"Move!" he shouted at me, flicking on the cabin light and frantically searching on his hands and knees.

I had seconds, a minute maybe, before he figured out how to restart the boat. I backed my way toward the stern and looked into the inky black water, and then in the distance, at the faint dark red of the last buoy we'd passed, and when Earle finally exclaimed that he'd found the switch on the floor, I jumped overboard.

* * *

When I surfaced, I saw the lights on the boat

fading into the distance, and I heard the whir of the motors. I was alone in black water. Or was this my dream? If I sat up or opened my eyes, would Pepper be lying beside me in my king-sized bed? I shut my eyes tight and opened them. Nothing changed. I did it again, shutting them harder this time. Nothing. Nothing but cold black water. My teeth chattered and my heart pounded. I could feel the pulse in my ears, the sound of my own panicked breathing. I could tread water only so long. I *had* to get to the buoy.

My legs were heavy in my jeans, my arms felt constricted by the jacket I wore, and I thought about removing it but it might provide some warmth *if* I made it to the buoy. The red light of the beacon mocked me and wobbled with the low chop. I didn't feel like I was making any progress, gaining any distance. What was worse: being tired in cold black water or being on that boat with Earle Davidson? Too late now. I had to think about something else. It was Thanksgiving. Were they all sitting at Aggie's enjoying turkey and the trimmings? Would this be my last Thanksgiving? Would they even come looking for me? I *had* to get to the buoy.

As I swam toward it, there were moments when it looked like the light had gone out, just as the light in me was fading. If I let go now, I'd see my father again, my husband, everyone who had gone before me. Maybe even Nat. It was tempting. If I fought, I'd see Ags, Bugsy, Hagen, and

Richards. I'd see Jack and the gang again. I'd have a heck of a story to tell them at the next poker game. I *had* to get to the buoy.

Closer now, I reached out and grazed it with my fingertips. My fingers smooshed into the algae below the water line and my hand slipped off the steel. My fingers were so cold I could barely feel them, barely grasp when I reached out. I needed something to hang onto. Salvation felt so close and yet so far away. I could literally reach out and touch it. I'd seen seals on these things countless times; they had no trouble getting on top. Tired, cold, angry, I lunged up to grab the metal angle iron and my hand, half numb, became pinched in the frame. *Dammit.* The pain was excruciating, and I let out a primal scream that morphed into crying. I bobbed there for what seemed like an eternity, one hand pinched in the metal frame of the buoy, the weight of the water pulling the rest of me down. I built up for one last try. "You can do this," I told myself, and in the next moments, as though I were being pulled up by my beltloops, I found myself on the platform of the buoy. I let out another scream from deep within, extracting my hand that had been caught in the metal. I brought it to my mouth and huffed on it. I crawled into the framework, the cold steel warmer than the water. *I had made it to the buoy.*

EPILOGUE

I was told later that when Johnny Fleet gained consciousness, he ran to Aggie's where someone called the police and they spotted me with a FLIR camera. It was Hagen's first dispatch on the marine unit. They also spotted Earle Davidson. He'd run out of gas down the coast about forty minutes after I'd jumped and was adrift on the ocean. He is presently in the Marysville jail charged with kidnapping, assault, four counts of burglary, and I suspect that the Hamilton police will be charging him with criminal mischief in the sinking of Jack Albright's vessels. The *Gee Spot* left port two days after Thanksgiving. It came back to Marysville one day later to return Sefton, the stowaway. Russ Shears stayed long enough to earn the money to pay back his private financer in Vegas and last Ags heard he was back in Ohio, working at his parents' hardware store. Jack Junior and Lisa broke up a few weeks after I was rescued. She had stayed overnight and Jack got his first look of her sans Spanx and other enhancers. The last I heard, Roddy had pawned his watch and he and his mother were on a singles cruise. Speaking of boats, two days after I got back to the Marysville Marina, I signed a lease agreement with Bugsy and he took up residence on the *Splendored Thing.*

The End

ABOUT THE AUTHOR

Maggie Seacroft is thrilled that you've dropped in on the second Alex M. Mystery and she hopes that you enjoyed Mystery #2 Buoy just as much as you did Mystery #1 Ahoy!

Maggie was raised around boats (and a lot of quirky 'boat guys'), and admits to being a sucker for good mysteries and 1940s hunky actors (don't get her started on her trip to see William Holden's home town!) One day while walking by the water on her way to the marine brokerage she owns, she decided to combine these ingredients, and thus was born the Alex M. Mystery series.

Maggie lives in Port Dover, Ontario, could listen to Christmas music all year round and has some seriously sassy tendencies.

Stay tuned...there are plenty more Alex M. mysteries to come!

Made in the USA
Middletown, DE
04 May 2022

65244148R00196